THE KISS
G.A. HAUSER

Prologue

"You don't have to tell me he was gorgeous," she said, "I wrote the book! Look, having co-owned a male modeling agency for the last fifteen years, I've seen every breed of male form imaginable. Out of the hundreds of resumes and photos we receive, only two percent were what I would call, truly outstanding.

"You have to understand this business. Luckily everyone has his or her own perception of what beauty is. Mine had to be what beauty could sell. And that old adage about 'sex selling' was never truer than it was with the male of the species in the twenty-first century. It was as if the world had gone through some black hole of male beauty in the eighties and nineties. Ugliness prevailed in the leading male category; on film as well as in print. Lovely men had gone out of fashion; made extinct by a male-dominated, homophobic brotherhood that detested anything that threatened their plump, bald existence. Pretty women were always in vogue. Lovely men seemed to come and go, like the fickle Paris fashions."

Stopping herself, she peered up over her poised water bottle, and said, "I tend to get on a soap box about it. It's a topic I'm passionate about, as you can tell. You see, life isn't always fair. And the battle of the sexes was never more one-sided as it was with male models. And more's the pity, as I have seen some models in my time that could have swept the big *screen like Monroe had done in the sixties. Women loved them, and so did men, though they were horrified to admit another male was 'pretty'."*

Flipping her hair back from her face, seeing the slant-eyed gaze of skepticism, she sighed. "No? You don't believe me? Go see for yourself. Ask any straight male if they think another male is attractive. Watch homophobia in action. I'm not a lesbian but I can give my opinion on the beauty of a woman. That's acceptable, you see."

"Maybe that was why we were both single and living together, my brother and I. It just worked out that way. I moved to New York from Seattle ten years ago, hating that wet moldy place and craving my bite of the Big Apple. Scott decided on interviewing with my agency though in his heart he wanted to be an actor. We did supply a few men for television commercials, but print was our specialty. After living in Los Angeles for a while, trying to break into film while seeing some blonde bimbo named Fifi, Scott gave up on Hollywood and flew here to stay for a week, then two, then...well, I didn't mind him here. It was company. And he was my little brother, after all.

"Scott is tall, very well built, and yet, not what I would call pretty. He filled the fifty percent niche in modeling. Not extraordinary, not ugly. He did silly jobs like those extras you used to see in the old Columbo movies. A quick stroll across a mock up village in a studio and he was handed his meager paycheck. Though his acting lessons continued, we both knew his aspirations might never be met. I was making enough to support us, so I didn't push him to get another line of work. I loved him. Why destroy him that way? Mom and Dad already had."

She paused, thinking about what she was going to say, then came into focus. "You're not going to write all this down, are you? I mean, isn't anything off the record?"

After pondering the answer, that 'nothing was off the record', she continued more cautiously, "Separating my life from my work wasn't easy. Coming home with my portfolio bulging with photos and faces to assign, I had the habit of spreading them all out on the polished wood flooring of my three-bedroom loft apartment. It was huge and sparsely furnished and I liked it that way.

"And he would crouch over the selection of black and white snapshots, helping me decide which male should go to which interview. Appreciating the input, I often wondered why he had an opinion at all, when men, as he said, 'weren't his thing'.

"So, testing my theory on whether men can actually see one another as sexual beings, or just see walking beer advertisements, I began this chain of events that I never expected would amount to much more than one day of silliness, and not the circumstances that followed. Unbelievably, in the end I was proven right. They do see each other and assess their beauty. And sometimes in a sexual way, though not always but, most certainly judging it against their own value and taste..."

Again she paused to gather all her thoughts on how she wanted to proceed. When she took too long she was prodded to continue. "Stop bugging me. I told you I would get to the point. Now, in my opinion, it all started one evening over Chinese food..."

Chapter One

The meal they had ordered over an hour ago was late. Both their stomachs were growling in the silence. Echoing gurgles, symphonies of bubbles and hisses, intensified by the quiet of the interior. Claire normally put on a CD the moment she stepped into her apartment, loving her old classic rock music, the louder the better, but that night she was so overwhelmed with work, she bypassed the stereo and immediately dumped out the contents of her briefcase onto the floor. Moments later, Scott lay next to her to sift through the faces.

"Him?" she asked, pointing to a black and white eight by ten. "Which one?"

"I'd send him to Ralph Lauren. He has that…uh, I dunno, some stuffy English Country Gentleman kind of thing." His voice reminded her of someone who had just woken from a deep coma. It was low and lacked any kind of accent. All sense of belonging to a region was erased by his drama elocution lessons. He neither sounded like a Seattleite nor a New Yorker. She thought it was a bit bland, but he liked the way he enunciated his words and paused at punctuations. Having so many other reasons to tease him, she left that one alone.

"Yeah, all right." She set the photo aside, noting on the back in pencil his thoughts.

The shushing noises of the prints sliding on the spotless slick wooden flooring were in competition with their stomachs growling. Concentrating on the list and her thoughts about it, she lost track of Scott, who had found one male of interest.

About to ask him to get her another glass of much needed wine, she suddenly noticed his odd expression. With the print elevated in his hand before him, his eyes were riveted to one of her new model's amazing faces. Hesitating, wondering how long he would ogle, she began to laugh to herself at how hypnotized he had become.

"You like him?" she asked.

Then something happened that she had never seen before in all the times they had lain on the floor together sifting through male bodies and faces. He blushed and had no snappy reply.

Stunned beyond belief, she sat up and ripped the photo out of his hand. She had to see which one of her accounts caused such a bewitching reaction in him. Hungry to identify him, she pushed her long brown hair out of her eyes to get a look, and then gazed at the suspect male model in curiosity.

At first she thought she had made a mistake and this wasn't one of her clients for one simple reason. It appeared to be a woman's portrait. Doing a quick double take to focus on his features, she remembered who it was. Ian Sullivan, fresh from the United Kingdom and hoping to make it here in the United States. All his stats were on his compcard. Six feet tall, one hundred and seventy-five pounds, brown hair, green eyes, twenty-one years of age, shirt size seventeen, waist thirty-two, inseam thirty-six, shoe size ten and a half.

After refreshing her memory with those notes, kicking in the brain cells to recall him completely, she found her brother's very odd expression.

"Wha-at?" She flapped the photo at him. "Hello? Scott to earth!" She thought it was hilarious, his blank stare, his expressionless void, and his refusing to comment either way. Scott was such an easy target to get a reaction from. Some days a simple good-morning would churn up a 'what's good about it?' And now? This guy was rendered speechless? Impossible!

The door buzzer scared the heck out of both of them. Famished, he hopped up on his feet like the floor was on fire and answered the door.

As Scott dug out his wallet and searched for cash, Claire became mesmerized by Ian's lovely face. It was that long hair of his—down to his shoulders—and those fine delicate features that set him apart. Ian Sullivan looked like a gorgeous young woman in that photo. Intrigued by his dark long eyelashes and full pout, Claire sighed at how impossible Ian was to categorize.

Because of it, she had a miserable time placing him. Pretty men were only just making a comeback, and one this exceptionally lovely would scare the prospective advertising agencies to tears. "*No, no,*" she could hear them now, "*We want someone rugged. A man's man—*" How many times had she heard that lame excuse when she had some fantastic male beauty to share? It was hard to be sympathetic when no one was willing to admit these fantastic males existed. They were not the stuff of fairy tales. They actually were flesh and blood and she wanted to show them off!

The tantalizing aroma of shrimp fried rice and sweet and sour chicken filled her senses. As Scott carried the bags to the table, she motivated herself to get up off the floor and help him. Digging through the silverware drawer noisily, she found two pairs of chopsticks, then dropped some napkins on the table.

Once they settled in and were stuffing food into their starving mouths, she asked, "Did you think he was attractive?"

"Who? The delivery guy?"

She snickered to herself; the boy was so transparent it was sad. "Who!" she laughed.

"Oh…you mean that guy in the photo…him… Uh, he was sort of attractive."

"Is that right?" she smirked.

Anger flashed quickly in his brown eyes. "I still wouldn't

want to fuck him!"

She let it go without an argument simply because it wasn't the first time she had teased Scott about his sexual preference. And, well, why not? He never stayed with a woman for longer than a few months, and they were all the same exact type. Empty-headed blonde bimbos. It almost was as if he hated them but felt obligated to keep one around for show.

"You fit the damn profile! Single, cute, built, and an actor! Hello!"

"Shut up!" he growled defensively. With his pout directed back on his fried rice and chopsticks, Claire just smiled in satisfaction. It was rather callous of her to push his buttons. Their dad always had that job. And he did it so well.

Later that evening for no apparent reason, she awoke. Checking the alarm clock by her bed, she read the time. Four fifteen a.m. Annoyed she had woken up, she decided to go and relieve herself since now that she was up it would be all she was thinking about. After that task, she heard a noise in the living area. The apartment was twenty floors above the traffic, so the sounds of the sleepless Manhattan streets didn't affect it in the least.

Peering into the dimness of the living room, she was surprised to find Scott, who suffered with chronic insomnia, seated on the couch. Her briefcase had been rifled through and a photo removed and placed in his hot little hand.

As he sat in his Jockey briefs, reminding her to call them about a model she had in mind, she knew whom he had in his hand. But she was speechless.

Wanting to genuinely embarrass him was out of the question, so she ducked out of sight and crawled once again into bed. As she curled the blankets around her, she strained to listen to the movements outside her door, trying to hear when he would go back to his room to sleep.

What the hell was Scott doing staring at a picture of Ian? Was he gay after all? Was he daydreaming about meeting him? Thinking about masturbating over him? Or maybe just fascinated by a boy who looked so androgynous? It was all very intriguing. She thought she knew her brother inside and out.

Her ears perked and alert, as if she were a little child frightened of ghosts, she pulled the sheets over her head, afraid to find out some hidden truth. But when she thought about the implications, an ironic smile emerged on her lips. She would find out. Oh, yes. She would find out.

Chapter Two

Taking a cab the ten blocks to her office on Fifth Avenue, she checked the time on her Cartier tank watch over and over and couldn't have told you the hour if you had asked. When the elevator doors opened, the glass-encased offices of Spencer & Epstein Modeling Agency appeared. Her sensible leather Joan and David shoes trod over the unobtrusive mauve colored carpets past potted ferns and molded plastic chairs. She barely nodded to Tara, the receptionist, as the girl waved messages in front of her like she was a sinking ship with SOS signals. Claire knew exactly how she felt.

Gripping the handful of paper as she passed by, she slapped down her armload on her desk and threw her Tuscany hand-made leather coat on a chair by the wall. The sun was dazzling at the moment as the span of windows revealed the rest of the towering frozen city of glass, concrete, and metal—a contrast to her last view of the Cascade Mountain range. This was her new mountain view; she would announce proudly, adding with a twinkle to her eye, but with a lot less green. Since the Twins fell, only the Empire State Building seemed important. And the sight of it made her glad she wasn't staring at the tacky Space Needle in Seattle any longer.

The moment her partner, Jenine Spencer entered her office, the phone rang. Claire shouted to her secretary to grab it, and then shut the door for privacy. Jenine looked smart in her tight business skirt and blazer, while Claire preferred slacks and a button down top.

"I have to make some calls. You got anyone for Felix Nicholls at Jaguar?" Jenine always seemed as if she were running on a treadmill. The earth kept spinning, but she never made any progress. Her movements were so quick you could imagine dust and bobby pins flying off of her from the centrifugal force.

"Yes…hang on…a handful." Opening her briefcase, Claire dumped out the contents like her desk was a construction site and the papers a pile of rubble. Sorting through the files haphazardly, she handed some to her. "Top one is the best."

Opening it for a peek, Jenine nodded. "Right…next … Calvin?"

"Long shot, but I don't know where else to send him." She hunted for Ian's photo.

The phone rang again and was automatically transferred to her secretary; both women lost their train of thought wondering who it was.

As Claire double-checked her briefcase in confusion, she had a sudden thought about the file. "Son of a bitch."

"What? You forget something?"

"No, I think my brother snagged one of my photos." She sorted once again through the pile she had placed on her desk. The heap expanded in girth but still didn't give up its mystery.

"Scott? What for?" Jenine let out a sarcastic laugh.

Almost blurting out the reason, Claire bit her lip. "Uh, I think I'll just check with Ben and see if he has a few extra copies."

"Okay. Who are you sending them?"

"Ian Sullivan."

"Which one's he?" She leaned to look at the mess on the desk even after Claire had told her he wasn't there.

"Pretty one, long brown hair, English."

"Hmmm, I didn't see that one. How pretty? Calvin isn't doing that right now. Back to brawn I'm afraid."

"I know, I just thought this one had something special."

"You see him in just his briefs?"

"No, his body shot was with slacks, but great suggestion!" Claire's smile broadened at the thought.

As Jenine headed out, she yelled, "If you're sending him to Calvin, get a look at him first! You don't want any ugly surprises!"

"No problem! The one thing I can count on with that gem is his beauty!" Claire laughed to herself, *'God, I love this job'*. After Jenine had gone, she sat down, inhaled deeply, and rechecked her briefcase. That damn head shot photo was not there.

Having managed to get through the morning of setting up interviews and getting packets together to mail out, she had a salad delivered and ate at her desk. After sipping some of her preferred bottle of Buxton water, she dialed Ian's number. He was staying temporarily at a hotel.

"You're there!" She was stunned he answered the phone and checked the time again mechanically.

"So I am! Hullo, Miss Epstein."

Even his voice was charming and enthusiastic. "Stop it! Claire! Call me Claire! Just because you have an accent doesn't mean you have to be formal."

"Yes, I'm sorry. Claire. Do you have anything for me?"

"I was thinking of sending you to Calvin. You mind underwear?"

"No. Not in the least. I've been seen in my pants before, I assure you."

"Lovely. But, before I send you to them, I do need you to

11

come in and…"

"Show you what's under the jeans?"

"Oh, not only are you gorgeous, you're clever."

"You want me now?"

"Yes. I'd love to get you there tomorrow, but I want you to go with the right photograph in your hand."

"Brilliant! Give me as much time as it takes to grab a cab."

"Good boy! I'll reimburse you!"

"See you soon, Miss Epstein!" he said, with a very sly laugh.

She hung up the phone, smiling wickedly. That damn English accent. It was so frickin' endearing she wanted to die. Regaining control, taking another bite of her chicken Caesar, she actually felt a warm flush up her neck and cheeks thinking about him. Very unusual. When people asked her how she felt about working with the most beautiful men in the world, she compared it to working in a chocolate factory. Think of having eaten so much chocolate you were sick to death of it. Then one day someone comes in with a strawberry and you're so relieved it's not another truffle, you cry.

A tap on her door followed and she raised her chin to see Scott peering in shyly. He came to her office occasionally, if for no other reason than for the agency to remember he existed and to keep him in mind constantly for jobs. "Scott!"

"Oh, you've already eaten. I thought we could get together for lunch."

"Yeah, sorry. I'm swamped. I couldn't have gotten out anyway. Here, you want some?" She held out the bowl.

He moved across the room and eyed her meal. "Caesar?"

"Yeah, not half bad. Try it." Knowing he'd eat just about anything imaginable, she handed him a plastic fork as he took off his coat and sat down in front of her desk. "Guess who's coming in for photo shoot…in his undies," she smirked, as she scrutinized his features.

"Dunno, who?"

"Your favorite Spencer & Epstein icon. Ian."

"Ian who?" He became involved in the art of consuming lettuce leaves covered in heavy dressing.

"Oh, come on...remember that guy last night that you found in my photos? Scott, don't play stupid, it doesn't suit you."

Eating the salad faster than she thought humanly possible, it was down to a scrappy piece of dressing covered limp greens in seconds. "Why should I care who the fuck's coming in? For Christ's sake, Claire, I'm not fucking gay!"

She moved around her desk to sit on it and stare at him. Smug written all over her, she folded her arms across her chest and watched him as it seemed he was making sure he ate every possible bit of food in the bowl and ignoring her. She said, "I know you're not gay. But! If a boy that pretty got on his knees and said—"

He stopped hunting for more food in an empty bowl and snarled, "I still wouldn't have a guy suck my cock!"

"No?"

"Christ, Claire, would you let another woman go down on you? Especially if she looked like a guy?"

Flinching involuntarily at the thought, she shouted, "It isn't the same. Women who look like guys are ugly. This boy is very attractive."

"So, you're saying you would let a pretty woman munch on you?"

He was trapping her with her own logic. Her first instinct was to cringe and shake her head in revulsion, and he knew it. So, she covered for herself, and said, "Well, I wouldn't kick Madonna out of my bed."

"Oh, give me a break. You're so full of shit." He tossed the empty bowl into the trash and then hunted for more food. The roll was next in line for ravenous consumption.

"Okay, look…" She headed back to her chair, leaned across the mass of paperwork, and said to him, "Just for fun I thought you might want to sit in on his shoot."

Something mysterious sparked inside him. She saw it as well as felt it.

The roll being bitten and swallowed as quickly as the salad, he raised his head as casually as he could and managed to get out between chews, "Can people do that?"

"No, *people* can't. But, you're my brother. Interested?" Knowing he was dying to, she grinned like the Cheshire cat with yellow feathers in her mouth.

She smiled as she watched him taking his time, leisurely looking at the photos of the models on her walls as if he were counting the proper number of seconds in his head to not seem too anxious.

He mumbled, "I—I always wanted to see what you guys did… I mean, it's different when you're in front of a photographers' camera in his studio, and not here at a top agency… I didn't get much out of it from your end of the biz. Only posed, you know, for a few shots…so, ah…" He never once made eye contact with her, and Claire knew he was having trouble making any of this sound convincing.

"Uh huh." *Humor him, yes, humor him.* she thought.

"I have time, I mean, my afternoon is free…unless you or Jenine found something for me—"

"Sorry, babe, not today. You know I look every day…"

"Yeah, I know. I don't expect…" He bowed his head.

"Good, so you'll stay for it?" This was intriguing her to no end, and she had no idea why. What if? What if the right situation arose, the right male appeared…and was willing? For years she had the feeling Scott was too timid to dive in. To admit he may have preferences the other way. The poor man couldn't manage even one successful female relationship. This boy needed a push! She hated to admit the idea absolutely inspired her.

To her knowledge he had never been with a man sexually. Never. Fifi was the typical blonde ditz with big tits. He screwed her. That's what women like that were for. But he couldn't talk to women, relate, communicate, care deeply, and that's where big sister came in. He had no trouble talking to her. But she was non-threatening kin, and not girlfriend material. Could he relate in any deeper sense to a man?

"Is that all you ordered for lunch?" He was still scavenging.

"What are you hungry for? I'll have Rachel order something."

"No. Don't bother anyone. I'll be all right till dinner...uh, what are we having?"

"Is food all you think about?"

He laughed shyly like a little boy. "No. Not all..."

As he giggled, she thought about asking him about that missing photo of Ian's when someone tapped at her door.

Rachel stuck her head in to announce, "Ian Sullivan is here."

The minute she said his name, with acute instincts Claire diverted her attention to her brother's reaction. He flinched. It was involuntary and unpreventable, yet completely unmistakable.

"Is he? Wow, he made great time. Tell Bill and Randy to get the studio set up for some full body shots. We'll be right there. Oh," she stared back at her brother again before she purred, "and send him in."

The moment she finished her sentence, Scott jumped to his feet and started wiping his palms on his jeans like they were sweaty and he was at an interview. His focus was on that door, ajar and about to open, and if she had to guess, she would say

15

his heart rate elevated to a rocket launch.

She was stunned.

Both of them were riveted to the gap, and when the door moved, she held her breath. She had met Ian before and thought he was very special, one of those top two percent, but she didn't fall over her tongue. Maybe she was just used to pretty boys.

Scott, on the other hand, wasn't.

When Ian Sullivan stepped into her office, she was so annoyed she had to be polite and address him properly, when all she really wanted to do was be a fly on the wall and watch her brother's unbelievable behavior.

"Miss Epstein!" His wonderful smile warmed her instantly as he nodded and went to reach out to shake her hand. "So, we meet again!"

He was tall and sleek and marvelous. His photo didn't do a thing to communicate his amazing aura of sex appeal. "Yes, my dear, and you made excellent time."

"Ran the whole way!" His tongue firmly planted in his cheek he let a chuckle escape. She thought it was completely in character for his shining little boy smile.

"And didn't break a sweat!" She winked.

"Well, I didn't want my pants to stick, you know." He pretended to be bashful suddenly, then seemed to notice another male was in the room. His emerald green gaze lit up in delight.

Meanwhile, Scott was mute. He hadn't taken his eyes off Ian since he strut in. When Claire could, she finally introduced them. "This is my brother, Scott. Scott, this is Ian Sullivan."

They were almost the same height. Scott had him by two inches. The most noticeable difference was the length of their hair. Scott's was more conservative, neatly cut, very thick and full on top, but not too short by any means. Ian's was so long and shining, it flowed down his shoulders in shimmering waves, like the women in the Pantene commercials.

"Brother? I see!" Ian reached out for Scott's clammy hand.

"Cheers, mate. Do you model?"

Covering her mouth with her hand to hide her perverse grin and stifle what was fast becoming a hysterical laughing fit, she stared at her brother in amazement as he stammered and shied away from Ian's curious gaze. Never, and she repeated in her head, *never*, had she seen Scott act that way in her life with another man, or woman, for that matter.

"I...uh...I do...model...some acting...a little...you? Oh, that's stupid, duh...never mind." No cliché gesture was lost on him. Stuttering, kicking his shoe into the carpet, fussing with his hands, rocking side to side. He was the picture of frayed nerves.

And in contrast, boldly confident, Ian stood still and firm. "Lucky you to have a sis in the business... You must be swamped with work."

"No, actually, not swamped." Meeting Ian's eye finally, Scott seemed to melt. Claire imagined he'd lose his outer shape, his spine weakening, and fall to the floor like a bowl of pudding.

"I don't see why not. You're fabulous. Don't you think your brother is fabulous?" Ian leaned back as if to appraise Scott's virtues.

Scott chuckled awkwardly, "God, I love your accent!"

Both Ian and Claire exchanged surprised looks. In moments, Ian burst out laughing and twisted away from his bewildered gaze.

"What?" Scott's cheeks were burning red. "What? Did I say something stupid?"

"No, mate..." Ian tried to recover, "Just that all you yanks say that!"

"All right, we can socialize later." Though she was enjoying every minute of this tête-à-tête, they had work to do after all. "Come, gentlemen, this way."

As she led them out of her office, Ian turned back to Scott to ask, "Are you coming to watch the shoot?"

"Uh, yeah, you mind? I don't have to. I just thought it would be interesting—"

"No, I don't mind a bit." He softened his features and gave Scott a charming smile.

As if he weren't red enough, Scott's blush deepened from the attention.

The spotlights were already on making the tiny room an oven. With the windows concealed with white canvas, and another matching canvas covering the back wall, the studio seemed as sterile as an operating room. Adding to that the clutter of cameras, lighting umbrellas, spots, stools, and humans, the E.R. ambiance continued to prevail. Not to mention, the one appearing about to be surgically opened seemed to be Scott, not Ian. Claire shouted for someone to turn on the air conditioning and then sorted through some packs of Calvin's underwear. "Large, my dear?" she seductively hissed, giving him a wicked smile.

With her brother hiding behind everyone else, she heard Ian's laugh. "Of course!"

"Oh, this ought to be good," Randy quipped sarcastically as he checked out his camera and then the lighting once more.

"Shush, photographers are to be seen and not heard," she scolded him. Handing Ian a pair of new briefs, she pointed to a changing room, which was nothing more than a large closet with a full-length mirror. He nodded in understanding and disappeared into it.

When he was out of sight, she found Scott ducking and diving to keep from being seen. "You don't have to hide! Come here!" She waved him to some high stools behind Randy's tripod.

"I don't want to be in the way." His hands were deep in his pockets. Mouthy Scott was turning into a shy introvert before her eyes.

"You're not. Sit down, silly." She bopped his head with the empty underwear box.

More self-conscious than she had ever seen him, Scott managed to sit in a chair like he was the size of a peanut. It was getting more and more bizarre.

As they waited and Randy fussed with his camera lens, Ian made his grand entrance and strut boldly before the small group like none of this mattered to him. Claire knew if she were in *her* undies in front of six strangers, she would at least blush.

"Okay, Randy, dear, he's all yours." As if she were leading the orchestra, she waved dramatically, then sat next to Scott and tilted her body so she could watch both the action and him simultaneously. At this point Scott was all knotted up. His legs and arms were crossed, and his head was tilted down, as if he were averting his eyes from the very reason they were all there.

When she gazed back up at Ian, he was trying very hard not to burst out laughing.

"What now?" she shouted, almost in exasperation.

"Did you call him 'Randy'?" He pointed rudely at her cameraman.

"Yes, dear." She tried to be calm and see the significance.

"Rrrrandy!!" Ian said, as if he was an engine turning over, and he couldn't stop laughing.

By now the real Randy was getting upset. "What's the deal?"

"Alright, I'm alright, I'll stop laughing..." Ian tried to put on a straight face, but little giggles kept slipping out.

His laughter was catching. Scott started to chuckle for no reason.

"Stop it!" she hissed at him.

"I can't help it," he laughed and then covered his mouth.

"Okay, stand straight, arms to the sides!" Randy shouted, trying to get the job done.

As Ian settled down and obeyed his command, Scott and Claire relaxed and began to enjoy it. The moment Ian's face grew calm, he shook back his hair and thrust out his pelvis. Claire's eyes widened in delight. "Oh, my fucking god."

Scott shifted uncomfortably and ignored her comment about Ian's obvious protruding bulge.

"You are hung like a horse, sweetie!" She couldn't resist voicing her thoughts.

Checking his own crotch curiously, Ian said, "No, you think so?"

"Stand straight!" Randy shouted in irritation.

"All right, Rrrrrrandy!!" Ian burst out laughing and Claire couldn't help but crack up with laughter.

Scott was rolling in hilarity, wiping his eyes.

"This is costing money, Claire!" Randy reminded her of something she usually yelled herself.

"Yes, I know! My money. Come on, Ian, try and think of something else."

"Sorry…" Instantly turning on his professionalism, his focus became distant, his features passive, and he relaxed again.

As the camera whirred, she leaned over to Scott, and whispered, "Well? Isn't he amazing?"

He shrugged, but he never took his eyes off him.

As the sun dimmed over the skyscrapers, it threw elongated shadows across the frosty streets. December was only a quarter of the way through and the threat of snow came blaring from every radio station. Claire was thinking of packing up and calling it a day when Rachel asked her if she would mind taking one more phone call. Nodding she would, she lifted the receiver.

"Ms. Epstein, Harold Lewis from *Men's World* magazine…"

"Yes, Harold, what can I do for you?"

"What have you got for me that I can use on the cover of my next issue? I need a good set of abs ASAP."

"No problem. Any other specifications?"

"The usual, twenties, good looking, clean shaven...obviously fit."

"I'll make some calls. You want their photos and comps first?"

"Please. If you can get a few together. I'll phone you if I think one is suitable."

As she scribbled on a pad she nodded. "Great, first thing tomorrow."

Hanging up the phone, she made her notes more legible, and then mulled over some likely candidates. Her brother sprang into her mind for that one.

A smile played across her lips as she recalled the events of the day. After the shoot with Ian, they gathered again in her office. As part of her little experiment, she deliberately kept quiet, letting the men get better acquainted. Ian, being more assertive, asked her brother question after question about his experiences interviewing and going out on casting calls. And her brother was happy to share his limited information with one who had none.

As the two of them communicated, they forgot momentarily she was in the room. Male bonding in action. She had to admit something to herself she didn't want to admit; at first she was amused, watching them, then something darker managed to sneak in. Jealousy. Finding that emotion completely absurd, she put it into a compartment in her brain that was the equivalent of the recycle bin on a computer screen. Then hit delete.

Clicking back to the present, and her exhaustion, she decided she had enough ringing telephones for the day. Packing a handful of likely candidates to send out to the numerous clients who were hungry to prepare for their spring catalogues, she crammed the leather case full and then grabbed her coat.

Passing by Jenine's office, Claire noticed her blonde head was bowed over her desk, exposing suspiciously darker roots, the phone on her ear, Jenine still pecking away at her 'to do' list. When she heard Claire come in, she signaled for her to wait one minute with her index finger.

Claire nodded and sat on one of the cozy brown leather chairs in front of Jenine's desk, eavesdropping in on her conversation. Jenine handled mainly the commercial and television contacts, while Claire handled everything else. After her usual assurances to whomever she was speaking with over the phone, she hung up and made a face at Claire, indicating she was exhausted.

"Go home!" Claire shouted at her playfully.

"I am..." Pushing her hair back from her forehead she seemed to be remembering something. "Oh!! You wouldn't believe what I need next."

"A hot bath and a massage?" Claire smirked.

"Yes, but that's not essential..."

"Bull shit...but, go on..."

"I got this call from Andre Surah at Minty Fresh Gum..."

"Yes?"

"They want me to provide two males to do a kissing scene. The first gay kiss in a commercial! I swear I almost died. Gum advertising... Don't you love this business?"

A flash of brilliance washed across Claire's face. She sat up eagerly, leaned on Jenine's desk, and asked, "What are they looking for?"

Surprised at her partner's enthusiastic interest, Jenine rummaged around, finding her notes obviously amused by this whole advertising concept. Finally locating the correct piece of paper, she read, "One male with long hair, any color, pretty, the other, attractive but more masculine, short hair, all American—"

The Kiss

Cutting her off, Claire gushed, "Oh, Christ, it is too fucking perfect!" She sat back in the chair, her briefcase still on her lap, her coat crunched around her and beamed at Jenine in amazement.

"You perve."

"No! Jenine! Let me pick the models. Please! I know it's your thing, but, for me. This one favor!"

Slanting her eyes suspiciously, she leaned over the desk to her and whispered, "What are you up to?"

"Trust me. Can you do that? Please?" She was begging. If she had to get onto her hands and knees she would.

"Claire Epstein, what on earth!? You have to at least tell me!"

"No! Yes! Oh, my god, it's perfect!" Something inside her was jumping wildly. It was as if fate had a momentous event in mind and she was simply the messenger.

Sitting mute, Jenine's eyes widened as she gazed at this woman in wonder. And all the while, Claire couldn't wait to put her plan into action.

Chapter Three

While seated in a taxicab, she used her cell phone to call Scott. "I'm on my way home. What are you hungry for?"

"Anything, I'm starved!"

"Well, give me some suggestions. I'm at a loss. My brain is fried."

"Where are you?"

"In a cab, almost home actually, but I can detour him."

"Pizza?"

"You're too easy. Sicilian?"

"Yes!"

"See ya in a bit."

With her grin devious, and about to burst into another laughing fit, she asked the cab driver to stop at Ray's pizzeria first, and then promised him a huge tip if he waited. He actually did.

Balancing the pizza box as she came down the hall, Claire noticed the door to her apartment opened before she even put her key in it. Scott had been waiting, staring out of the peephole.

"Ahh, hungry?" She laughed as he sniffed at the warm box.

"Famished! Damn, that smells good."

As he took it from her grasp, she was able to set her things down and remove her coat.

After he put the pizza on the table, he shouted, "Wine is already poured."

"I love you!" She laughed and joined him, sitting down across from where he had already put out place settings. In complete relief she lifted that glass of wine to her lips, then stopped him before he opened the pizza box and started wolfing the contents.

"What? Claire, I'm starved!" he whined in feigned agony.

"Before you eat, stand up and lift up your shirt for me."

"Shut up. You are so weird."

"You shut up! I am not weird. I got a call from *Men's World* and they want abs on their cover."

He jumped to his feet and raised his shirt, tensing up for her.

"Not bad. I'll send him one of you."

His shirt falling loosely over his jeans again, he went for the pizza with more control than a moment earlier. He gave her an affectionate wink. "You're the best!"

"You know…there are some things coming in that I have been considering you for."

Half of one of the large square pizza slices was already in his mouth when he tried to answer. A mumble of incoherent sounds came out, but she knew what he said.

"Yes! Several things!" she assured him.

Barely chewing, swallowing quickly, he faced her with a very serious expression. "What things?"

The excitement in him was palpable. It was as if he were jumping up and down in his seat, though he wasn't moving a muscle.

"A television commercial. How's your acting class?"

"Oh, god! Really? Claire, you're not shitting me?"

"Look, that acting class you had at Juilliard, do they teach you to play all sorts of roles?" She nibbled her pizza carefully, for under the cheese was steaming hot sauce and she hated getting those annoying skin flaps on the roof of her mouth from burning it. As kids they used to call them 'winkies'. She had no clue why.

He set his slice down and glared at her. "What? Am I in some gorilla suit?"

"No! Oh, god, no. They will see you. No costume."

"What's the product?"

"Gum. Minty Gum."

"Gum?" He deflated. "Oh, well, sure, why not." His eating resumed.

She let it sink in. It was obvious he was imagining the shoot. Unwrapping the gum and smiling as he chewed. Some classic version of what had been done decades before. When he went for his second slice of pizza she laid down more land mines. "Though it sounds like some dull ad, it could get you noticed."

Flapping the box closed to keep the pie warm, he let out a sarcastic chuckle. "Yeah, right. I'm sure Tom Cruise's big break came after advertising gum."

"It's a very controversial ad." Lifting her wine to her mouth, she was so close to that laughing fit again she had to bite her lip painfully. The one thing her brother wanted was fame. And for the last three years, though he had clawed and scratched for a piece of it, he got nothing, and now even the ads were few and far between. In his mind she knew he would do anything, or at least almost anything he needed to do to get that lucky break.

"Controversial how?"

"It's a kiss."

"So? Kissing in gum commercials is common!" He began consuming once again.

"Not this kind of kiss."

It dawned on him finally. "No... Oh, come on, Claire!"

"Look, it's one of those once in a lifetime deals where it is so risqué that everyone will be talking about it. You will get noticed. Of that I assure you."

He threw his food down in disgust and cried, "Everyone will think I'm a fag!"

"Not necessarily. Look at all the leading actors who played gay characters and aren't gay! No one can assume that!"

Lifting the slice back up, staring at the grease dripping off the cheesy pizza, he was thinking seriously about it. She only needed to add one more tantalizing detail.

"Oh, and the other guy...the one you're meant to kiss..." Seeing him holding his breath in disgust, she knew he waited as visions of fat, smelly beasts flashed through his head. "I was considering sending them Ian."

The look on his face was worth everything she owned. If she thought she would shock him, she had. After digesting what she had said, he tried not to be obvious with his thoughts or expectations. As casually as he could, he tilted his head to her and replied, "This is all just a gag to wind me up, right?"

As she refilled her wine glass she kept smugly silent, grinning like she knew damn well it was real, and so did he.

When she didn't answer, he ended up releasing a long exhaled stress-filled breath. "Sis, I have no idea what you're playing at...but, if this is true...then yes, I'll do it."

"I thought you just might." Her grin widened.

"But I'm not gay!" he added quickly.

"No, of course you're not." She smiled, a devilish twinkle to her eye.

She couldn't sleep that night. Half of her felt like a demon and an instigator, which was nothing new. She had been her whole life. The other half, an angel for salvaging his career and possibly opening a new door in his life. And as she tried to sleep, both tiny creatures were doing battle against each other in her head.

Lying on her bed, thinking of how they made a one-office business into a Fifth Avenue high-rise mega-company with a list of almost five hundred male models and a thousand ad agencies to send them to, she was astonished. But where there was a niche, there had to be a market. And there was. Female beauty was done to death. Almost to the point of exhaustion. But dominant male beauty was only big in Italy and Greece. In the U.S. and U.K markets, men were invisible. It was about time retailers realized that pretty men sold to women more, (the greatest consumers), gay men, (the ones with the disposable incomes), and to heterosexual men as well. Don't even mention the young adult female market. They clipped and hung almost every ad they supplied a model for. The demand for posters and calendars was another spin-off of their success. It was as if all of a sudden advertising agencies remembered men existed. And not just fat ugly caricatures of men, like they used to use. Non-threatening beasts, which they never realized turned everyone off their product. Suddenly pretty men were the rage. And thanks to Spencer & Epstein, these men were being paid six figure salaries. It was a lovely time to be where they were.

Tossing and turning all night with all this mash in her head, she had no idea Scott was enduring the same punishment. Insomnia ran in their family. Their dad had it and so did they. It was a punishing genetic defect. Not as obvious a trait as a big nose or large hips, but brutal none the less.

Sweating from the thermostat being too high for his liking, Scott shoved the blankets off and punched the pillows, angry he could not sleep. Peeking at the clock, he rubbed his face and yawned. With his eyes closed, he searched the dark room with the slatted blind covered windows for his desk. On top of that desk sat a folder. Inside that folder was a photo.

The Kiss

Blinking open his lids, visually checking the door and the secure lock, he spun his legs around to the floor to find the carpet under his soles. Then naked, as he always slept, he walked to that desk and flapped back the folder. He was crazy to take it. She would know it was missing. Why did he snag it?

Lifting it to admire, the dim moonlight not nearly enough to see by, he flipped on the lamp on his desk and squinted at the sudden rush to his irises. When he could bear the glare, he opened his eyes. He just could not get over it. That photo. Fuck. The man was unbelievable.

And in his head he could still hear that contagious laughter and that attractive accent. But, he wasn't gay! This is just some idle curiosity. Some weird fascination with the 'dark side'. Yeah, that's all.

About to set it down again, he paused to check one last thing. Those lips. They were full and parted as if they were inhaling a rose-scented breath. Did he want to kiss those lips? He simply didn't know what he wanted. That was the problem. Life was a never-ending string of confusion and denial. It just never seemed to turn out the way he had envisioned it years ago. By now, at the age of twenty-five, he was supposed to be an actor in Hollywood. A name they all knew. Maybe people would recognize him on the street when he passed. He'd attend movie premiers with a starlet on his arm. That's what it was supposed to be about. Not living with his sister, broke and anonymous. Why didn't things in life ever go as planned?

Chapter Four

"Morning, Scottchula!" Claire warmed the croissants in the toaster oven. "Help yourself!"

As he scuffed his feet, his plaid terry cloth robe covering his nakedness, his hair pointed and spiked from a bad night, he collapsed onto a chair at the table and stared off at nothingness.

"You need to look sharp, my love. Interview with Mr. Minty Gum."

"Coffee," he mumbled and pushed back from the table with an effort to get himself a cup.

She averted her eyes and cringed as he went by. "Wear some fucking underwear. I don't need to see my brother's balls."

"Yeah, yeah, you probably liked it," he chuckled as he poured coffee into his favorite Yankees' mug.

"What's with you today? You feel okay?"

"Slept like shit." He scuffed back to the table, sat down, and stuffed a croissant into his mouth.

"Join the club. Still, you should try to look your best."

"How long have I got?" He checked the cow pattern clock over the kitchen counter.

"Half hour."

"Right." He inhaled the food and downed the coffee. She

had never seen anyone eat as quickly as he did. No matter how much bigger his portions were than hers, he was always done first. The boy took amazingly large bites.

"Shit." She just remembered she needed to call Ian. Rummaging through her purse for her electronic address book, she found his number and sat on the couch to dial. After it rang five times, she was beginning to get discouraged. Just when she was about to hang up, he answered, out of breath.

"Uh oh, bad time?"

"No, I was just in the shower! Glad I heard it. Is this about the Calvin shoot?"

"No. I haven't heard back on that yet. We did get the photo out in the afternoon mail, so they will get it this morning...shit, unless this Christmas rush fucks it up, oh well, never mind. I have something else to offer you."

"Do you? You're brilliant! I knew you were the best in New York. What have you got for me, Miss Epstein?"

"Well, it's only a possibility, but it's a commercial for gum."

She heard him laugh at the disappointment. It didn't sound very impressive from the description. But she knew the secret. "Look, it's better than it sounds. Meet me in my office at nine-thirty, and we'll be at the interview by ten. Got it? Oh, shave close, leave your hair loose, don't put it in a ponytail or anything, and wear a button down shirt, two top buttons open. Oh, and tight black slacks. Got it?"

"All this for chewing gum?"

"Trust me. Will you do that, gorgeous?"

"I will do that, Miss Epstein. See you at half past nine."

As she hung up, she pictured him naked and dripping wet. Shame on her.

Seated in a dirty salt and mud stained cab, her attention

was on Scott as he stared out of the window at all the rainbow colored lights and decorative window displays down Broadway's overwhelmingly crowded width. Costumed Santas rang their bells at storefronts as children gathered at Macy's to watch the animated snow scenes.

"Penny for your thoughts?" she whispered, though she could guess. Three letters came into her mind. I-A-N.

"Hmmm?" She could tell he was a million miles away.

"You okay? You still feeling crappy after last night's insomnia?" She touched his knee with her black leather gloved hand. His leg had been moving up and down in almost a manic gesture of nervousness.

"Yeah, fine."

"Look, if this is stressing you out too much—"

With his teeth bared, he cut her off with a curt, "It isn't!" then she could see he regretted his tone immediately. She was his ally, after all. "Look, it's been a while since I interviewed for anything live. I've done nothing since California, and I don't even count those stupid extra rolls. It's just normal nerves. I don't want to fuck it up."

"You won't. Will you trust me?"

Clasping his hand over her glove, he gave it a squeeze and then lost himself out of the window once more.

When they arrived at her office, Ian was already there, seated in the lobby flipping pages of a magazine anxiously. Heeding her advice to a tee, he was the picture of loveliness; soft, alluring, and very appealing. As she stood near him, Claire could tell Scott's mouth went dry instantly, and getting him to talk was impossible until they were all in the cab together.

As they rode to Park Avenue in the light snow, Ian's electric excitement was contagious.

"The two of us? Chewing gum? Fancy that!" he laughed.

Scott glared at Claire through slanted eyes. "He doesn't know?"

32

"Ah, no. I was going to tell him on the ride there."

Giving up a loud sigh and scratching his chin in anxiety, Scott once again gazed out beyond the foggy condensation dripping down the backseat windows to the frigid streets.

"Sorry? What don't I know?" Ian asked, rubbing his hands together for warmth.

"It's a kissing scene. A chewing gum ad with a kiss." She smiled impishly.

"All right…"

"Well, supposedly, you will be kissing each other." She waited, grinning at him. The cab driver's bushy-eyebrow-gaze darted to the rear view mirror when he overheard.

"Wha-at?" Ian was laughing. "You're taking the piss!"

Not making eye contact with a soul, Scott was trying hard to disappear, curling over himself to hide, his hand still covering his mouth, his glazed stare still out of the window.

As he looked from Claire to her brother, Ian's smile dropped from his face. "I'm supposed to kiss him? In an advert for gum? Are you certain?"

"Well, that's the premise. I don't know the details. That's what we're going to find out."

With his hands clasped and dangling loosely between his tight slacks covered thighs, he glimpsed first at Claire, then at Scott.

Scott never met his eye.

"Will you do it?" Claire asked. It never occurred to Claire he wouldn't.

He opened his mouth to reply, but never did. Claire wondered if he was trying to get his thoughts to come out correctly and not speak before he had the chance to decide.

"Look, it's very controversial and I thought the two of you would be spotted because of it. I've been in this business for over ten years and I know controversy sells and gets publicity."

"But, what kind of publicity is good for us?" Ian asked more seriously than she expected.

"Any kind, my love. Remember Hugh Grant and the hooker? Come now, trust me."

They finally looked at each other. Claire thought it was an odd exchange. Almost as if they were trading sympathies.

Finally, Scott said flatly, "She knows this business."

"I reckon she does," Ian agreed reluctantly.

A shiver passed over Ian's length, Claire assumed from the freezing air coming in through the driver's cracked open window. The bitterness of the temperature was something Ian was struggling with. He had mentioned to her he hated the cold.

"Hey, neither of you have gotten the part yet. Let's take it one step at a time. This is a simple interview and we just don't know what the guy is looking for. Maybe once he lays down the script and storyboard, we'll understand it better and can make a more informed decision. Okay?"

Suddenly, to her confusion, they exchanged wicked little boy smiles. Ian turned back to her and said, "Yes, Miss Epstein."

"Good. Now shut up and let me do the talking."

When the cab parked out in front of the building, she thought both men were going to be sick. Their nerves were shattered, and she didn't think it was because of the kiss. She believed it was just the stress of the interview and wanting something you didn't yet have in your clammy frozen hand. After paying the driver, she stood on the sidewalk and fussed with Ian's hair and Scott's shirt collar. As they stood side by side, allowing her to take control and make decisions for them, which was her job, she couldn't help but see them as a pair. Almost as a couple. An eerie chill ran up her spine. The fact that they looked perfect, absolutely beautiful together and seemed to compliment each other's appearance, was astounding. Thinking she had gone mad at that mind-bending image, she shook it off as nothing more than the icy draft that screamed painfully between skyscrapers.

"Let's go, men, onward and upward." She led the charge into the lobby, where they checked the names on the wall directory to make sure they had the correct information. As they ascended to the tenth floor, Ian kept giggling in spurts. Unfortunately it was spreading like the flu. "Stop it!" Claire shouted, stifling her own laughing fit.

Bowing his head at being scolded, he stared down at his shoes, only to attempt to polish them better on the backs of his black trouser legs. They were gleaming already, so it was more out of nerves than necessity.

When the doors opened, she read all the walls of names as they displayed their companies proudly. Minty Gum seemed odd near all the architects and accountants.

The two hovering behind her in mortal panic, she advanced like a general from the cavalry to the receptionist and announced boldly, "Claire Epstein, director of Spencer & Epstein Modeling Agency. I have an appointment with Mr. Surah."

"Yes, have a seat and I'll let him know you're here."

Spinning around to the dynamic duo that were standing idly, hands in pockets, weight shifting from one leg to the other, looking at the photos of gum ads on the walls, she nodded for them to sit down. They both seemed unreasonably tense, but like good little pups, they sat on command.

"Look at you two! It isn't the last time you'll get a chance at something! If it doesn't work out, I'll find you another! Calm down!"

"I need a valium." Scott shivered in anxiety.

"Yes, please…" Ian laughed nervously.

"Your job is to look the part. If you're a quivering mass of nerves, you will not impress him. Now, pull yourselves together." Waiting as if she expected some dramatic change in them suddenly, she added, "If you don't fall on your faces, I'll buy you both a lobster dinner."

Like Pavlov's dog, she could see Scott's mouth started watering as Ian's eyes widened in surprise at the generous offer.

"You're the best, Miss Epstein."

"Christ, you make me sound like I'm your kindergarten teacher. Stop calling me that!"

"You don't look like my teacher." He grinned invitingly at her, then tilting to Scott, he whispered in confidence, "They were all nuns."

Before either she or her brother was able to give him a quick retort, they were called into an office.

The secretary had them seated in a conference room and offered coffee. Claire rejected the offer for all of them. They were tense enough as it was, not needing a caffeine buzz, and just asked the woman for water. She nodded and went to attend that task.

As they sat silently, toes and fingers tapping irritatingly around her, she caught sight of a storyboard with a sheet of paper hiding the contents. Biting her lip and checking the door, she snuck to it and lifted the corner.

Her heart jumped into her throat as the door opened and Mr. Surah came in with his water-toting secretary behind him.

Spinning around and regaining her composure, she shook his hand and introduced him to her two studs.

The look on his face when he caught sight of them was enough to tell her she didn't do half bad. As she jabbered on about how perfect they were for the parts, she slid their photographs and compcards in front of him casually, explaining the virtues of her two charming models and their professionalism and reliability.

Balding and Middle Eastern in descent, his dark eyes lit up mischievously.

Claire sat down finally, trying not to act as nervous as the silent sentries behind her, and asked, "Now, what exactly are they expected to do?"

The excitement in his face when he rose up to flip the concealing cover from the cartoon board was as if this were show-and-tell time in nursery school. "It's a wonderful little story. You see here, we have the first man," he gestured to Scott, "coming into a movie theater with his girlfriend. They sit, the room gets dark."

Claire glimpsed back as two sets of wide eyes followed his pointed finger as he moved it to the next frame.

"Now," he continued, "man one opens a package of gum and secretly puts it into his mouth to freshen his breath. As his shoulder is turned, his girlfriend leaves to the lady's room."

Through the tail of her eye, she found her brother fidgeting as Ian kept still as stone.

Mr. Surah flipped to the next page of the presentation. "The vacant chair is now being filled in the darkness by man number two." He gestured to Ian. "Man number two and his girlfriend sit down, eyes on the movie screen. Man number one still thinks his girlfriend is sitting there next to him. His long hair is the same length as his girlfriend's." He paused to laugh at Ian and said, "Perfect! So perfect!"

Coming to attention again, Ian shifted in his seat and tried to smile sweetly.

"Now! You see what is next!" He pointed to the storyboard again. "Man one places his hand behind man two's head to bring him for a kiss with his fresh breath. Man two is bewildered until he is kissed. Suddenly, man one realizes it is not his girlfriend, and leans back to gape in amazement. Man two is now smiling sweetly, chewing the gum. The only dialogue is when man two smiles and says, 'Nice'. Meaning, the gum."

"Brilliant!" Claire shouted, clapping her hands in a gesture of applause that was over the top but she didn't care. "I love it! Let me tell you, Mr. Surah, these two models are perfect for it. I assure you, you need not look any further."

Sitting down with them at the table, he rested his elbows on it, leaning toward the two men. Several gold rings came into view distracting them from his words. "I ask you both…"

Acting as if this was a secret classified CIA mission, they mimicked his posture to hear him, very stern expressions on their faces.

"You have no objection to this kiss?" His black marble eyes flitted from one man to the other.

Claire's hand was making its way back up to her smirk. It needed hiding. As she watched the two of them thinking faster than they could possibly speak, it was really all hilarious. But the ad was a winner, anyone could see that.

Scott cleared his throat before he could squeak out a reply while Ian shook his head and said, "No, sir."

"Are they gay?" Mr. Surah asked Claire aside, as if the men couldn't hear him.

Lowering her hand to answer she said, "Does it matter? They're actors!"

Pausing, eyeing them again, he shook his head. "No, it doesn't matter." His attention diverted to their photos and he took a moment to assess them, reading carefully the information on the back and their compcards. It was dead silent as he did. Claire didn't want to keep rambling. The beauty of her men should speak for themselves.

Checking the time, he rose up and said, "Follow me."

They all stood up immediately and the noise of chairs and the rustling of coats drowned out everything else. As he hovered in front of his secretary's desk they tried, but they couldn't overhear what he was discussing with her. Claire kept silent and hoped the boys were behaving behind her back.

"I like you. I want you to sign the contracts."

Having no idea they had made such a strong impression, her eyes widened in surprise. She took the paperwork quickly before he changed his mind. "Can I look these over?"

"Sure, go into my office. Take your time." He nudged her elbow and escorted her to a lush room with leather furniture and an antique desk. The boys followed her in while Mr. Surah shook his head at them, smiling ear to ear.

When the door shut behind them, she gaped at the men in an exaggeration of excitement. "We got it!" she mouthed.

It was hard to tell if they were pleased or too stunned to react. As she let them digest it, she sat down and read the fine print. They were standard contracts and held no secrets. Before she signed them, she wanted last minute assurances so no blame could ricochet back on her. "Okay, boys. You saw the ad. You up for it?"

After a sheepish glimpse at each other and shrugs of indifference, she said, "Look, you wanted to break into television. This is it. You *will* be noticed."

"No kidding!" Scott sneered sarcastically.

Feeling as if they were ungrateful for the opportunity, she was about to get upset. She stood up defiantly and faced them. "Fine. I'll tear it up. He'll have a stream of guys coming in here to be the ones all the fuss is about. Do you have any idea how much press this is going to get? Airtime? Scandal?"

Ian's chest swelled in pride, "I'm ready! Sign me up!"

"Scott?" she asked, trying not to be unreasonably irritated.

"How much?" he asked quietly.

She read over the numbers and then said, "Twenty thousand, split between you and we get twenty percent."

"Okay, I'll do it."

"Gee, good idea." She shook her head, returning his complacency with sarcasm. As she signed her name on the dotted line, she glanced up to see them staring at each other. Possibly they were judging each other's beauty, or their courage. As their focus remained glued to two dazzling sets of eyes, one chocolate brown, the other jade green, she had no idea what thoughts may have been passing through their heads, other than dollar signs, that is.

Chapter Five

As promised she booked a table for three at the Hudson Café. With a spectacular view of the George Washington Bridge's lovely battleship gray cables, lit up gloriously with spotlights and appearing to be an enormous skeletal dinosaur, a very small man in a tuxedo and red bow tie showed them to a table.

After the interview, she had taken them both back to her office to arrange with the studio when they wanted to begin rehearsals. Scott stood by with her on the sidewalk as they gave Ian their cab to get back to the hotel. Waving for another yellow taxi in the freezing snow, Claire managed to get one for Scott quickly to take him home. Both men had been silent the entire drive back to her office. She didn't know what she expected. A thank you would have been nice.

Later that afternoon when she arrived back at the apartment, Scott was napping in bed. It took forever to rouse him and she knew it was because of the lack of sleep the night before. They picked Ian up at his hotel and the three of them where once again back inside a cab on their way to the restaurant. No one had broken the odd silence that had surrounded them. Deep inside some crevasse of her mind, Claire was unnerved by the blank soulless gaze they aimed out into the deepening December evening.

Once seated at the table, the lavender cloth napkins on their laps, Claire tried to be patient as she scanned the menu and craved booze.

"I should get a bottle of wine...you both want wine?" Two tight-lipped, no eye contact nods were all she got. This was getting ridiculous.

Her patience tried to a frazzle, she waited for the waiter to take their wine order and then crossed her arms over her chest angrily. "What the hell's the matter with the two of you? It's a hell of a way to say thank you! What the fuck is wrong with you?"

Scott ran his hand back through his hair nervously.

"Nothing is wrong...not really..." Ian stammered, uncharacteristically nervous.

Holding back a full-blown growl, Scott corrected Ian's comment. "Yes, there is something wrong. All my friends are going to see me kiss a man on television. And Mom and Dad, too, for that matter!"

"I don't know if the west coast will get that shot," she said casually. "And besides, Mom and Dad will be so relieved you found work, they won't say a thing."

Grumbling under his breath, Scott said, "Is that right? Not a thing? You know Dad! He'll go ballistic. He's completely homophobic. And another thing! Will I be type-cast?"

"From a frickin' gum commercial? Oh, Christ..." She gave him a very sarcastic laugh and then nodded to the waiter that they were ready to order their food as he poured wine for them. She was so angry about this pettiness she was about to explode. If Ian hadn't been seated at the table, she would have unleashed a string of accusations all pointing to Scott's pathetic existence and lack of motivation.

After the men ordered the most expensive item on the menu as revenge, two Australian lobster tales with shrimp and crab appetizers, she tried to find out what the real issues were. Other than the obvious anxiety of kissing each other.

The Kiss

A half glass of wine passed her lips, and a deep exhale to calm down, she said, "I thought I was doing you a favor. Sorry for trying." She decided Jewish guilt was in order.

"No! I don't mind! I'm thrilled actually!"

She smiled to herself as Ian fell prey instantly. Scott was more accustomed to the tactics. "You should be! Oh, and by the way, Calvin was a no. They found some Aussie they fell in love with, sorry."

Grinning shyly, Ian met her eyes, "No bother. This was better than I expected."

"And, Scott, my love, Harold Lewis wants your abs for his cover."

"Oh!" His mood brightened considerably.

Two offers in one day after months of barren desert, the one thing he shouldn't be doing was complaining, she thought.

"Thanks!" he said finally.

"Well done!" Ian grinned at him, patting his shoulder. "So, you've a nice set of stomach muscles on you?"

Stumbling off the curb once more, Scott cleared his throat and blushed miserably at the attention. "Uh, yeah... I work out a lot."

"You better, with the amount of food you eat!" Claire laughed loudly.

"Shut up!"

"No, you shut up!"

Ian stared at them in horror.

"Don't worry, we're just teasing each other." She winked at his very nervous expression.

"Oh, right." A tentative smile appeared.

As their salads were set down before them and the wine glasses were refilled, she thought back to the story line again in her mind. Picturing her brother kissing this fantastic pretty boy was doing odd things to her. Grossing her out being the least

43

likely. She was strangely turned on, yet that deleted pang of jealousy returned. She was thirty-two. Ian was eleven years younger than she was. Maybe getting to know him on a deeper level than she had with any other model in that agency was the problem. Though his looks were incredibly sensual, he had an innocent quality to him that made her want to strip him and have her way with him. Bad Claire! Bad!

She didn't think Ian was gay. Not at all. So, the jealousy thing…that was just some passing mood. Wasn't this whole experiment just a product of her boredom? And it really was so damn amusing. What would happen after they had the experience of kissing each other? Most likely, absolutely nothing. But, she was dying to know.

Even Ian looked stunned at how quickly two large lobster tails could be devoured. Scott was like a magician when it came to food. Claire imagined peering under the table to see if he was feeding the restaurant's dog. But no doggie existed. He was devouring food like he normally did, in two seconds flat.

To her surprise as they stood in the softly falling snow, the wind calming to a wispy stream of spinning flakes, Scott asked Ian if he would like to come back to the apartment for a nightcap. He quickly agreed.

Trying to unsuccessfully catch her brother's eye to smirk at his offer, they once again rode in a yellow taxi, silent but for Ian's occasional comment about the lovely Manhattan Christmas decorations and its comparison to Regent Street.

Vaguely Claire wondered as she paid the fare if the cabby thought she was some horny old lady bringing two lovely young men up to her loft to assault. Leaving him to his own imagination, she hooked their arms and smiled in delight at the doorman who obviously recognized her brother.

After another silent moment in the elevator, Scott unlocked their door and deactivated the alarm. Ian paused as he stepped in and admired the décor. The living area was open plan, hardwood flooring. On his right was the minimalist dining table and chairs, a single aluminum light fixture hanging over its center. Behind it, up one step, was the steel and marble kitchen. Directly before him was the vast expanse of the living room. Only a small section of it had a leather couch, loveseat, and chair with a hassock, coffee table, and small colorful area rug. The rest was wide open to the wall of uncovered glass windows. On his left were the three bedrooms; Claire's with its own toilet and shower, and the second bath with a tub between the other two bedrooms.

"For fuck's sake," he sighed as he took in its size.

Scott threw his leather jacket on the couch. "Amazing what money can get you."

"This is lovely! I'm quite sure downtown London has flats like this, but I've never seen one." He wandered in, admiring the few original prints on the walls.

"Give me your coat, have a seat." Claire reached out for him.

Shaking his head as he took it off, he kept searching the place carefully, as if memorizing its details. Gathering up the coats in her arm, pretending she was the maid, she hung them up as she shouted to Scott to get Ian something to drink.

"More wine?" Scott asked him, "Or coffee?"

Ian shrugged and followed him up the one step to the kitchen, admiring the spotless stainless steel appliances. "Aye, wine is fine. Do you cook?" he asked Claire.

"Oddly enough, I love to. The only problem is I have no time!" She moved toward them as Scott set three stemmed glasses on the counter.

"We're the king and queen of take-out," Scott said as he poured.

"Right. I understand. Been to the Indian myself for a kabab more than once." As he took the glass handed to him he thanked Scott. "It must be nice," he mused.

"You'll get there." Claire smiled at him, knowing he had

every chance to earn a top salary.

"Right, by kissing a bloke on a gum advert." This obviously amused him because he burst out laughing at the sick irony.

"Stranger things have happened, Ian Sullivan!" she warned, wagging her finger at him.

Gesturing with the hand that held his glass, Scott said, "Go have a seat."

As he and Ian sat together on the couch, Claire headed to the stereo to pick out a music CD.

While Ian continued to absorb the details around him, Scott took the opportunity to openly stare at him. Claire could only imagine what he was thinking. The more they hung around Ian, the more incredible looking he seemed to become. Not a shred of conceit was in that boy. It was truly remarkable.

Sensing a soft moody vocal sound from Jann Arden was appropriate, she lowered it to a nice hum of background music and then joined them, sitting on the love seat perpendicular to the couch, tucking her leg under her after kicking off her shoes.

"So, tell me about England," Scott twisted his body to face him, also nudging off his shoes and then even opening another button of his collared shirt.

"What do you want to know?" Ian got rid of his shoes as well.

Claire asked, "Your Mom and Dad okay about you being here?"

"Yes…they're well pleased I've this opportunity. Mum said New York is where to make it. So they enrolled me in the Juilliard School."

"Oh?" Scott perked up. "I'm an alumnus!"

"Are you? Well, I could use a mentor. If I get overwhelmed can I count on you?"

"Of course!" The sparkle in Scott's eyes was like he had

found true love. Claire had never seen him behave this way before.

"Cheers! Thanks, mate!" Ian raised his glass to him.

"Cheers." Scott tapped it with his.

"I noticed you don't have a Christmas tree. No time?" Ian checked around again. "You certainly have the space!"

With a sheepish grin Claire was looking to Scott to explain. He did without hesitation. "We don't celebrate Christmas. We're Jewish, Ian."

"Oh! Fancy that!"

"I thought about getting a tree. I have had one before," Claire said, "But it is the time factor. I just can't seem to get organized."

"I do miss the holidays with Mum and Dad..." His eyes misted over.

"We can get a tree," Scott offered. "You can help us decorate it."

Bursting into warm laughter, Ian said, "I don't want to be a bother! Really, you don't have to on my account!"

"No bother. No, bother at all, Ian." Claire smiled at him.

"The two of you have really been quite wonderful to me. I can't tell you how bleak the idea of sitting alone in that hotel room on Christmas has been."

Scott's eyes met Claire's instantly. And she knew what he was about to say. Though it seemed logical, since they had a spare room, she hesitated for so many reasons, the foremost being getting to know her clients on too personal a level. Before she could voice her negative impulse, Scott had already made the invitation.

"Stay here! We have an extra bedroom! And you'll save my sister's business tons of money on that fancy hotel they have you in."

As those words fell into the air, with Jann Arden singing

her accusing and expressive '*Insensitive*' song behind it, Ian met Claire's eyes as if making sure it was a mutual invitation. When that gorgeous face with its darkly lashed green eyes met hers, she had to admit, 'No' was the furthest thing from her mind. Instantly she had image flashes of him strutting nude or with a tiny towel around his hips from the shower.

"Sure, why not?" But even as she said it, something in it smacked of lacking common sense.

The excitement on his face echoed by her brother's was irresistible. And she always had been a sucker for pretty faces.

As the midnight hour struck and their conversation grew mixed with yawns, Scott suggested Ian sleep over for the night and then when they could, they would collect his things from his hotel room and move him in. It seemed reasonable, since sending someone out into the dark streets at that hour, especially one as lovely and foreign as Ian, could mean disaster. The snow was increasing in density as thick swirling drifts leaned against the window sills.

After checking the spare bedroom to make sure it was complete with towels and items to attend him, including a new toothbrush, Claire kissed them both on the cheek and went to wash up and sleep. The day was catching up to her and she could not stay awake another minute.

Leaving her brother and Ian alone together as they set the glasses in the sink and tossed the empty bottle into recycling, she wished once again she could have been a fly on the wall and watched them without being present. The possibility that they would touch each other sexually was minimal, remote at best, in her opinion. At least if she was any judge of character at all she would guess both to be heterosexual, and extremely intimidated by the kiss alone. Rest assured there would be no butt-fucking in that apartment that night.

As they watched her disappear into her little feminine boudoir, they paused until the door had clicked closed, sealing her in like a vault.

"I should really be in bed, too. I'm exhausted." Scott wiped his hands on the dishtowel and then ran his fingers back through his hair.

"Yes, I'm knackered as well. I just don't know if I could sleep yet, though."

"Jet lag? Or do you have insomnia, too?" Scott moved out of the kitchen and back into the living room.

"No, I'm over the jet lag, I'm sure. At times I do have sleepless nights, but not chronically. Do you?" Ian followed him.

"Yes, unfortunately. My dad told me to try sleeping pills, but I don't want to feel groggy in the morning."

"Too much on your mind?" Ian sat next to him.

"Yes! That's the problem. I think non-stop. Mostly about how to make a living doing this. Modeling and acting is what I want to do most. I just can't picture myself doing anything else. You know what I mean?"

"Of course I do!" Ian's face lit up with his laughter. "Why do you think I left England and placed all my hopes on this agency?"

"How did you find Spencer & Epstein way out there?"

"On the net. They had a great web-site and seemed to really have their shite together. I sent in my photo and resume, then got a student visa and auditioned for Juilliard. It seems to be all falling into place...at least I think it is." Sighing, he said, "I'll tell ya, mate, if things go bad here, I'll be on that plane from JFK airport to Heathrow faster than you could throw a pint."

"Yeah? You'd head back? Just like that?"

"Yes, I would! I reckon my chances are about the same over in London if I blow it here. It was a gamble, coming here, mate. Me mum said New York is where models are made. If it pans out, chushty, if not..." he shrugged.

"Huh," Scott replied, "I never thought you'd give up on the USA that quickly."

"Miss me mum," Ian teased, winking at him.

"Yeah? I miss mine, too, sometimes. Oh, too bad about that Calvin ad. You would have been really great for them. I'm surprised they didn't snatch you up."

As Ian paused to stare at Scott intently, the light seemed to grow dimmer in the silence of the room. Finally, he smiled warmly at the sincere compliment. The glittering headlamps of a low flying plane passed beyond the large windows on the east side of the apartment flickering a silver sparkle into the gloom. A low rumble like distant thunder was heard from its jets.

Finding Scott's shining but tired eyes, Ian whispered, "Not to worry. I do have something else on my plate. Chewing gum." He chuckled.

Scott echoed the laughter, but added nervousness to it. A yawn crept over him and he stretched his arms over his head. "Fuck, I'm tired. I hope I can sleep."

"Yeah, you should do. You look cream-crackered. Come here...turn around." Ian spun his index finger in the air.

"What?" Scott asked, "Turn around how?"

"Face your back to me. I've had some massage therapy lessons. Maybe this can de-stress you."

Pausing, Scott then turned his back to Ian and waited.

"Take off your shirt, mate. I can't do it over it."

Scott slowly he rose off the couch, still facing away from Ian, and began unbuttoning his shirt. In the back of his mind he wondered what would happen if Claire came back in and caught sight of this type of behavior. She was so quick to assume the worst, this would give her ammunition for weeks. Trying not to care, or at least appear he didn't, he tossed his shirt over the back of the chair, and sat down once again, waiting patiently.

"I really need massage oil, but, I'll give it a go without." Kneeling behind him on the large couch, Ian laid both his hands on Scott's shoulders and began to massage them.

"Oooh, fucking hell...that is wonderful..." Scott moaned in ecstasy.

A small laugh emerged from Ian. "Christ, you're tight."

"I bet you say that to all the girls," Scott whispered wickedly.

The minute Ian got it, he roared with laughter. Joining him with relief, Scott tried to control his chuckle of nervousness. As Ian calmed down and focused on rubbing him, it was silent except for some soft sighs coming from Scott's lips.

"You've a fantastic body..." Ian murmured quietly.

His eyes blinking as they focused on the door to Claire's bedroom, Scott swallowed down a dry throat and didn't answer. Maybe this kind of honesty was an English thing. He shouldn't read too much into it.

After fifteen minutes of a very nice neck and shoulder rub, Ian stopped and said, "There, how's that?"

Not intentionally meaning to be seductive, Scott looked back over his shoulder and said in a very sexy hoarse whisper, "It was great...thanks, Ian."

Ian reached out and touched Scott's hair softly, toying with the dark thickness with his fingertips. "Good. My pleasure, for your hospitality."

Pausing a moment to enjoy the hypnotic effect of the petting, Scott managed to get upright and say, "Bed."

"Bed," Ian agreed.

They waved goodnight to each other as Scott closed himself into his room. He hesitated a moment, listening to the eerie silence, then flipped open the folder on his desk. That photo didn't do him justice.

Chapter Six

The first to bed, the first to rise, Claire was up at seven with the birds. Saturday had finally arrived and she promised herself she would not work the next two days. Not even at home.

The coffee dripping, the orange juice squeezed, she found the morning paper outside her door. As she waited for the men to come to life, she decided to cook them breakfast instead of just preparing toast and jam.

Within the hour she heard some movement and to her delight, Ian scuffed out of his room in just his slacks. "Hello, gorgeous!" she shouted.

"And a good-morning to you, Miss Epstein." He smiled and shoved his unruly hair back from his face.

"What would you like for breakfast? Eggs?"

"I don't want to be a bother. Coffee is fine."

Getting up to pour him a cup, she said, "No, I insist. How do you like them?"

"Scrambled, please…"

"Great. Have a seat." Then she spun into action and started some soy bacon and sausages frying.

As he tipped in the milk and a spoonful of sugar, he yawned, looking adorable.

"You sleep okay?"

"Hmmm? Yes, fine, thanks." He noticed the paper and gazed at it with some interest.

"What time did you guys get to bed?"

"Not long after you." After preparing his coffee to his liking, he stood and leaned on the counter near her to watch her cook. "You certain you don't mind me moving in? I wanted to ask you without Scott here."

Facing him straight on, and with her expression as serious as possible, she said, "I do not mind." And in her head she was imagining them meeting in the night for some wild sex. Though in reality, that was kept to her fantasy life.

"It's really quite generous. I'll pay you when I get my first check."

"Don't be a silly billy. You will not pay me." She poured the mixed up eggs into the pan and they made a lovely sizzling sound, smelling of browned butter.

"All right then, if you ever come to London, I'll put you up."

"Oh? You have your own place there?"

As she tilted the pan to get the egg covering it, he said shyly, "Well, not exactly. I still live with me mum and dad."

"Ah, I see." She smiled to herself. *Christ, he was so young.*

"But, they wouldn't mind at all," he added.

"Of course. Thanks for the offer." Stifling the laugh in her head, she imagined meeting his parents and sleeping in some spare bedroom while they kept vigilant over their son's virginity.

"What is that?" He pointed to the fake meat.

"Soysages and fakin' bacon. Don't worry. They taste really good, and they're better for you."

"Oh, you can't eat pork."

"No, it's not a religious thing, it's a health thing. I do spoil myself with real bacon on occasion, and I did eat a lobster last night."

"You must think I'm terribly ignorant. I'm sorry. I don't know a thing about being Jewish."

"Don't be silly. Ian, I don't think anything at all. This Jewish thing, it's just what we were brought up as. Neither of us practices it."

"Oh! Like the Church of England!"

Laughing softly, Claire agreed, "Yes, just like that."

Raising her head to a noise, she figured the minute the aroma hit the air, Scott would follow his nose. "Good-morning, sunshine."

"Are you making breakfast?" He scuffed in wearing a pair of tiny black gym shorts.

"Yesss. How do you want your eggs?"

"Over light!! Excellent!" He found the third mug and poured some coffee for himself.

"You sleep all right, mate?" Ian asked. "Nice abs!" he laughed as he admired them.

"Err, thanks." Scott rubbed his hand over them, in a reassuring gesture, then said, "Yeah, really good for a change. You?"

"Yes, like a log."

When the phone rang Claire asked Scott to get it. He checked the caller ID and shouted, "Out of area!"

"Could be Mom and Dad..." She checked the time.

"Hello?" Scott lifted it quickly. "Hi, Mom! Yeah, Claire just said it must be you, but it's so early! It's almost eight here now, isn't it?...Why are you up so early?"

Ian sat at the table as Claire set his plate down. "Where do they live?" he asked.

"Seattle."

"Yes, I did get some work. Claire got me a cover for a

men's fitness magazine."

"He won't tell them about the commercial," she whispered to Ian.

"No, I shouldn't think he would." Stuffing some food in his mouth, he brightened up and said, "This soy shite is all right."

"Good!" She laughed as he gobbled it down and went to check on Scott's eggs. "You're almost done, dear."

"Okay...I'll give you to Claire. Breakfast is done."

She laid it out on a plate for him and said, "When there's a choice between food and family, well..."

"Shut up!" he said.

"No, you shut up!" she laughed and took the phone from him. "Hello? Hi there, early bird. Yes, everything is fine...ahh, hang on, let me see." Walking with the cordless phone, she leaned against the large glass panes facing the east side of the city. "Yup, it's snowing right now...I haven't been out yet today, but by the look of the streets from up here it's all white..." Even though Scott had sat down after him, he had managed to finish his food before Ian. Ian watched in awe.

"We've a guest staying..." They both whipped their heads around to her smirk. Scott started to mouth frantically not to mention the commercial. "A nice English man from the agency. He was staying at the hotel, but we thought it was cruel for him to be on his own through Christmas. He's lovely...you should see his hair, Mom."

At that comment, Ian laughed again. Scott shook his head in disbelief.

"Dad? Are you on now? Hi, Daddy...yeah, things are great...I was just telling Mom about our lodger!"

"She can't keep her mouth shut!" Scott grumbled to Ian.

"Am I a secret?" Ian asked.

"No! I didn't mean it like that...she just tells them everything."

"Twenty-one, six feet tall," she grinned as she described him, looking straight at him. "Long shoulder-length brown hair and the loveliest green eyes. Mom, you would die."

At the gushing, Ian went beet red. "Criminy!"

"I told you!" Scott warned.

"Well, I sent him to Calvin for underwear, but even though he's hung like a horse, he didn't get it."

"Fucking hell!" Ian choked as Scott hid behind his hands as his sister continued to embarrass them horribly.

"I've something special lined up for them both now..."

"No! No!" Scott rushed to his feet and began waving in front of her frantically.

"A commercial! Yes, TV!"

"No! Please! Claire! Please don't say it!" Scott was on his knees pleading.

"Oh, I could tell you all about it, Mom, but it's getting late and I have to get to the office. Of course I'll get a tape for you! You bet... Love you! Bye!"

As she hung up, Scott was gnashing his teeth in anger. "You suck!"

"I didn't tell them!" She twisted away with that expression of superiority he detested, and headed to the shower. "Clean up, boys! I cooked, you clean!"

As she left she knew Scott was still steaming. *Hey, you get to kiss that lovely thing, you get tortured! That's just the way it is!* she thought smugly.

Chapter Seven

Over the weekend they managed to accomplish several things: clearing out Ian from the hotel, moving him in officially, and getting a wonderful Noble pine tree and covering it with lights and balls. The fragrance alone was worth the effort, not to mention how warm and cozy it made the place with its flickering colored lights and gleaming tinsel. Curled up on the chair with a hot chocolate, Claire allowed the boys to do the honors as Scott seemed as excited as Ian to get the tall stately fir decorated and lit up. And for a couple of regular guys, they did a wonderful job.

In the free time they had, they wandered the crunchy snow covered streets of New York, showing off the sights to Ian who was delighted, promising them the same when they visited him in England. Every time he extended that invitation, Claire had a remarkable vision of she and Scott sharing a single bed in some tiny two bedroom flat, in a London suburb. 'Mum' Sullivan would be offering tea on a regular basis, and they'd sit in some parlor trying to be polite. It wasn't her idea of a vacation to London. But it would be ungrateful and rude to mention she'd prefer a five star hotel in downtown Soho.

One brilliant blue frosty afternoon they found the time to skate at Rockefeller Center, something Claire hadn't done since she was a child. Scott was the only one to fall on his butt. And unfortunately for Ian, his skate was caught up in the avalanche and he came crashing down with him. Doubled over in laughter, Claire didn't do much to help their egos, nor their wet backsides. Like comic geniuses, they slid precariously reaching to haul each other up, only to crash down again and again. And each time, Ian would shout, "Bollocks!" causing everyone to turn and stare at this lovely foreigner. Claire would have given her kingdom for a video camera.

Sunday evening brought a blushing peach twilight and shimmering constellations overshadowing the deep freeze of the dropping thermometer. After a change into warm dry clothing, they were sated with more of Claire's home cooking as the aroma of lasagna filled the air, as well as their hungry bellies. Ian was very flattering of the meal in comparison to his mother's bland meat and potato diet, while Scott ate it so quickly, and so much of it, Claire doubted he tasted a thing.

Slouching around the living room, the television playing *It's a Wonderful Life* for the tenth time, the black and white version which Claire preferred, they were content to just be there together. Warm, snug, and secure.

"You were adorable today at the skating arena, Ian." Claire smiled. She had been staring at his profile critically as he watched television. It was perfect and linear, as if he were pure white marble.

"Why, thank you, Miss Epstein, but I should hardly think I was adorable, flat on my arse!"

Scott and Ian always sat on the couch, while Claire curled up in the leather chair with the ottoman, one she claimed as hers ever since Scott moved in years ago.

"And what a tight lovely arse it is!" Claire grinned devilishly.

"Hey!" Scott interrupted the conversation. "I'm watching a movie here!"

"Oh, come on! How many times have you seen it? You could recite the lines by heart!" Claire shouted, trying not to pout at the scolding. She liked when Ian giggled and attempted to make him smile as much as she could. Something wild would shine in his emerald colored eyes, and she wanted that wickedness from him very badly.

"Would you lasso the moon for someone, Scott?" Ian asked, pointing to the television screen at that moment when the drawing of George roping the moon for Mary flittered across it.

After watching the scene, Scott gave Ian a very personal glance.

Instead of responding verbally, Ian gave a similar smile back. That one, facing Claire, was caught and stored in her memory. Trying her best not to second guess what she knew for a fact about them, that they were both straight, she ignored their interaction, and set her gaze back on the snow covered streets of Bedford Falls.

"Now, let me just say something right here." Holding up her hand to emphasize her point, she continued, *"It's one thing to think about their kiss, and an entirely different thing to witness it. Believe me, I had no idea what I was in for. Let me just say that knowing and seeing where as far apart as the earth from the surface of the moon. But, you saw that commercial, didn't you? Yeah, I thought so. It seems everyone has…"*

Chapter Eight

Monday morning arrived and Claire had the job of rousing the troops for battle. Though Jenine usually assigned subordinates to the task, Claire wanted to make this one her special project. Besides, if these two were going to kiss, she was going to see it!

No time for cooking, Claire, Scott and Ian consumed the store purchased muffins and instant coffee before scampering to the lobby to hail a taxi and start their extraordinary day.

"You guys excited?" Claire was and had no trouble expressing it.

Stomping his feet to keep warm as they waited for a ride, Scott shook his head at her in irritation. "Yeah, thrilled."

"Your first kiss! I'm so excited!" Claire teased, trying her best to torment them.

"First?" Ian made a very confused face.

"She means with a guy," Scott snarled. "Stop being so excited about it. You're too weird wanting to see your brother kiss another man."

"She wants to see us kiss?" Ian's expression of astonishment and confusion didn't change.

"No, never mind. She's just warped. Watch her."

"Oh, I do. Every chance I get."

The Kiss

At that comment, though the taxi pulled up in front of them at the curb, Claire caught Ian's impish smile. "Do you, Ganymede?" she purred.

"Most definitely," he answered, a provocative grin on his face.

"All right, I'm about to barf." Scott shoved them both inside the back of the cab roughly.

Silence reigned again as she thought about the comment. *Hmmm, maybe she wasn't too old for a tumble under the sheets after all.*

Scott again gazed out of the window in silence.

Driving directly to where the commercial was being filmed, they had been instructed to go to a movie house uptown. It appeared they were hoping to keep costs low and shoot it in one day. It seemed reasonable considering how simple it was and the lack of dialogue.

When they entered the theater, they were immediately inundated with a hundred young people. Most were extras used to make the movie house appear packed, hence the robbing of the seat in the sketch. The rest were cameramen, stage crew, make-up artists, the director, the works. The noise was the first thing Claire noticed as they made their way through the chaos. With how nervous she was feeling, and the early hour of the day, the friction of the disorganization made her grate her teeth in annoyance at all the teeny-boppers cackling like geese.

The moment Claire was spotted she was waved to the front of the audience quickly. The director wanted a look at her two men.

"What are they wearing?" He set back from them and assessed their casual but smart attire, then asked someone behind him. "What do you think, Paul? They seem all right to me."

"They're fine. Get them brushed and powdered."

As Scott gave Claire a last nervous glance, she threw him a

kiss and made herself scarce. *Not only does he have to kiss Ian, he has to do it in front of a house full of teens! Oh, this is divine*! she thought wickedly.

Disappearing into the crowd, Claire found the two female models that had the jobs as their pretend girlfriends. Amazingly enough, the one that was to play Scott's girlfriend had the exact same hair as Ian. It was a marvel of advertising and casting. Somehow she imagined they would rather be the ones who were doing the smooching of these gorgeous fellows, but that was tough luck.

The rumble of voices succumbed to the shouting of the few, who tried to get everyone who was an extra seated in the area of the theater which was going to make it into the background of the shoot. Realizing she was not going to see a thing from the back, Claire crept her way to behind the cameras, yet still far enough out of the way to avoid being yelled at.

As he was being directed, Scott was nodding. A fresh package of gum was handed to him. This was just the first rough take. No one was filming yet. They just wanted to go through it to get everyone where they should be. He nodded again, looking surprisingly calm.

In the quiet of the room, Scott, holding hands with his Ian-look-alike girlfriend, made it down the aisle of the movie theater and into two seats, leaving only one free seat on the right side of the woman. Claire called her "Gigi", thinking it fitting because Fifi had blonde hair. She had no interest in her real name. Male models were more her thing. She was sick to death of female covers on magazines. 'Sick to death' being an understatement. More like on the verge of spurting bile at every plastic female face.

Moving through the motions, Scott and Gigi sat down as if they had the last few seats in a very large sold-out theater. On cue, Scott started fussing with his pocket opposite Gigi to get at the gum. It was supposed to be a long, awkward pause, long enough to get her out of the row and up the aisle and lovely Ian in. The director shouted, "Okay, the lights go out now!" though they didn't that time.

Whether it was on purpose or not, Scott was convincingly fumbling with the wrapper as he turned his shoulder to the action behind him. Passing each other in the aisle, Ian and his girl, Claire called her "Bambi", squeezed in. As everyone waited, Scott stuffed the piece of gum in his mouth and chewed quickly. Moments before the 'act', Claire got on her tiptoes in anticipation. When Ian found his seat behind Scott's back, unbelievably, Scott shouted to the director, "Do you want me to really kiss him this time?"

A rumble of stifled laughter surrounded them like 'the wave' at a football match. Claire had to turn her back to stop her outbreak of hysterical laughter.

"Not unless you want to, dear," came the campy response.

Scott cleared his throat awkwardly and nodded, as if the question was legitimate and he wasn't mortified by it.

"Okay, where were we?" came the next shout from behind the camera.

With Ian trying his damnedest not to bust a gut laughing, Scott turned to face him, placed his right hand behind Ian's head, digging into that luscious hair, and pulled his seductive lips close enough to…almost kiss.

With perfect timing, Ian pretended it happened, and his eyes went wide as he feigned panic, then he sat back and breathed with uncommon sensuality, "Nice…" pretending he was now chewing the gum.

"Okay, people! That's all there is to it! Let's try one on tape!"

As they were getting up to re-start the scene, Claire read Ian's lips as he whispered, "Now you have to kiss me," with the most devilish smirk she could have imagined. This was first class entertainment as far as she was concerned.

Scott's cheeks went into one lovely red flush as he coughed

and tried to appear normal while that pretty boy teased him. And the tease Scott was enduring was even lower than his red cheeks. He seemed completely aroused.

Like dominos moving in reverse, everyone stood up as they scooted back out of the row.

Vainly trying to appear seductive and alluring to a man who was completely preoccupied with something masculine and British, Gigi was waiting at the top of the aisle for Scott. As he ignored her, he habitually ran his hand through his hair, was scolded, and re-brushed once more. Powder was applied to his face as his sweat from heightened nerves made him glisten. He spit out the chewed gum, handed it to someone, then took a fresh pack, and shoved it into his left jacket pocket.

With more intensity than before, the scene was made official as "Take one!" was shouted and then, "Action!"

Holding hands once more, Gigi and Scott made their way down that aisle while the soft rumble of scripted stage conversation hummed around everyone. As planned, they scooted into the row with the last three unoccupied seats and sat down. Instantly the lights went out. On cue, Scott began digging into his pocket. So far it was perfect, a piece of gum in his mouth, Gigi gone to potty, Ian moving in for the kill.

Squinting through the dimness, Claire could see Scott take a very deep breath. Somehow it seemed appropriate as he would need that courage to kiss his chick. But Claire knew damn well it was real.

As if in slow motion, he sat back, raised his right arm over the back of Ian's chair and with complete affection, dug into that glorious head of hair and gently urged that pretty boy's mouth towards his. When Ian's face turned his way, Claire was biting the inside her cheek in anxiety. Ian was wearing an expression that he actually had to change. At first Claire caught some loving affection there, then the actor part kicked in and his panic-stricken look appeared. When their lips met, even she felt a charge of electricity. No peck on the lips was this! Her brother was sucking his face! As the seconds ticked away, she almost expected the director to cut and shout that the kiss was too long. Finally they separated and Scott gave his expected gape at Ian in horror at the realization. That wonderful sensuous grin appeared on Ian's lovely face as he said, "Mmmm, nice..." (Improvising the 'mmmm') as he chewed seductively. Then, just when it was almost a complete take, he leaned over and pecked Scott on the lips. In astonishment, Claire choked and widened her eyes in awe. "Oh, my fucking god," she mumbled to herself.

Shouting ensued as they cut the scene, and the director screamed at Ian, "What the hell are you doing?"

He shrugged, matter-of-factly, and said, "Felt right."

"Well, no matter how much you turn each other on, stick to the script! You can make out later! On your own time!"

By now Scott was folded in half with his face in his hands, hiding from the humiliation. Claire gave up holding it in and burst out laughing. Hearing her voice, Scott instantly sat up and glared at her. It was mean, but she loved it. *Time to kiss again*! she thought, giving him a big intimidating grin.

They were told, with some annoyance, to do it once more. As they exited the aisle, Claire noticed something unexpected happen. Very secretly in the distracting chaos, Ian reached back his hand and made contact with the inside of her brother's thigh, very close to his crotch as they scooted out of that row. It was quick, it was discreet, and it was unbelievable. Her jaw hung open. She must have been the only one who noticed it because things just simply progressed as usual.

'Take two' was shouted, then instant replay began. A silly thought ran through her head. Would Ian keep mucking it up, simply to keep having the opportunity to taste her brother's lips? And what about her brother? Giving that lovely man a kiss worth remembering? One thing she was certain of: they did not hate this contact. Not once did they cringe, look disgusted, wipe their mouths off. Nothing that would indicate this was distasteful to either of them. It was completely baffling.

As she contemplated the depth of the male psyche, they walked down that aisle again. Blah, blah, blah, it was all a bore until that damn piece of gum was in his mouth. Once again Scott took a very deep breath and turned to caress the back of Ian's hair with what was becoming familiarity. As Claire stared in awe, Ian parted his lips to receive Scott's mouth. It was really getting wild between those two, and yet it seemed only the three of them were aware. Or so Claire hoped.

As Scott's forehead and eyebrows creased in absolute pleasure, she wondered again how long of a kiss they had anticipated. Left to do their thing, would their lips be connected eternally? The amount they were savoring that luscious forbidden contact was truly amazing to her. After what felt to Claire was a ridiculously long make-out session, they parted and went through the rest flawlessly. The director yelled 'Cut', and they took a break as they rewound the tape to take a look at it.

Distracted by the videotape as it played back the scene, Claire glimpsed between cameras to again find a subtle hint of things to come. Ian's hand squeezed her brother's knee affectionately, then quickly released it and hid itself in his pocket.

"Perfect, gentlemen!" the director shouted, "You've done it in two takes. Congratulations!"

As Scott exhaled with relief, Ian got a very mischievous look on his face. Grabbing Scott's head in his hands, he planted one on his lips, a freebee.

When everyone noticed, a roar of laughter and clapping followed. Claire felt miserable for Scott, and knew he'd be mortified. As Ian pulled back to laugh in his face, instead of rage, Scott was smiling at him, shaking his head.

"Well, fuck me..." she mumbled, totally amazed and ever so slightly sick with jealousy.

The crowd, which Claire found were mainly made up of students who had volunteered, mulled about, giggling and whispering like giddy juveniles at the risqué scene. The director hollered over the din that they were sworn to secrecy and could not let out the nature of the kiss before the commercial was aired.

With Claire moving as close as she could to the men to meet them and ask them how they felt, she found Gigi asking Scott in pouting disappointment, "You guys really lovers?"

Claire anticipated a very volatile reaction from her brother, including possibly a punch in the nose, but he simply lowered his head shyly and whispered, "No." This was not the Scott Andrew Epstein she had been brought up with. The old Scott would have had a panic attack and fit right there, screaming in horror that she was insane. Claire's fascination was peaked, and the green-eyed monster was beginning to rear its ugly head again.

Coming around the cameras to meet her excitedly, Ian got sidetracked as he glimpsed the ad running again on a video screen and paused to watch it. On his way to do the same, Scott stood behind him, and as they both stared at it in a trance, Claire moved to be able to overhear any delightful or incriminating comments.

Oddly, they were completely absorbed at what they looked like kissing each other. It was one thing to do it, and obviously quite another to witness yourself doing it.

When Ian leaned to Scott's ear Claire heard him whisper, "The bird looks like a slapper sitting there. She doesn't even know her boyfriend is snogging another bloke!"

Slapper? Snogging? Claire assumed the latter was kissing, thinking the former was some derogatory term for a female. She did love those English idioms. At least she imagined he meant kissing. Snog? Were they dueling tongues in there?

With Scott knowing exactly what he meant, and appearing a bit light in the head after the sensuous rush of Ian's lips, he chuckled as the scene was finished and smiled sweetly at him. "I don't know what the hell you just said, so is it okay if I just nod and smile to keep you happy?" he teased playfully.

G.A. Hauser

With his bright eyes wider than normal, Ian burst out laughing, "Oi! You just keep up that handsome smile, mate."

Standing behind them with her arms folded, silently listening, she was very surprised at the affection growing between them. When they finally turned around they found her grinning at them mischievously. At some hidden message from her smirk, they both seemed shy to her gaze suddenly. "Uh huh...I bet you were upset with yourselves to be so professional and only do it in two takes. Shame on you. You could have had a whole day of...snogging."

"Shut up!" Scott said, but this time with a big smile on his lips.

"No, you shut up! Christ, was I right?" Claire had actually asked that out loud and Ian overheard. She was dying to know if her brother was now hot for this English stud.

"Right about what?" Ian asked curiously.

"Nothing. She's delusional." Twirling his finger by his head, Scott tilted at her in an obvious gesture.

"Careful. I'm your bread and butter, honey."

"Is that it?" Ian asked, pushing those long locks of his back from his adorable face.

"I think so. You guys can get lunch if you want." She dug through her purse for some cash.

"Where are you going?" Scott took the money without a second thought.

"Back to the office." As she said it, she found her cell phone and called Jenine. "I can't play hooky the rest of the day, though I wish I could." While they walked back up the theater aisle on their way to the outside streets, Claire's phone finally connected to Jenine's. "Hello, sweetie. We're finished here. Those lovely boys did it in two takes."

"Did they? Wow, that's great! You coming back? I'm sinking here."

"On my way now." She hung up the phone and stuffed it

68

into her purse as Scott attempted to flag down a taxi.

"You get the first one." He nodded.

"Thanks…see you guys home? Dinner time?"

"Yup." Scott opened the cab door for her.

"See you later, Miss Epstein." Ian waved.

"You will, you gorgeous cherub." As the cab rushed back into traffic, she watched them lean against each other to whisper something. About her, she had no doubt. She only hoped it was complimentary.

Back in the office, she headed straight for Jenine, who had her ear connected to the phone and appeared tremendously relieved to see her. The minute she hung up, Jenine said breathlessly, "That was Andre Surah. He loved the damn thing! He's pushing it to air Super Bowl Sunday! You have any idea how expensive those slots are?"

"Oh, my fucking god! And the amount of people that will be watching?"

"He's planning on leaking the story line to the Times, and *People* mag. I cannot believe it. Can you?"

"Oh, this is fantastic! You know everyone will be calling him to see where he got those two gorgeous men from. This will be great for us, lady. And I will bet you—just bet you— that both of those boys get an offer after this."

"Tell me about it! What was the kiss like?" When the phone rang, Jenine hurried to her door, shouted for her secretary to grab it, then shut it quickly. "Well? Dish!"

Shoving her coat onto a second chair, Claire sat down and waved her to her desk. "Girl! They swapped spit! I mean, full on! Open mouthed! Took their damn time! I cannot get over it!"

Jenine breathed, "And? You think this is the start of some kind of gay fling?"

Sitting back, a smug look on her face she said, "Wager?"

Having landed in a pizzeria, Scott and Ian demolished their food quickly, sipping their soda through pink flexible straws. Checking the other occupants of the restaurant before he began, Scott wiped his lip on a napkin and said, "So, you like New York pizza?" He was well aware they had avoided talking about the actual kiss and neither wanted to be the first to comment on it, either way.

Still munching the last of the crust, Ian nodded, "Fandabbydozie. Better than London. But we've got better Indian."

"Fandabbydozie?" Scott shook his head. "You are so weird."

"And you're the dog's bollocks..." Ian laughed.

"Speak English!"

"I thought I was!"

"Then speak American!"

With his eyes lighting up devilishly, Ian did his best impression of President Bush, "We're ganna have ta git those folks!"

"Shut up!" Scott burst out laughing.

"No! You shut up!" Ian challenged happily.

"I've created a monster..."

"Come on, let's piss off out of here!" Ian threw down his napkin, slurped the last of his soda, and then rose to his feet.

As they walked through the frosty air, their shoulders brushed together softly. Leaving the chatting to Ian, Scott was content to listen to him, loving the way he spoke. Occasionally smiling and nodding for encouragement, his mind was flashing over and over again at what contact with his lips felt like. In complete distraction, he would lose himself on his mouth, the fullness of it, the fact that his lips appeared painted and glossed though they weren't.

The Kiss

"What did you think about the commercial?" After two hours to let it sink in, Scott wanted to gauge if the kiss had any affect on Ian. It most certainly had on him.

"It was quite easy. I was very surprised how quickly we did it. A little earner, too. Twenty thousand dollars! Why, that's about fifteen thousand pounds! That's a fair bit of wedge for less than two hours work."

A little disappointed that all Ian was referring to was the profitability, Scott tried to smile and nod. "Yes. It was easy. I could have done a few more like that. I hope Claire gets us more work after it airs."

"She will. Try not to upset yourself." Ian patted his back warmly.

By three p.m. they found their way to the apartment house. Coming in, shaking off the cold, Scott checked the thermostat to make sure it was warm enough in the flat, then threw his coat on a chair. After he did the same, Ian moved to the stereo equipment and investigated the music selection.

"Play anything you want," Scott said, kicking off his shoes.

"I hardly know any of them."

"They're mostly British bands, for Christ's sake!" Scott teased.

"They are? You're taking the mick!"

"Taking the—? Oh, for crying out loud." Kneeling next to him, he tugged out several as proof. "Look, Emerson, Lake and Palmer, Led Zeppelin, Black Sabbath, Jethro Tull, and here! The fucking Beatles!"

"Oh! Yes, Beatles! I know them. No ABBA?"

"What? Oh, don't even say that when Claire gets back. You'll never hear the end of it."

"Why?"

Pausing, Scott just stared at that bewildered innocent expression. "Are you stoned, or stupid?"

About to burst out laughing, Ian said, "Both? Possibly?"

"Oh, my god, you're mad...a mad Englishman!" He backed away comically.

"Yes! And you're in a flat! Alone with him! Ha ha!"

As Scott scrambled to get back from him, Ian leaped on him to pin him down. Wrestling to gain superiority, Scott managed to get on top of him and press his shoulders into the wooden floor. Ian gave up and panted to catch his breath, his long hair covering his face in irritation. "Uncle! You win! You brute!"

Satisfied he was the stronger of the two, Scott released his grip and sat back. As Ian removed the hair from his eyes, Scott's attention was diverted to the contact they were making from the waist down. Finding their genitals connected, he stood up quickly and straightened out his shirt. When the phone rang, he jumped out of his skin as if he had been caught in a lurid act.

Sitting up to watch him, Ian bit his lip as Scott pranced over to it and read the caller ID. Lifting the receiver he said, "Oh, it's you, buttface."

"Is that anyway to talk to your sister?" Claire said, "Did I catch you two buttfucking?"

"Oh, here she goes again..." Scott didn't even look back at Ian that time.

"Look, the reason I called was because tomorrow I have you scheduled for that shoot with *Men's World*. So, do some sit-ups or something. Tighten that belly up."

"Will you shut up! No! Don't say it!" He prevented the obvious response. "What time is the meeting?"

"Early. Nine a.m. You remember that studio where I took you to redo your head shots for your portfolio?"

"Yes. West Sixty-eighth Street."

"Right. There. Okay, sweetie? I just wanted to give you advance notice. I found out this minute."

The Kiss

"I appreciate it. Thanks."

"You guys okay?"

This time he did turn to see Ian still sorting through CD's. "Yes. This limey doesn't even know British music."

"Well, it's your chance to educate him. You can play teacher and teacher's pet with each other."

"God! Enough already!"

"Okay, see you tonight."

He hung up and exhaled in annoyance.

"You all right?"

"Hmmm?" Scott turned back to look at him. A child-like expression was gazing wistfully in his direction. "Yeah. It was Claire."

"So I gathered."

"She wanted to give me the heads up about that ad I have to do for that men's mag."

"Oh?"

"It's tomorrow morning."

"You ready?"

Scott unbuttoned his top as he walked to the mirror in the bathroom.

With Ian scampering behind, he tossed his shirt on the floor and stared at himself in the mirror, flexing his stomach muscles.

"Fuck, you're built," Ian sighed.

"I need to shave."

Ian checked Scott's jaw for the day's growth as Scott shook a can of cream and spread it all over his sparse chest hair.

"Oh, blimey! You mean your chest?" Ian burst out laughing.

"Yes. They expect it."

"Christ! Don't cut yourself!" Ian leaned on a wall to watch

73

this ritual.

"I won't. I've done it a ton of times before."

"Have you? I never have. I don't have much." He tried to raise up his shirt, then decided to pull it off over his head. As he checked out his own chest hair in the wall-to-wall mirror over a double sink, Scott found a new disposable razor and hovered over himself, deciding on his shaving tactic. Before he began, he lost his concentration as Ian rubbed his palms curiously over his own rounded pectoral muscles, feeling for hair.

"Give me that cream." Ian reached out his hand.

"Why?" Scott started laughing. "Are you going to shave?"

"Yes."

Scott handed him the can and then began shaving his own chest in the mirror's reflection. He kept being distracted as Ian rubbed the white foam all over himself.

"Do you have a spare razor?"

"Yup, hang on." Scott grabbed a plastic bag with a dozen of them inside and handed it to him. "They're brand new so be careful."

"Right, I shall." Ian took one out and uncapped it. "Right, okay. So, how does one begin?"

"I do it top down."

"Top down. Right."

As Ian watched Scott shave off his chest hair, he began stroking the razor over what little he had.

Trying not to get too absorbed in Ian's actions, Scott finished and started rinsing off the remaining shave cream, running his hand over himself to check for any missed spots. Scott rummaged through the medicine chest just as Ian finished up shaving.

"That's me done now." Ian rinsed the blade under the tap and then started wiping the rest off with a washcloth. When he was through he gave his attention back to Scott. "Well, what do you think?" He stuck out his chest while Scott was busy digging through medicine bottles "What are you doing now, mate?"

"Looking for the tanning shit. It's a bronzing cream." Scott found what he was after and shook it vigorously.

"Fancy that! How do you manage to coat all of you?"

"I do the best I can."

"Give us the bottle, I can do it."

Widening his eyes in horror, Scott shook his head. "No! I always do it! It's okay!"

"Don't be a wanker. Let me help." Pulling the bottle out of Scott's stunned hand, Ian poured a blob into his palm. "Now, just rub it on?"

"Yes. Evenly please. And not too much or I'll turn orange."

"Ha…orange."

"I mean it. Literally orange!"

"Keep your hair on! I'll be careful!"

Exhaling a sigh of annoyance, Scott stood facing him as the cream was applied. He watched Ian's hands as they spread the tanning lotion over his upper chest and neck. In the meantime, Scott used what he had left on his own fingers to rub over his face. Then when those British hands lowered to his waistline, Scott found their reflection in the mirror.

"I'm going to get it on your slacks. Take them off."

"What?" Scott asked flatly.

"I said, I'm going to bugger up your slacks! You're behaving like a dipstick, ya know?" Ian laughed to soften the insult, while holding up his messy hands.

Clumsily opening the snap and zipper, Scott stepped out of his pants and hung them over the towel bar.

"Good. How low do you need this tan to go?"

"I—I was going to do my whole body," he swallowed nervously, "I don't want to look patchy."

"Including your helmet?" Ian grinned.

"My what?"

"Your helmet! Your one-eyed trouser snake! Your knob!" Shaking his head, Ian said, "You are a bit thick, you yanks, aren't you?"

Scott tilted his head, completely lost.

"Your dick, you plonker!"

"No! Not my dick!"

"Your bum?"

"Ahh…" As Ian stood with a blob of cream, ready for a direction, Scott said, "Do my legs first, let me decide."

"Right. I reckon you're not shaving those…"

"No. Not my legs."

"Right." Ian knelt down and started spreading the lotion down each thigh.

As Scott peered at the top of his head, he had an image flash of Ian sucking his cock. Closing his eyes for a moment to decide whether to savor or remove that image from his thoughts, he then turned his face away in humiliation. His gaze moved back to the mirror. From there he could see Ian's determined expression in profile, trying to do the job perfectly.

"Turn around…okay, what did you decide? Your bum?"

"Uh, yeah, all right." Scott tugged his briefs down and gave Ian his back.

Starting at his shoulders, Ian worked his way down.

As if tickled with a feather duster, Scott's skin began to tingle, and it had nothing to do with the tanning gel. As his bottom was coated with confident strong strokes, his dick rose against his will. Turning his eyes upwards to the ceiling and the line that divided the wall from it, he wondered if he had gone completely mad.

As Ian knelt down behind him, he ran his palms over the two tight rounded balls of Scott's bottom, then his thighs.

"Fuck, you're built," he mumbled again, then slid his hand to the inside of Scott's legs, brushing under his balls.

Scott kept repeating the same question he wanted to ask Ian. *Are you gay?* As if that made things clearer and he could make a more informed decision from there. But, no matter how he rehearsed it in his head, he couldn't force those words to pass his lips.

When Ian's hands slowed down and concentrated solely on the inside of Scott's inseams, the sweat broke out on Scott's face. As discreetly as he could, he stole a peek at the mirror. With rapt attention, Ian was massaging those large thigh muscles, his lips as close to Scott's backside as they could get without touching it.

"Oh, god..." Scott breathed.

Ian heard it. He quickly finished up his task and stood, capping the bottle and setting it aside, then turned on the tap to rinse his hands.

Scott had no idea what to do. If he had any resources to cope with this odd predicament, they had drained down the sink with the rust colored gel.

"I think that's us done. Check if I've missed a spot, would you?"

Slow to react, Scott made a small gesture of looking himself over, keeping his erection facing away from Ian, though Ian must have already spied it in the mirror's reflection.

"I...I think you're all right. I mean—I'm done. Thanks."

"Good. Brilliant...I'll-uh..."

As Ian shifted anxiously, Scott struggled to find the courage to face him full on, showing him how excited he was, for no other reason than just to see his reaction. Turning around, holding the sink for support, Scott imagined reaching out and taking Ian in his arms, kissing him like he had in the theater.

The moment Scott moved, Ian backed out of the bathroom. "I'll leave you to it then."

Standing by himself, the mirror his only company, Scott exhaled a long breath. He had no idea what was going on in his own head, let alone in Ian's.

Chapter Nine

She didn't know what she expected to find as she came through the door with a bag of sushi-to-go, hoping Ian liked it, knowing Scott did. There wasn't much Scott didn't eat, if she thought about it.

With her imagination running amuck, she opened the door as quietly as she could. Disappointed she was wrong in her theory, yet slightly relieved to find them both slouching on the couch watching television, she let out a long exhaled sigh. "Hello. Did you eat dinner yet?"

The right word spoken, Scott jumped to his feet, wearing nothing but a pair of microscopic black gym shorts, and started sniffing hungrily. "No. We're starved. What have you got?"

"Sushi...good boy for getting ready? You look great." As she set the bag of food on the table, she said, "How the hell did you get the tanning stuff on so well?"

Peeking behind him sheepishly, catching Ian's eye quickly, he mumbled, "Ian helped me."

"Did he?" *No kidding*, she thought, feeling slightly betrayed though she wouldn't admit it to herself. "Well, that was nice of him." She leaned back to see him crunched over on the couch. For some reason the news on the television was fascinating him suddenly. "Ian?"

Acting paranoid, he seemed to force a smile. "Yes, Miss

Epstein?"

"Do you like sushi?"

He hopped off the couch and headed over, the Christmas tree lights shimmering in silent rainbows behind him. "Yes. Some of it. Not the smelly raw fish, but I do fancy the ones filled mostly with rice and veggies."

"Great. Scott, go get some plates and something to drink."

"Can I help?" Ian asked.

"You can shut off that awful news and put on a CD. How about that?" She smiled sweetly so it didn't seem like a complaint.

Happy to oblige, he spun around and found the remote control. While he was occupied, Scott was setting down some plates near Claire. "You guys do anything exciting today? Other than rub lotion on each other?"

"Geezuz! Do you ever stop?"

"No. At least not until you say I was right."

"Well, you aren't right! I'm not gay!" The loud exclamation resonated around the space they occupied.

Both of them twisted to see if Ian heard the last comment. Busy sliding a CD in, it was obvious he either didn't or was ignoring it.

"Is he?" she whispered.

"I've no clue, and I'm not going to ask." Scott resumed his task of setting the table and went to get some glasses and napkins.

"Warm up some sake, okay?" she shouted to him.

"We have a bottle?"

"Yes, top cabinet over the sink. Unopened, unless you've already tapped into it."

"I haven't." Pulling open the tiny wooden door with the stainless steel knob, he found the bottle still in a cardboard box and took it down.

The Kiss

Emerson, Lake, and Palmer music started playing and Claire smiled as she heard it. "You know my taste, Ian," she said.

"So I've heard. Best of the British bands. And you hate ABBA."

"ABBA?" she laughed sarcastically. "Right, whatever you say." She had no idea where that one had come from, but she suspected it was something Scott had warned him about. "Okay, why don't you guys go sit down? I'll keep an eye on the sake."

"It's okay, I've got it." Scott waved her back to her chair.

While she handed out the chopsticks and packages of soy sauce, Ian sat down across from her, scratching his chest through his shirt.

"You okay?"

When he raised his head to meet her eyes, a flash of guilt passed before he could hide it, then he pushed his long hair behind his ears and nodded, "Yes, brilliant. Okay, what should I start with?"

"These are California rolls. You'll love them." She nudged the package to him as Scott came to the table with a cloth around the bottom of the sake bottle. "Who wants some?"

Since they all did, Claire set the three cups in front of him.

Silence followed as they ate hungrily, until Claire asked Ian, "Did you let your parents know you have moved here? From the hotel?"

"No. I haven't spoken to them for about a week."

"You can call them…you should call them."

"I didn't want to make a phone call to them without checking with you first. I was afraid it would cost too much," he said, then shoved another piece of sushi in his mouth.

"Well, if you want to save me a few cents, I think I have one of those ten, ten, numbers."

"A ten-ten?" Ian tilted his head curiously.

G.A. Hauser

"Yeah, ask Scott to show you how to do it."

"Why didn't you say something? I would have helped you call them earlier today!" As usual, Scott was consuming the food so fast, Claire rushed to grab a few more of her favorites before he did his magician act on them, and made them disappear.

"Oh, I guess I just didn't think of it. They're five hours ahead. What time is it now?" He searched for a clock.

Claire checked hers. "Six o'clock."

"Naaa, it's too late now. They'll be in bed."

"Remind me tomorrow, before I go to the shoot." Scott hunted for anything left edible on the table.

"Right, cheers." Ian nodded.

"Oh! Shit, I almost forgot!" Claire chewed quickly and swallowed. "Guess when that commercial is going to air?"

They both froze and stared at her in horror.

"Super Bowl Sunday," she gushed, "And they are leaking it to the *New York Times* and *People Magazine*! You guys will have it made."

The redness in Scott's face was amazing. Even through the fake tan, he blushed brightly. Suddenly losing his appetite, he pushed his plate aside in disappointment. Claire wished she had thought of it earlier when there was more sushi left. At the news, Ian didn't blush, but stayed very quiet.

"Uh...okay. I expected something. A comment? A bit of excitement?"

Scott scooted his chair out and decided to start clearing the table and tossing the empty containers into the trash.

"Scott Andrew Epstein! What the hell is the matter with you? You can't still be worried the world will think you're gay from one frickin' commercial ad! Grow up!"

"Fuck you!" he roared defensively, as he slammed some things around.

82

The Kiss

Completely bewildered, Claire looked at Ian for his reaction. There was none.

Thinking she was becoming unreasonably warm from her irritation, sweating as a hot flush raced over her, she suddenly realized it was oven-hot in the apartment. Claire gaped at Scott in frustration wondering if he had turned up the heat so he could lounge around in a state of almost nudity, after having the boy rub him with tanning lotion. And he wondered why she was reacting this way? As he strut around, showing off his body to Ian, in hopes of…what? Turning him on?

About to attack with another nasty comment, she rose up and checked the thermostat. He had it set to almost eighty degrees. She lowered it and glared back at him, about to explode with fury.

It was more than their ungratefulness, more than the cranking up of the heat, it was the fact that they were hiding things from her, as thought they had dirty little secrets.

It was Ian who finally broke the silence. Clearing his throat, he rose up with his plate and went to set it in the sink. "I'll load the washer."

Remembering they had a guest from another country staying in their home, she forcefully changed her demeanor, trying not to allow him to see their seamier side. "Great, thank you, Ian," Claire sighed. It was with some relief that she felt she had one normal man in the place.

When Ian made his generous offer, the guilt forced Scott into joining him. With the three of them clearing, washing, and putting away things in complete silence, it was done quickly.

As she wiped her hands on a towel, she sighed and said under her breath, "I'll be back. I need to change out of my work clothes. I'm fucking roasting to death!" Sneering the last line directly at her brother, she felt their eyes on her watching her go, having no idea if they made any exchange behind her back as she kept moving. The only thing on her mind was changing, now that it was as hot as the Bahamas in there.

Hanging up her shirt, standing in her bra and slacks, she heard a light rap on her door. Thinking it was Scott coming to apologize, she said, "Come in."

When Ian poked his head in and spotted her, he grinned in pleasure at her state of undress. "You have time for a chat, Miss Epstein?"

"Yes, Ganymede." She searched for something to throw on as he came in.

"Don't cover up on my account." His smile was wide and a bit flirtatious.

Since she was having a hard time finding something appropriate anyway because her intention had been to take her damn bra off and slip on a tee shirt and shorts, she gave up and sat on her bed. "Come here and sit down."

Closing the door behind him, he tried not to stare at her black Victoria Secret undergarment and the breasts they covered. "Very hot," he said as he seated himself next to her.

"Thanks…so, what can I do for you?"

"Other than the obvious?" he grinned.

Again it caught her by surprise. This was most certainly the words of a heterosexual male. No mistake there. She guessed her little experiment was a failure. "You naughty boy! I'm ten years older than you are!"

Shrugging gently, he whispered, "Think I give a shite? Fancy a shag?"

"Ian Sullivan, you bad boy!" But the idea excited her. An instant image flash of diving on him, shoving him back on her bed and covering him with kisses made its path across her conscious mind. "What did you want to talk to me about?"

As he gathered his thoughts, he reached up to toy with her brown hair. It was slightly longer than his own, and wavy. "Do you think my staying here is causing problems between you and your brother? Because if it is—"

"It's not. We're not getting along any differently than we

had been before you came. I don't mind you staying here, Ian. On the contrary." A shiver passed over her as he tugged gently on her waves.

Seeing that little quiver, a very delighted smile emerged on his lips. "It's just for the winter break. I'm sure once I start winter session, I can move into the dormitories on campus."

"If you haven't made arrangements already, I wouldn't count on it." He had scooted closer, his body brushing hers, his hand still twisting a lock of her hair around his fingers.

"Oh. Well, I have been remiss then. I'm sorry."

"How many times do I have to say, I want you here?"

"How badly do you want me?"

This was moving in a direction she wasn't sure she was ready for. She had never had sex with a client. Though they were tempting, gorgeous, and willing, she decided the first day she started the business never to mix it with pleasure. Besides, most of these pretty boys were out for what they could get, period. And he was only twenty-one! Did she just want a tumble with him? And if they had sex, and he remained living there, and he found a little ditzy girlfriend? Oh, lord, no, what a mess.

Backing him up by his shoulders, smiling to soften the blow, she said, "Look, Ganymede, I want you here so I can stare at you and fantasize about fucking your brains out, but, not to actually touch. Okay? I have a rule about my models, and I will stick to it."

Dropping his hand to his lap in disappointment, he nodded. "I understand perfectly, Miss Epstein. I wouldn't dream of making you break any of those rules."

"Oh. Good," she said without emotion, hoping he would have put up a better argument for her to do just that.

As he stood, he grinned wickedly. "You have lovely tits, Miss Epstein."

Laughing in surprise from such a direct comment, she shouted, "Get out before I change my mind!"

Staring at her for as long as he could as he inched backwards, he finally faced the door, leaving her to sit and think about it. This was a test for Scott! Not for her! Wasn't it?

Cozy under her fluffy blankets, about to drift off, the clock reading ten p.m., her door once again started moving. Staring at it intently, she wondered if Ian came in, stark naked, with that big hard-on, if she would really be able to resist him. Debating that in earnest, she was a little disappointed it was Scott.

"You still up?" he whispered.

"Yeah, what's up, cookie?" She managed to sit higher on the pillows and flip on a low light that was on her nightstand.

Coming to snuggle in bed next to her like he did as a little boy so many times before, usually after nightmares, he crunched the blankets around his chin and sighed heavily. A lot was on his mind and she was partly to blame, if not entirely.

"Talk to me, Scottchula..." She shimmied down so they were nose to nose.

"I don't know really. I just can't sleep."

"You never can. You, Dad, and me. It's the family curse."

"Yeah, I suppose..."

She paused, staring at his sad face, then pet his hair back gently. "Is it Ian?"

Rage flashed, then vanished to exhaustion. "I don't know."

"Now, don't get mad at me if I ask you some things. Okay?"

"What things?" She could tell he was already furious at the implications.

"Forget it. What did you come in here for?"

"Just for the comfort."

"Okay, baby, go to sleep." She kissed his forehead and shut the light.

The Kiss

Unknown to either of them, Ian was tiptoeing to Scott's room.

Opening the door quietly, he closed himself inside with the intention of having a quiet private chat with Scott, then squinted at the empty bed in disappointment. As he paused, wondering if he was possibly in the bathroom and would return at any moment, he struggled to remember if the door was closed when he walked by. Moving around in the dimness, he eyed the contents of the *simple bedroom curiously. A double bed, disheveled, a desk, covered with papers, a full bookcase and a three-drawer antique dresser. No clutter. Clean and minimal. Moving to the desk, he noticed a corner of a photo sticking out of a folder. Imagining it was one of Scott's shots, he opened it, choking in surprise to see his own portrait. At a sound behind him, thinking he heard someone coming, he spun to the door in paranoia. Then after slowing the beating of his heart, realizing it was no one, he gazed back again at that photo. His head shot. The one he sent to Spencer & Epstein with his application. Why was it in Scott's bedroom? It was a mystery.

Closing the cover gently to conceal it once more, he stared at the bed. There was something he was dying to ask Scott, only he couldn't think how to phrase it. Was Scott gay? It wasn't an easy question to ask. But the reason he came into his bedroom tonight may have been for that answer. The more he thought about it, the more it plagued him.

By now he figured Scott was in the other bedroom with his sister, talking. He wished he could be a fly on the wall and hear what they said. It would all make sense to him suddenly, knowing Scott was homosexual. It would account for so much of his odd behavior.

Headed back to his own room, he dared to lean his ear against Claire's bedroom door. Not a sound could be heard. Shrugging to himself, he went back to bed, and fell into a deep slumber.

"Do you mind if I drink another bottle of water? I'm dying of thirst." She waited as an assistant hurried to get her one.

"Look, about seeing them kiss. It was a shock to my system. I don't know what I expected... Oh, thanks for the water." She uncapped it and drank it down quickly. *"Ah, that's better. Now, where was I? Oh, the kiss.*

"Well, in my mind I kept asking myself what they now felt for each other. Now that they had touched each other sexually and were still living side by side. That whole business with the tanning lotion was another thing I didn't get. I couldn't even imagine Scott allowing Ian to touch him that way. You see, Scott was not himself back then. I'm convinced he was very nervous around Ian and he could not stop thinking about how attractive Ian was.

"When Ian propositioned me, I knew it would be a big mistake. I had to keep reminding myself of my position, and then of course, the attraction my brother was beginning to feel for him. I never would have actually gone to bed with him with all that up in the air. I could see the relationship between them blooming and wondered why Scott couldn't, or didn't openly admit it. But, I'm afraid it took a little longer for my brother to admit he was falling in love. Though I could see it myself, I would never have said it to him at that time."

Chapter Ten

When the alarm screamed rudely, Claire realized she was in bed alone. Scott must have woken up during the night and climbed back into his own bed. Yawning and stretching like a feline, she made it upright and back to the world of the living. The pummeling body massaging showerhead steamed hotly and felt wonderful to her groggy senses.

Dressed, made up, and blown dry, she hurried to make sure Scott was awake and ready to go to his shoot. He was still asleep, the blankets twisted horribly showing her what a bad night he had. Regretting she had to wake him at all, she rubbed his shoulder to rouse him. "Okay, baby, rise and shine."

A groan of agony escaped him. With an effort he rolled to his back and tried to open his eyes. "I swear the best sleep I get is between five a.m. and seven."

"I'm sorry. I would love to let you sleep in, but you have that shoot at nine."

"Yeah, I know." He sat up and pushed the covers back.

Seeing he was completely naked, she cringed, spun around, and made herself scarce. Closing the door behind her, she thought she heard the shower in the second bathroom. Leaning her ear against it to be sure, she did indeed. So, body number two was upright. Good. She headed to the kitchen to start a pot of coffee.

As she decided between frozen waffles or toast, the bathroom door opened and lovely Ian came out with a towel wrapped around his narrow waist. Scuffing his way passed him, was Scott, who was too tired to say good-morning, and closed himself in for his turn to shower. While Ian and she watched, smiling in sympathy, they exchanged greetings.

"Morning, Miss Epstein!"

"Good morning, gorgeous! You hungry for breakfast?"

"Yes, please!"

"Okay. You go and get dressed before I fantasize that towel falling off, and I'll have your coffee poured. Two sugars?"

"Yes, Miss Epstein." He paused.

Right before she turned her eyes, he twisted to go back to his room, dropping the towel so she could see his lovely backside before he disappeared into the guest room.

"Flirt!" she yelled, imagining him laughing his head off over it, which he was. "Christ, I must have the will power of a fucking saint!" she grumbled to herself. "He's not gay, though I suppose he could be bi." She chuckled as she shook her head. Experiment gone bad. Oh, well.

Trying to tidy up the kitchen as the time was running short, she grabbed her purse and keys and shouted to ask the boys if they were coming or she was on her own in a cab.

Scott was racing around anxiously, his nerves kicking in for his appointment. "Go! I'll lock up!"

"What are your plans, Ian?" Claire said, the doorknob in her hand.

"I don't know."

"Okay, well, call me if you need anything. Bye!"

As she closed the door, Ian stopped Scott's mad pacing and said, "I'll come with you."

The Kiss

It took him by surprise, then he sighed, "Thanks."

"It's all right. Come. Off we go."

As Scott posed in a pair of clinging white gym shorts, he wondered what the other men in the room thought of him bringing along such a pretty-boy. Asking himself if he cared if they thought he was gay or not, he found it was mattering less and less to him. Having someone like Ian associated with him, in any manner, could only be a plus point. The boy was so incredibly beautiful. He turned heads. Literally. No matter where they went, people craned their necks to see him. Out of self-preservation, Scott imagined it was more to double-check his sex. At times Ian appeared to be female, but, more times than not, he was just a very good-looking young male. As they walked down the Avenue of the Americas together, Scott hated to admit he liked Ian by his side, was proud to be there with him, and loved the jealous stares and admiring gazes, especially from pretty women. Loved it!

And now, that gorgeous man was smiling at him with that adoring grin of his. With the lights bright and hot, the camera whirring and clicking as he flexed his oil-coated abdomen, and moved side to side for the best shot Ian never lost interest in gazing at him. No longer feeling humiliated by his attention, Scott was actually savoring it.

He loved the fact that Ian had chosen to come along, wanted to stare at him at length, and offered his help and opinion. Even if this relationship was not physical, he was certainly growing fond of that man beyond his wildest dreams. It had been since high school, back in Seattle, that he'd had a best male friend. He was overdue.

And then, just when he had forgotten the world existed and absorbed himself in the work, that masculine kiss would haunt him. His taste, his lips, and that tongue. That mischievous tip of his tongue that had snuck its way into his mouth when no one was aware. Why else would he have done that if he weren't interested? It was the present reason Scott could not sleep.

With Ian's vacant smile and glazed-over green eyes attached to some spot low on his body as he posed, what was he to think? What would happen if he came on? Did he want to? Prove Claire was right and touch a man sexually? She wasn't right! She couldn't be! This was absurd!

With that same argument playing in his head like a broken record, he could not stop obsessing over Ian, and not knowing the answers to his questions, especially the most obvious one, was literally driving him mad.

The session over, his street clothing back on concealing his muscular body, Scott escorted Ian out of the studio and into the cold December air.

"I love this city!" Ian raised his eyes to the narrow stone-faced skyscrapers, like a child filled with the wonder of the season. "Every building is so 'uge!"

"Better than London?" Scott asked, smiling.

Pausing, a shy grin on his lips, Ian said, "No, mate. Not better than London, sorry." Nudging him as they walked, Ian sighed, "There is nothing like my city. You must come there with me."

"Where? London?" Scott gasped in excitement at the thought. "Really?"

"Yes! Really!" Ian laughed at Scott's wide-eyed enthusiasm. "It's fantastic! The London Eye, the Tower, the Thames... I'd show you a great time."

"I'd love that! Thank you, Ian!" His mind working feverishly, Scott was wondering when they could book a flight. The idea of leaving New York and spending time alone with Ian was extremely exciting.

"It's the least I can do. You and Claire have been so kind."

As they continued to walk silently, Scott wondered if he went to London with him, would they sleep in the same room?

Same bed? And man, did he want to go! He'd been to Paris once, a few years ago with his parents. He felt odd, hated being seen with them, and wished he'd never gone. Going with Ian would be an entirely different experience, one he would savor and cherish for the rest of his life.

Then another intruding thought occurred to him. "Do you have a girlfriend back there?"

"Hmm? Me? No." Ian laughed in a cough. "No bird waiting."

Trying to read more into it, Scott almost formed the question. 'The Question'. Then chickened out and wished he'd had more courage.

"You mind if we head back to the apartment?" Scott asked, "I slept like crap and I need a nap."

"Knackered? No, I'm not bothered. It'll give me a chance to call me mum." He checked his watch. "And I could use a lay-down meself."

"Oh! Okay."

They came through the door shaking off the cold from the icy draughts that whipped violently between buildings. After Scott tossed his jacket onto the chair carelessly, he dug through a junk filled drawer in the kitchen. Throwing his own jacket on top of Scott's, Ian waited by the telephone in the living room patiently.

"Got it!" Scott brought out a little card and read the instructions. "Okay, dial this number, then the country code, then your own number."

"Bloody hell!" Ian shook his head. "Right, let's give it a go."

As Scott watched in fascination, Ian dialed the United Kingdom.

"Ringing?" Scott asked.

"Yup!" Ian answered brightly, "Cheers, mate!"

"Mind if I sit here? I could leave." He made like he was getting up, though he didn't want to.

"No! Don't be daft!" Ian waved for him to sit back down. After a pause, Ian said, "Mum? Ian!"

Reclining back in the soft leather chair, Scott leaned on his elbow and gazed at Ian as he explained his new living arrangements and his excitement at being able to explore New York City with someone who knew it well. Scott thought he was so damn cute he could die.

"I've been to Central Park, the Empire State Building—" Cupping the receiver he asked Scott, "What was that skating place called?"

"Rockefeller Center."

"Right!...Mum? And Rockefeller Center, where we skated on ice. Yes! I've me classes lined up, I'm all sorted. They're lovely. Switched on to it all, you know? Claire and Scott Epstein, brother and sister. Oi! Who's takin' the piss! They are!" He winked at Scott though Scott was struggling to understand most of the conversation. "She's me boss. Stop winding me up! Are you listening to me at all?" He rolled his eyes at Scott as his mother questioned him. "Oi! Don't be 'orrible to me! I'm not a bleedin' little one. Yes, Mum. I do know. Yes...uh huh..." Taking his ear from the phone he made a silly face at Scott and then went back to it to nod and give her one-word reassurances. "Yes, Mum. Yes, Mum...I don't know. I reckon some time. It depends on the housing at the school. No, they like me! Of course!" He whispered aside to Scott, "You do like me here?"

"Yes!" Scott laughed and almost hit him playfully.

Ian flinched back and said, "Oi! I'm about to be boshed. No, he's just playing! Right! I will, Mum! I love you, too. You take care and tell Dad I'm sorry I rung whilst he was working. Oh? Yes, hold on." He cupped the phone. "Can she have your number here?"

"Of course! Ready?"

When Ian nodded, Scott recited it and Ian repeated it. "Got it? Good. Bye, Mum!"

After he hung up, Scott was smiling at him warmly. "You miss her?"

Sheepishly, Ian nodded, "Would you think I'm a plonker if I said yes?"

Scott burst out laughing, "No. I don't know what a plonker is!"

"Never mind. You going for a lay-down?" Ian stretched and yawned.

"I should. You?"

"I could use a siesta."

"Right. Come on." Scott patted his knee and rose up, reaching out to haul him up.

Ian said, "You looked great at the shoot. Blimey, wearing those tiny little things."

Scott spun around, smiling at the encouragement. "You think? I never know if I look stupid."

"You look anything but stupid!" Ian laughed.

For some reason, the words that were being spoken at that moment caused the expression on Scott's face to fall. Having no other thoughts on his mind, and not knowing why he was even doing it, he impulsively reached behind Ian's head, into that long wonderful hair, and pulled his lips close for a kiss, just like he had in the commercial.

At first Scott felt Ian tense up, as if he were about to reject it. But a moment later, Ian wrapped around Scott's body and returned the hungry passion, connected to his lips.

For a long leisurely moment, they stood still and kissed, exploring each other's mouths with hungry tongues. Small noises were escaping, moans of yearning and lust that started soft and slow and were gaining in urgency.

Driven wild by this pretty boy's mouth, Scott started tearing open Ian's clothing, yearning to feel the heat of his silky skin. And as Ian continued to kiss Scott's mouth, he aided him, stripping off his own shirt and slacks, never releasing the connection to him.

Finally gasping for a breath after at least fifteen minutes of kissing, Scott groaned, "Oh, god," in agony.

Ian urged him back into his bedroom, undressing Scott this time, licking and sucking at his mouth as he did.

With a trail of clothing leading to the bed, they fell back on it, clinging together, wrapping their legs around each other.

"Oh, my fucking god..." Scott moaned, "You feel so fucking good! It's unfucking real!"

"You, too...oh, for Christ's sake, baby, you are unbelievable!"

Squirming, rubbing on each other, kissing over and over, Scott finally pulled back to stare at him. "Okay. What do I do?"

"What do you do?" Ian ran his hands down Scott's warm sides. "I don't know what you mean."

"How do we do this?" Scott tried to make it clear.

"I don't fucking know!" Ian laughed.

"You don't?" Scott could not catch his breath.

"No!" Ian leaned up on his elbows to see Scott more clearly.

"Aren't you gay?"

"No! Aren't you?"

Staring at each other in complete astonishment at that revelation, they burst out laughing. Ian rolled off of Scott and they both lie on their backs, roaring at the hilarity.

Trying to calm down, wiping his eyes, Scott kept saying, "Oh, my god..." in disbelief.

"How hard can it be?" Ian sat up and grabbed Scott's cock in his hand boldly.

The Kiss

"Fucking hard!" Scott laughed at the pun.

"I can see that! Do we screw? Or just wank each other off?"

"I don't fucking know! Would you let me butt fuck you?"

Ian paused as he thought about the option, still playing with Scott's cock. "Uh, can I do it to you?"

At that comment, Scott's laughing renewed. "Oh, Christ, this is so fucking funny!"

"All right, so neither one of us will get shagged this time. You want to suck me?" Ian tilted his hips up, showing his cock.

"Uhh," Scott considered the possibility remote. "Not at the moment."

"Bloody hell!" Ian laughed. "Two fucking straight guys who don't want to touch each other! How the bloody hell do we manage this?"

"I want to touch you!" Scott wrapped around him and squeezed him close. "You have no idea how much I want to touch you... And kiss you." He made a trail of kisses up his neck to his ear.

"Yes...oh, baby...that's it." Ian shivered.

"Jerk me off," Scott whispered.

"I can handle that." Ian leaned back and exposed Scott's cock, then began working it. "How's that?"

"Fucking great!" Scott lay back and spread his legs. "That's it..."

"God, you're beautiful!" Ian squirmed all over the bed as he masturbated him. "Come, baby, come for your Ian!"

"Ah!" In moments Scott shivered and shot cum all over his chest.

Still massaging him gently, Ian stared at him in awe. "You are so fucking built!"

"Oh, my fucking god..." Scott groaned.

"I have an idea." Ian started gathering up all the spent cum from Scott's body.

"Uh oh…what's your idea?" Scott watched him nervously.

"I'll just stick it between your thighs."

"Oh. All right." Scott opened his legs as Ian coated himself with Scott's cum and climbed over him.

"Now tighten those fucking thighs up, baby."

Clamping his legs shut, Scott felt Ian's hard cock sliding between his legs. "Feel good?"

"Oh, fuck yeah." Ian leaned up over him and pumped furiously.

"That's it, baby. Come for me. Come for me, you gorgeous creature. I want to see your face when you come."

When Scott cupped Ian's chest in both hands, then pinched his nipples, Ian gasped and came between Scott's thighs.

Staring up at that sight, Scott could not believe how beautiful he appeared at that moment. "I think I love you."

Ian blinked his eyes open, gaped at Scott, then they both burst out laughing.

"God! Don't tell Claire! Please!" Scott begged.

"Oh, bloody hell, no! Are you mad?" Ian breathed.

"Good. Thank god. Okay, we're agreed. Our secret."

"Yes! Are you fucking insane? You think I want people to think I'm gay?"

Scott's eyes widened at him in awe. "Exactly! I feel the same way!"

"Good!" Ian lay down along his side and exhaled in relief.

"Good."

Then the two of them started shaking with laughter again.

"I didn't know you weren't circumcised." Scott grinned wickedly.

"Yes, o'naturale. See you've had your helmet clipped."

"Yes, dear. It's called a briss."

"Ouch."

"I don't remember it hurting."

"I should hope not!"

Turning on his side to face him, Scott said, "I really do love you, Ian."

His smile full of affection, Ian faced him to say, "And I think I love you, too, Mr. Epstein."

The phone driving Claire crazy, the work piling up, she decided to stand and stretch her legs and get away from her desk. Instinctively heading to Jenine's office, she leaned on her doorway and stared at her as she had her phone to her ear, and her secretary about to hand her more notes for phone calls to come. Claire sighed deeply and tried to catch her eye. After acknowledging her, Jenine held up her index finger, indicating she was almost done on the call. Out of ritual boredom and idle curiosity, Claire wandered to her desk and nosed through her piles of photos. The commercial and television men tended to be different from the models she handled. They were more rugged. She had no other word to describe it. Not pretty in the least, but not ugly either. Just men's men. She liked her androgynous boys much better.

"Christ!" Jenine shouted after she disconnected the phone. "I don't know what in hell they want! They ask for a male who's in his twenties, tall and handsome. I send them ten to browse through and I get a call, 'But, he needed to be clean shaven!' Why didn't they specify? You know, I swear, Claire, they are such idiots. They don't know what they want!"

"Yes, dear. Take a break. Send Patty out."

Turning up her nose, Patty stood up and headed to the door as Jenine yelled, "Two minutes and I'll talk to you about those calls!"

When the door shut Claire sat down and they took a moment to catch their breath.

"I need a vacation." Jenine rubbed her hand over her face.

"Most companies close between Christmas and New Years. What do you think?"

"I'd love to…fuck them. Let's just do it."

"Good. I agree. I need more than a day off."

"Good. Let me tell Patty—" as she reached for the phone, a hand stopped her.

"Later," Claire interrupted.

"Later." She inhaled and sat up straight. "Okay, what's up?"

"Anything back from Mr. Surah on whether the spot is going to be played for the Super Bowl?"

"No, not on that, but! I got a call from *People Magazine* and they want a shot of them kissing for their article. They called Andre and asked for a still frame from his shoot, but he refused. He's being very tight about what he allows out before the actual airing."

"Then we can't. How about just two head shots?"

"Hmm, I don't know. Never mind. I'll tell them it's all we've got. Oh!"

"Oh?" It always seemed to Claire that Jenine's mind was working in four directions at once, and her conversation and train of thought seemed on opposite poles.

"I don't know how I forgot to mention this!" Her excitement grew to an explosion. "Calahan! Calahan wants them on his talk show!"

"No fucking way!" Claire gasped.

"Yes! He wants them after it's aired. The first taping after the football match! Live!"

Covering her mouth at the shock and coming hilarity, Claire said finally, "I told them it was their in."

"Nationwide interview! I think the exposure is going to get our phones ringing off the hook for them."

The Kiss

As they said those words, they heard the phones already doing just that. Claire rolled her eyes at the ironic comment.

"Well, more than what they are," Jenine clarified.

"You know, Calahan's got a nasty reputation. You think they'll be all right?"

"Sure! They're big boys. Besides, what can he do to them that won't already be done coast to coast? They're not gay, Claire. So, they'll handle it just fine."

"You don't know my brother."

"What do you want me to do? Tell them to pass this one up? I can't! It's exactly the publicity they and we need. They're going."

"Okay! Okay!" Claire held up her hands in case the verbal assault was continuing. "I just know that Calahan has two sides. He can be the sympathetic angel if he's dealing with a young cancer patient, and the devil with something this juicy."

"Will you just stop worrying?! You're worse than a mother hen!"

"All right. I'll stop telling you I'm worried, but I won't stop worrying."

"Whatever!!" Jenine started to get back to her phones.

"I was thinking about having a cocktail party at the apartment. I want to do it as a Christmas/New Years thing for the office and some close colleagues."

"Great! When?"

"Saturday before Christmas. You think it's too late notice?"

"Yes. How about the Saturday between Christmas and New Year's?"

"Okay, whatever...who do you want there?" Claire searched for a scratch paper as Jenine handed her a pen.

"None of the employees. You can't select. You have to have all or none, so we'll have an office do for them separately."

"Right. Of course. Clients?"

"You have any favorites?"

"It's a problem. If I invite my favorite male models, then the ones who are snubbed and get no invite have a chip on their shoulder."

"Okay, no clients. How about ad agency contacts?"

"Yes. I would like some there. I'll go through my Rolodex and pick ten. You do the same."

"Shame, really. We should have some models mixing with them. You know."

"No, I don't know. The models tend to get some eggnog in them and they act like asses. I think we'd be better off leaving portfolios around. The less they know about the way the men really behave the better."

"How can you say that? I'm sure they'll act like gentlemen! Especially if they find out the names of the clients there!"

Claire leaned over the desk to her and stared into her eyes. "Okay. Look. If you want some of your men there, be choosey."

"Deal. What's the limit, number wise?"

"Ten again. It's a big place, but too many will be uncomfortable."

"Okay. You better get on the catering fast! Your time is running out."

"Right!"

When she came through the apartment door, they were in their spot, slouching on the couch, the bowl of fruit consumed and all of the cartons of juice empty. That was why she didn't buy junk food and pop. It would be eaten as quickly, and with her brother's profession, he couldn't afford to binge like that.

"Hello, boys."

The Kiss

"Hi." Scott barely made eye contact.

"Hullo, Miss Epstein! You all right?"

"Yes, Ian, I'm just swell." As she came in and took off her coat, Ian stood up and started clearing away the banana peels and apple cores.

"I'm starved. I'm sick of rabbit food. What are we going to eat for dinner?" Seeing Ian was showing him up, Scott grabbed some of the garbage as well and followed him to dump it all in the kitchen trash.

"I have no clue. My brain is mush. You guys decide."

"You too tired to go out?" Scott set the glasses in the dishwasher.

Pausing to decide if she was, she did feel on the verge of dropping dead. "I don't know. Can't we call for delivery?"

"Chinese?"

"Anything. You decide." She scuffed into her bedroom to change into something casual.

Scott found the paper menu and sat down waving Ian over to help him choose.

Her jeans and tee shirt replacing her slacks and blouse, Claire rejoined the men as they went back and forth between egg rolls or shrimp toast.

"Your usual?" Scott asked her.

"Yeah, why not." She went to the refrigerator and found only a dribble of wine left. "Christ, it's like living with two piranhas."

"Sorry." Ian apologized. "If you tell me where a market is, I'll head out and get you some things."

Softening her irritated tone, Claire smiled and caressed Ian's face. "That's okay, lovely. I didn't mean to make you feel bad. We'll take care of the shopping tomorrow sometime. Maybe I could make a list for you and Scott. What do you think? You guys have time?"

As she pet Ian's face and hair, Scott tried to hide his bristle of annoyance.

"For you, Miss Epstein...we can find the time." Ian grinned.

"You better stop that type of talk, you're liable to sweep a girl off her feet."

In annoyance, Scott cleared his throat and nudged between them on the premise of showing Claire the list of main courses. "You want an appetizer?"

"Uh, sure. Soup and egg rolls. You calling or am I?"

"I can. Ian? Do I have everything marked that you want?" Scott made eye contact with him to communicate his displeasure.

Ian cleared his throat. "Yes, you do." He nodded, then stepped back from Claire

"Okay." Scott headed to the living room with the list.

While he was busy dialing, Ian moved next to Claire again to whisper, "I want to pay you. I can't keep taking handouts."

"Don't worry, Ganymede. I've already taken the twenty percent from your first paycheck," she grinned slyly.

"That's not what I mean. Kipping here...eating your food—"

His eyes flickering back to the other two in the room, Scott said into the phone, "Yes, hello, I would like to place an order to be delivered—"

"Stop," Claire said softly. "Look, Ian, though your offer is very generous, and I'd be lying to say I wasn't glad you were thinking this way and wanting to give me something, it isn't necessary. You're staying here is not going to throw the budget out of whack, believe me."

"...shrimp toast, fried rice..." When Claire pecked Ian's cheek, Scott became flustered. "Ahhh..."

"Well, Miss Epstein, if there ever is a time you need a

favor, or I can somehow return the kindness, I do hope you won't hesitate to ask." Ian smiled gently at her.

Claire dug her hands through his long thick hair. "Don't tempt me, Ganymede," she purred.

"Yes, I'm still here!" Scott was being shouted at in Chinese. "Sweet and sour chicken and white rice for three. Okay?"

Ian set back in surprise to meet Claire's expression. "Tempt you? I thought it was taboo!"

"It is. Ignore me." But, with both her hands she cupped his jaw and gazed wistfully into his green eyes.

"Hey!" Scott shouted. He had finished the phone call and hung up, storming over to them in a huff, fists clenched, features hardened.

Ian backed away from Claire's hands instantly, lowering his head at the admonishment.

"Hey what?" Claire shouted back. "You got a problem, Bucko?"

"I...I just don't need to see my sister groping some guy."

"Some guy?" Claire tilted her head comically. "He's not some guy. He's lovely Ian Sullivan. Damn, don't you think he's adorable? I could eat him up!"

Succeeding in embarrassing them both, Ian and Scott could no longer look anyone in the eye. Ian scoured the vicinity for something alcoholic. "Is there anything to drink? Or have we demolished all the booze?"

"No, I think there's more in the cabinet." Scott pulled a chair out from the table and climbed it to dig through the cupboards.

Ingesting this unusual reaction and reading their unspoken signals, Claire leaned back to study them both. If she didn't know better, she would have thought they were reacting jealously. But, that was impossible. They were both straight. What the heck was going on?

The Christmas tree lights glittering in the darkness, the clocks reading the midnight bewitching hour, Ian crept out of his room and moved across the hall to Scott's room. As he passed the main corridor, he could see Claire's bedroom door shut tight. Leaning his ear against Scott's door, he listened, then tried the knob. As it gave way, he squinted in the blackness to see if he was awake or sound asleep. They had only been in bed an hour and Scott's insomnia was in action.

As the door opened, Scott grinned under the cover of the shadows. Some place in his mind he was dreading Ian making a left turn out of his room and detouring to Claire's. But now that he was inside with him, that didn't seem likely.

"Hello, Mr. Sullivan," Scott purred seductively.

"Good. I was hoping you were still up." He shut the door behind him.

"Lock it up tight, baby," Scott whispered.

Fumbling with the handle, Ian managed to identify the lock and flip it. Gradually making his way deeper into the room, adjusting his eyes to the dimness, Scott aided his blindness by clicking on a low light by the bed.

"Oh, cheers, mate."

As he drew near, Scott made room for him and peeled back his blankets.

Seeing Scott was naked, Ian shed his briefs and slid under with him.

"She asleep?" Scott asked, wrapping his arms around Ian's body to draw him near.

"I reckon so. The door is closed and there's no light coming from under it." He kissed Scott's jaw.

Pausing to listen, staring at Ian's face in the shadows, Scott pushed his long hair back and asked, "You're not attracted to her, are you?"

Pausing before he replied, Ian said, "Well, to be honest, I was. She's a lovely bit of stuff. Crumpet, actually." As he felt Scott stiffen up in irritation, he added, "But, she's a bit old, and well, I would rather have you, love. You know what I mean?"

Softening at that seductive smile, Scott whispered, "When you flirt with her, you make me jealous."

"Do I? I don't mean to. She's just like a mate. I like her. It would be rude to act differently. I mean, it's her wedge that's keeping us all afloat."

"Wedge?" Scott took a moment to decipher the riddle, then said, "Oh, cash. Yes, I know. So, you wouldn't fuck her if she offered?"

"No. Believe me. I had thought about it when we first met. She's very sexy. But, no. I won't because I do believe it would jeopardize our working relationship. I mean, imagine us shagging and then having a row! I'd be out of work. You see? And I couldn't do that to you, love. Why would I?"

Hearing what he was yearning to hear, Scott considered the reassurances complete. "I understand you being attracted to her. All the models are. But, she is very strict about keeping her pleasure separate from her business, though. And you're right. She's fiery and would hold it against you. Believe me. I've seen her angry. It's not a pretty sight, Ian. She can be either an angel of mercy or the devil incarnate."

"Oi! Oh, lover, I do believe you!" Ian laughed, then lowered his voice to purr, "All I need is you."

Snuggling closer, Scott sniffed at his neck and hair. "Good. I want you exclusively, Ian. I don't want to share you with anyone. I'm crazy about you."

"I know, love. It's amazing we feel this way about each other, I mean, since neither one of us is an arse bandit."

Biting his tongue to stop from laughing, Scott shook his

head. "Where do you come up with those sayings?"

Ian nuzzled closer into Scott's embrace. "You just love my accent!" he teased.

"Oh, yes, and your face, and your hair, and your body—"

"Speaking about my face…" Ian set back to see his eyes.

"Yes, you gorgeous creature you?" Scott reached down to find his crotch.

"I need to ask, sorry if it offends you."

"Uh oh. What?" Scott froze.

"My photo. You have my photo."

"You nosing through my shit?"

"Yes! Unintentionally, I assure you, but, yes! I thought it was one of yours. I found the corner sticking out, and well, imagine my surprise seeing my own photo."

Scott pulled back in humiliation, but Ian prevented him from getting away.

"It's okay, love. Really," Ian whispered, "I'm sorry. No need to explain."

"Good. Because I have no explanation to give you," Scott mumbled.

Grinning wickedly, Ian said, "You are adorable."

"Are you making it up to me now?" Scott's smile emerged.

"Yes! Is it working?"

"Yes. You were horrible to me." Exaggerating a pout, Scott stuck out his lower lip.

"And what does Mr. Epstein require as a consolation?"

Nudging his nose against Ian's cheek, he whispered, "Suck me."

Scott could feel a tremor of nerves mixed with passion run over Ian's body.

"Please, baby. I showered just before bed. Come on."

As Ian imagined the possibility, he said, "And? In return?

You'll do me?"

Knowing that was a strong probability, Scott swallowed his anxiety to say, "Yes."

"Oh? Promise? Promise you won't back out?"

"I won't swallow or anything!"

"Christ! I would never expect you to. I'm not about to, either."

"Then you'll do it?"

As Ian mused silently, Scott threw off the blankets revealing a very excited body part.

In the dimness Ian admired his form. "Fuck, you're built."

Kicking off the sheets, visually checking the locked door, Scott waited, begging with his expression.

"Right." Ian inhaled for courage. He moved lower on the bed staring at that large erect member.

As he loomed closer, Scott's excitement was peaked. In his wildest dreams he never imagined a lovely pretty boy doing anything like this to him.

Stroking it lovingly a few times, Ian made himself comfortable next to him and closed his eyes. As Ian took him into his mouth, Scott relaxed his tense body.

At first penetration inside that hot opening, Scott thought he would spontaneously combust. It was so wild, so risqué, it took nothing to get him to come. As it overwhelmed him, he whispered the warning to Ian so Ian could back up and allowed it to shoot out without getting a mouthful. Sitting back as Scott climaxed, Ian sat calmly, as if he were thinking about what they had just done. As Scott recuperated Ian found a tissue for him to clean himself up.

"Was it bad?" Scott asked, hoping he would say it was wonderful.

"No. Not as bad as I thought it would be." Lying flat, spreading his legs, Ian smiled. "You shall see."

"Right." Scott crawled on the bed and positioned himself between Ian's thighs. Ian ran his own hand over his erection a few times, then whispered, "It's ready for you, mate."

Leaning over him on his elbows, Scott gripped the base, closed his eyes and went for it. Without intending to, or thinking it even possible, he began to lose himself on the sensations, the tensing of Ian's muscles under him, his breathy gasps, and the vibrating shivers of the organ he had in his mouth. It wasn't nearly as difficult as he expected, and the thought of giving Ian that kind of rush sent an erotic chill over him as well. As Ian grew closer to an orgasm, he tried to warn Scott of what was to come. Scott didn't heed his advice purposely, wanting to see if he could swallow.

As if he couldn't prevent it, Ian came, shivering down to his toes.

Scott continued to suck hard and swallowed before anything hit his tongue. When he sat up to stare at Ian, he found Ian's eyes wide in astonishment and his breathing almost at hyperventilation pace.

"I tried to warn you! Sorry, love!" Ian panted.

"It's all right." Scott lay back down beside him and stroked him gently.

"You...you meant to do it?"

"I wanted to see if I could."

"And?"

"I did it, didn't I?" Scott grinned at him with so much pride in his accomplishment it left Ian speechless.

After a long pause, where Ian could not find any words to describe his feelings, he leapt on top of Scott and covered him with kisses. "You're fantastic! Absolutely bloody fan-fucking-tastic!"

And as Scott savored the wonderful praise, he crushed him as tight as he could and said, "God, I love you."

The Kiss

As they lie cuddled together, neither wanting to move, Ian lightly scratched Scott's chest as Scott reciprocated. Both had stubble growing that was intolerable.

"If I stay any longer, I'll fall asleep here. And you know Claire is an early riser." Ian stretched and tried to feel motivated.

"I wish you could sleep in my arms." Scott crushed him closer.

"You say all the right things," Ian purred.

After some passionate kissing, Scott raised off him to see his face. "You're right. We do need to call it a night."

"Yes. All right, baby. We'll do this again tomorrow, right?"

"Yes!" Scott squeezed him in excitement at the idea.

"Good. Right. I suppose I'll shove off."

Gripping him, resisting his impulse to let him go, Scott wrapped around him for one more kiss, moaning in agony. "God, I love you so much."

"And I you."

"Okay. Get going."

As Ian climbed out of bed, Scott patted his bottom and watched as he slipped on his underwear. Hating seeing him go, he sat up until Ian had let himself out, then sighed, shut the light, and stared at the dark ceiling.

Closing the door silently, Ian tiptoed to the bathroom to relieve himself.

Being a very light sleeper, Claire's eyes opened at the sounds. She blinked her lashes and listened to every movement. Hearing the stream hitting the water, she wondered which man was up and peeing. Mechanically, she checked the clock. It was three a.m. She grumbled in irritation and curled back into the pillows.

Chapter Eleven

The apartment was glittering with candles and shimmering luminaries. Classical music floated on the warm, cozy, food-scented air as guests lifted petite pastries from hired servants' trays. Claire's pale skin seemed florescent in contrast to her black velvet dress. Her hair was gathered up on top of her head as wisps slipped out softly to make her angular jaw seem less severe.

Claire made sure the food was served generously, the booze kept being poured copiously, and the guests were all charmed and wooed by her special selection of male models. She and Jenine exchanged smiles because it seemed to be going very well. Everyone was calm, smiling; no one was drunk. Yet. Her choice of models seemed worthy, and they were appreciative and chatty. So far, so good. It seemed nothing could go wrong.

"God, Ian, you're driving me insane." Scott pinned him against the back of his closed bedroom door, kissing him passionately.

"I know, you, too, love. But we must be sociable. Claire will be cross if we aren't." Ian held him back gently.

"I know. You're right. I just can't stand watching you out there. You are so amazing looking, Ian," Scott panted.

The Kiss

Ian caressed Scott's hair back with his fingers, smiling affectionately. "Tonight. After everyone is gone. I'm all yours."

"Mine. Oh, I love to hear you say that." Scott chewed on his neck, unable to resist, massaging the fullness between Ian's legs with uncontrollable hunger.

"Yours…yours…yours…" Ian sighed, closing his eyes, spreading his legs.

"Did you see Ian and your brother leave the room?" Jenine asked Claire quietly.

"No. Why? They must be bored. I'll bet there's some ball game on they're catching on the portable TV in Scott's bedroom." Claire refilled her glass of Bailey's and then offered Jenine more wine.

"Oh!" Jenine sighed, "I didn't think of that."

Curious at the odd comment, Claire set the bottle down and gazed directly into Jenine's face. "What did you think?"

"Nothing! It was silly. Forget it." She waved her hand and blushed in embarrassment.

"You sure?"

"Well…" Jenine took a swallow of her drink, then had a peek around first before she said, "I thought for a second they had some kind of look in their eyes. But, listen, it's ridiculous! Oh, look— Andre Surah just arrived!"

As Jenine flittered to the door to greet him, well before her partner had finished her cross-examination, Claire made a beeline for Scott's bedroom, trying not to sprint and cause attention.

"We have to get back out there." Ian straightened his shirt.

"Yes, I know Claire. She'll be wondering." Scott ran his hand through his hair and inhaled a deep breath.

As they opened the door, she was about to do the same

from the other side.

"Hullo, Miss Epstein." Ian smiled sweetly. "Come for a break from the dullness as well?"

Attempting to read something she was certain she would read, Claire studied them mercilessly. Scott said with a smirk, "We're still not gay!"

Ian choked and widened his eyes at them both at the comment.

But it was exactly what Claire didn't predict. Laughing, embarrassed by her naughty thoughts, she shoved them to get back to the party. "Smart ass!" Whacking her brother's shoulder playfully, she suddenly thought the idea of him and Ian touching each other sexually was ridiculous.

As they reentered the room, Andre Surah found them immediately and waved them over to greet them. Jenine was standing and chatting with him, and their giddy mood was contagious.

"Gentlemen!" Mr. Surah patted each one on the back, "I am so pleased to see you both again. This campaign is the best new gimmick my company has come out with since we switched from six sticks a pack to eight!"

The men nodded politely, not knowing how to respond. Claire was scrutinizing their every movement and comment as it seemed obvious to her that neither wanted to breathe a word in support of the commercial.

"I've paid a fortune to have it aired on Super Bowl Sunday, but it's worth it," he continued. "Several magazines said they will do a spread. Claire says most have already been sent your photos."

When he cupped Ian's jaw in his coarse, ring-covered hand, Claire noticed Scott tense up and look like he was restraining the urge to slap it away.

Ian's eyes widened in surprise at the touch.

"And you, my lovely Englishman," Mr. Surah purred, "will

be the next big thing."

As politely as he could, Ian backed from that grasp. "Thank you, Mr. Surah. I hope your prediction is accurate."

Grinning like a child, Mr. Surah turned to address the women, "Isn't he fantastic? Absolutely fantastic!"

With Claire loving every minute of it, she nodded in agreement that, indeed, Ian would be the next big thing.

Scott lowered his head and mumbled under his breath he needed another drink as Ian watched in frustration.

"Who is that gorgeous creature?"

Raising his head, Scott met the gaze of one of the male models from his sister's agency. One who was openly gay and quite proud of it.

"He's Ian Sullivan." Scott sipped his drink, glimpsing back at Ian as he smiled and fielded the many questions from his admirers.

"Damn." The model shook his head in awe. "He's a work of art. Isn't he?"

"Yeah, a regular Picasso," Scott grumbled sarcastically. Reaching out his hand politely, he introduced himself. "Scott Epstein."

"Sergei Molkov. Did you say Epstein? Like in Claire Epstein?"

"Yup. She's my sister." Scott moved his gaze to her as she kept a permanent grin on her face while her star client was captivating the crowd.

"You must get regular work, having her pitching for you."

As he spoke, Scott scrutinized Sergei's face, his square jaw, coarse with a black shadow, in contrast to his bright blue eyes. "No. Not as much work as you would think. She doesn't play favorites. She did, however, just get me into a commercial."

As if a light had gone on in his head, Sergei stared in awe at him and said, "You're the one she chose for that gum commercial?"

"Yes, me and Ian." Scott tilted his head to his lover.

Sergei leaned on Scott's shoulder and whispered, "How was that lovely kiss? We've heard so much about it. I'm green with envy. You two an item now?"

He had no idea why, but talk like this enraged him. As calmly as he could, he inhaled and said, "I know it looks like we're lovers, Sergei, but we're not. We're just friends. Okay?"

Sergei watched Scott as he walked away, heading to refill his drink once more.

"I grew up in Hertford, Hertfordshire," Ian explained, "Attended school there, and decided on acting instead of footy."

"Footy?" Jenine tilted her head. "Football? You wanted to be a football player?"

"You Americans call it soccer." Ian smiled sweetly and tried to keep track of Scott in the room.

The chairman from a cosmetic line laughed softly, and said, "I'm surprised you passed up on a career in soccer. Isn't that every young English boy's dream?"

"It is! Everyone yearns to be the next David Beckham or Michael Owen." Ian's glass was empty and looked around for more alcohol.

"Who?" Jenine asked Claire.

"I've no clue." Claire noticed Ian's anxiousness, first aimed at his empty glass, then the room.

The chairman smiled and informed the women, "The ex-captain of England's football team and one of their star strikers."

"Oh…" Jenine nodded, biting her lip.

"You'll excuse me. I need a topper." Ian raised his glass

116

and squeezed out of the tight circle to find Scott.

As the small crowd watched him leave, the women were hit with a barrage of questions as to when they could get Ian to come in for a shoot for one of their ads.

"You all right?" Ian leaned over the counter to get his glass filled with wine. Scott was already there, sipping and refilling his own for the fourth time.

"What do you care?" Scott growled, his lip curling in reflex.

"Oi! Don't bite me head off! Please, baby. Don't be cross with me. What have I done?"

Scott softened and lowered his head. "Sorry, Ian, I'm just a little tired. So, you're a real hit tonight with everyone, aren't you?"

Ian whispered, "It's just my accent! It's because I'm a Johnny foreigner. If you were at a gathering in England, the same would happen to you." As discreetly as he could, he touched his elbow.

Feeling the caress, Scott gazed down at the contact wistfully. "Yeah. Maybe you're right."

"Of course I am. Look, all I want is for everyone to piss off so I can get me hands on you."

His seductive smile emerged quickly at that wonderful comment. "Ditto."

The moment Ian was about to say something playfully obscene, someone was tapping him and asking him when he had time to come by for a chat about a new ad campaign. As Ian attempted to be polite and answer them, he kept peeking back at Scott in concern.

Not wanting to be the reason Ian was brushing people off, Scott refilled his glass for the fifth time and excused himself politely.

His expression knotted with concern, Ian could not help but watch him go as he ignored the offer for yet another job.

"Hey." Claire stopped Scott as he made his way out of the room again. "What's with the long face?"

"I'm just tired. I want all these morons to go home," Scott sighed.

"Morons? They're our bread and butter, sweetie. Go mingle! If you didn't look so fucking depressed, you might even get an offer."

"Is that right?" his spat out sarcastically, "No, I think I have to have an accent and long hair with this crowd."

"Meow! Pull your claws in!" Claire stifled a sad laugh. "Look, little brother, you have to allow Ian to blossom without your own jealousy! Don't you want him to succeed? Or would you rather see him fall on his face and crawl back to England a failure?"

As those thoughts struggled through her brother's mind, Claire was getting the idea that Scott did not want Ian to outshine him. But, why the intense reaction?

"You sure you're not falling for him?" she whispered. "I mean, this attitude—"

He cut her off in fury. "Fuck you! Leave me the fuck alone!" and stormed off to his room, slamming the door.

With her mouth hanging open, she spun to the rest of the guests to see who had overheard. Only Jenine and Ian seemed aware of what was going on. Claire thought the over-reaction was too much. With those thoughts in mind, she stared at the pain on Ian's face, growing more suspicious they were becoming attached to each other on some deeper emotional level. Even if they hadn't touched each other sexually, the concern was obviously there.

Ian's arm kept being tapped to remind him he was in the presence of someone who thought their voice should be harkened to with more consideration. This was the head of a very important advertising company and Ian needed to pay close attention to every word. There might be a contract in it if he did.

Ian could not keep his thoughts straight and the tapping was annoying. The moment Scott stormed off and Claire was left behind, Ian excused himself in the middle of another boring line of self-promotion to hurry to her and find out what had passed between them.

"Is he all right?"

Claire said,"He's a little uneasy with all the attention you're getting, Ian. I'm just not sure why. You have anything you want to tell me? To enlighten me?"

"No. But I do know how much he has wanted a break. And hearing them all offering me jobs isn't good for anyone's ego."

"No. You're right. He isn't the only model shooting daggers at you in here."

"Really?" Ian scanned the other handsome males in the room.

"Don't worry, it's normal. I should go see if he's okay." She looked for a spot to set her glass.

"No, allow me." He lowered his voice and said, "After all, it's my fault."

Cocking her eye at him suspiciously, she said, "Okay. You go in there and comfort him. That is what you're going in for, right?"

The polite expression falling from his face, Ian whispered, "I don't like what you're implying, Miss Epstein."

"No? I'll bet you don't."

"Do we continue this discussion after the crowd leaves? Or shall we draw daggers right now?"

Claire lowered her head to apologize. "No. I'm sorry, Ian. I think I just had too much to drink. Go. Go see how he is."

As Jenine loomed closer, she tried to get Claire back into the mix. The moment she made it into their personal aura, Ian walked away, leaving them staring after.

"You okay, Claire?"

"Hmmm?" She turned to Jenine and sighed, "Just ready for everyone to go home."

"They will be soon. It's getting late. Is everything okay between you, Scott, and Ian?"

"Yes. Don't worry. I think Scott is just feeling a little tired. Ian may be, too. It's all just wearing on us. You know."

"It was your idea to have this get together. You could have passed the idea up this year. No one would have cared."

"I should have. These things never end well." Claire sighed and walked back across the room to her clients. The commercial kiss was the topic of the night, thanks to Andre Surah's constant promotion. And several of them wanted more time to stare into Ian's handsome features before they left for the night.

Checking the handle first, then knocking, Ian found Scott's door locked. As he leaned his cheek against the wood grain he whispered, "Baby? It's me."

A moment later the sound was heard of the knob clicking. Pushing it back, Ian moved into the cologne-scented dimness and closed the door behind him. "Please. Tell me what I'm doing to wind you up so I can stop."

"Nothing. It's not you. It's me."

Navigating in the dimness with outstretched fingers, Ian made out his form on the bed, lying prone. As he sat near him, he reached out to lay his hand on his thigh. "What happened with Claire?"

"I said nothing!"

Ian flinched at the anger. "Was it a mistake, baby? Me living here? Us getting close?"

Frantic at the implications, Scott rushed to sit up and take him into his arms. "No. It wasn't a mistake. It was the best thing that ever happened to me."

"I'm not so sure. I don't know what I'm doing to give you the 'ump, but you seem very upset with me."

Setting back to make out his face in the dimness, Scott pushed his long hair aside to get a look into his light eyes. After letting go of a deep exhale, Scott said, "Look, you're out here for only a month and the attention you're getting is making me jealous. Okay? I admit it. But I do want to see you succeed, Ian. I really do."

"As I want to see you succeed, too, baby. It would be brilliant if we both got some major deal at the same time. But is that realistic?"

"No. Of course it isn't."

"Can we be happy for each other's victories? Or must we grow angry and short with each other?"

Completely disarmed by his softness and beauty, Scott's anger dissipated. "Come here." Wrapping his arms around him, he brought him lovingly to his lips.

As the cow pattern clock in the kitchen read one a.m., Claire finally began handing out coats to her guests. After they had disappeared for nearly thirty-five minutes, her brother and Ian materialized to say goodnight to everyone. The last to leave was Mr. Surah. As he stood shaking his head at the two men, he appeared about to kiss them goodbye.

Before he had his chance, Claire gripped his upper arm and turned him aside on the pretext of arranging a press meeting if he needed one.

The moment the large man was distracted, Ian and Scott backed away to oversee the tending of the apartment. Two maids were still on hand to dump the garbage and load the dishwasher.

Jenine waited until Andre Surah had vanished inside the elevator, then she leaned over to Claire to say, "I think it went well, considering. You just relax and I'll call you."

"You're a dear." Claire kissed her cheek and waved as she walked down the hall.

Finally shutting the door, Claire rubbed her forehead and hunted for the aspirin bottle as Ian kicked off his shoes and slumped over the counter to watch the clean up process dully.

All three were spent and tired of fielding questions.

"Thank fuck tomorrow's Sunday," Claire yawned. "All right, girls, you've done enough. Go home!"

The two maids happily set their dish towels aside and found their coats. As Claire sorted out their pay, Ian and Scott gazed wearily at each other.

"Still on for tonight? Or are you cream-crackered?" Ian whispered.

"Cream-crackered?" With an effort Scott managed a tiny laugh.

"Knackered. Tired," Ian translated.

"Yeah, I know. I am a bit, crackers."

"Crackered, you plonker." Ian giggled at him affectionately.

"Whatever. Can we take a rain check?"

"Of course!" Hearing the apartment door close, Ian glanced over his shoulder at Claire. "Well done, Miss Epstein. It seemed everyone had a splendid time."

"Yeah, yeah…see ya in the morning. Don't wake me up. I'm planning on sleeping in." As if shooing a fly, she waved as she scuffed her way to her room.

When the men heard the door click and lock, they made direct eye contact. It was one of those irresistible moments when you know the cat's away.

"She's having a lay-in tomorrow," Ian said, as if he was informing Scott of something he didn't know.

"Most likely till noon, I would figure."

"Still too tired?"

Wanting the idea to inspire him, Scott moaned in agony. "I don't want to be. I want to be awake for you."

Floating lightly over the waxed wood flooring, Ian met him by the single step that led to the kitchen. Scott was on it and stood tall over him. With very slow calming hands, Ian held Scott's warm sides and leaned to kiss his chest.

Closing his eyes at the tempting sensations, Scott swayed back unsteadily as the mixture of exhaustion and yearning crept with tickling fingers over his skin. Strong hands held him firm while a mouth found the gaps between shirt buttons and tasted the smooth hot flesh.

With both his hands Scott dug through Ian's hair as if he were made of silk.

At the sound of a click, they parted in panic and spun around to Claire's bedroom door.

"I thought you were both exhausted?" In her robe and slippers, she headed to the refrigerator and removed a bottle of water. "I'm so dehydrated. The alcohol and all that salty food! Blah."

"Yeah, we're on our way. We were just talking." Scott pretended he was busy wiping the counter as Ian backed away and leaned against the dining room table.

"Talking! Augh! I'm sick to death of talking!" she grumbled as she made her way back to the bedroom. "Go to bed and stop talking!" she shouted over her shoulder.

Trying to still their beating hearts, they waited, then glimpsed at each other, bursting out laughing.

"Ya know, it's somehow more obvious when I think back on it. I mean, at the time, I didn't even blink when they bought each other Christmas presents. After all, we all exchanged gifts that day. It seemed normal. The price tag was a bit high for the new leather jacket Scott gave to Ian, and Ian's gift of a day at a

spa for Scott seemed a bit over the top, but, once again, what could I say? They were fond of each other, and I was convinced there was still nothing but friendship between them. Try as I might to catch them at something, I never seemed to be in the right place or at the right time. They kept it well hidden. In their minds they had to. But, the strain sometimes was too much, and it began to show."

Chapter Twelve

Even though they tried to ignore it, New Year's Eve was upon them. Claire announced she was doing nothing. No parties, no clubs, no midnight horn blowing, nothing.

Ian and Scott were thinking of Times Square. Not once did they attempt to convince Claire to come along. Seeing how she expressed repeatedly her opinion on doing nothing other than going to sleep at ten p.m. defiantly, they didn't feel obligated to keep asking. And in reality, they didn't want her there.

December 31st at five in the evening, the three of them sat for a dinner of pasta and pesto sauce after Claire's hard day at the office.

"You guys are crazy! Times Square? Do you know how mobbed it'll be?" She roughly tore another piece of garlic bread off the loaf as if expressing her frustration on its crusty surface. "Okay, but don't say I didn't warn you. And Ian, the pickpockets are ruthless. Leave your wallet home."

"Yes, Miss Epstein." He laughed at her as he stuffed another green tortellini into his mouth. "She reckons I'm from some third world country," he said to Scott, whose plate was emptying rapidly.

"You mean England isn't?" His eyes sparkled impishly.

"You yanks. You're so insular!"

"What the hell does that mean?" Scott asked Claire.

"Narrow minded," she answered.

"We are not!" Scott puffed up in defense.

"Are to!" Ian shouted.

"Are not!"

"Boys!" Claire held up her hand to stop them. "Christ, it's Sesame Street in here."

"Oh, bollocks," Ian grumbled and ate the remainder of his pasta.

"You two are like a couple of old married people!" Claire snorted. "You spend too much time together."

"Get us more work!" Scott shouted sarcastically.

Throwing up her hands, she roared in irritation, "I've done more than enough! The two of you just need to wait until after the New Year for your offers, okay?"

"Yeah, yeah..." Scott snatched the last of the bread and wiped his plate clean with it.

"What an ingrate," Claire grumbled, trying to get a reaction.

"Oh, shut up!" Scott had enough and stood to set his plate in the sink.

"You shut up!"

"No, you shut up!"

"Aaaugh!" Ian screamed in frustration. "Back to Sesame Street we go!"

"We need to get out of the house." Scott rinsed his plate and stuck it into the dishwasher. "You done eating?"

"Yes, that's me done." Ian rose up and handed Scott his plate.

"Fine, leave me alone on New Year's Eve." Claire pouted.

"Don't even try that Jewish guilt shit with me!" Scott warned. "You said you didn't want to be sociable. If you've changed your mind, call Jenine."

126

"Oh, fuck you!"

Ian whispered, "Look, Claire, you're welcome to join us—"

"No! She's not!" Scott shouted.

"Scott…" Ian chided.

Claire took instant offense, "No…don't bother, Ian. He's being a brat and I don't want to intrude."

"Claire, it's not intruding—" Before Ian could offer another olive branch, Scott was cutting him off.

"No! God damn it! This is our night!"

As those words fell out onto the floor, both Ian and Claire gaped at him. After the moment when the three of them swallowed the silence like an icicle with a razor tip, Scott cleared his throat awkwardly wishing he could inhale that line and make it disappear, like his pasta.

"Your night?" Claire rose up, astonishment clear on her face.

"I knew you would take it that way!"

"What way, Scott? You mean, like you-two-are-a-couple-way?"

Ian shoved his way out from behind the dining table and headed to his room to get his jacket and his money.

As the other two watched him go, Scott was boiling mad. "You nasty bitch. You know how that shit hurts him? Isn't it bad enough you constantly torment me? Do you have to torment him as well?"

"I didn't mean—"

"You did mean! You know what? Have a nice night, alone!" He shoved a chair violently and rushed to catch up with Ian, grabbing his coat.

As Ian stormed out of his room, head down, jacket on, hands deep inside his pockets, Claire choked on what she wanted to say. "Sorry," was the only word to make it passed her lips.

When it reached his ears, he paused, raising his wounded expression to her. As the pain found her, she felt sick. "Ian, forgive me. I didn't mean—"

Lowering his dark lashes, he reached for the handle just as Scott fell in behind him, not looking back.

When the door closed Claire never remembered feeling so alone. She had to stop hounding them about this gay thing. It wasn't fair and was obviously wounding them both. Whether they were gay or not, she just had to cool it! Why was she so spiteful? Could it be that, lovers or not, she was being left out?

"Ian!" Scott rushed to keep pace with him when they hit the icy streets. "Ian! For Christ's sake!" Reaching out, he grabbed Ian's elbow and tried to halt him.

Ian reacted and jerked his arm back in fury. "Piss off! You're both so bloody fucked up. I can't stand it."

"Oh, god... Please, Ian. Don't do this to me."

"Do what? Live with accusations of being a fucking arse bandit?"

Knowing exactly what Ian was feeling, Scott wrung his hands in frustration, his heart breaking. "I'll talk to her. I'll tell her to lay off! Ian, don't let it affect us. I'm begging you."

As people walked passed, eyeing them curiously, Ian bit his lip.

Taking him out of the main stream of traffic, Scott led him to an indented corner of a building entrance, blocking them from the bitter wind. "Ian, I love you. I'm crazy about you. I thought you felt the same way about me."

"I do!" he tried to shout, but it all remained caught in his throat.

"Then calm down and talk to me."

Struggling, Ian twisted and turned in frustration. When

Scott gripped him to stop his writhing in agony, Ian said, "It's just the beginning! Don't you see? This flaming commercial! When that gets aired what do you think people will be saying? We live together, for fuck's sake! They will instantly call us a gay couple! I can't live with that, Scott! Think of our careers! Think of our families!"

It was all Scott had been thinking about, every night since the affair had begun. If he had more than three hours of sleep a night, he was lucky. With the tears threatening in his eyes, Scott was suddenly the one who was struggling for words. "I know. I know what you're saying, Ian, but, I can't live without you. We—we haven't even gotten the chance to make love or anything yet. If it's over, I'll go nuts. I will."

As Scott rubbed roughly at the few tears that rolled down his face, Ian sighed, "No. It's not over. Don't upset yourself. I just get crazy when the labeling starts. You know what I mean, baby?" Reaching out, he touched one of the hot salty drops before it made it to Scott's high cheekbone.

When someone walked passed, Ian whipped his arm back in paranoia. As they waited for a gap in the foot traffic, Scott got himself under control and wiped his face off with his hands, his back against the loud flow of cabs, trucks, and buses.

Peering over his shoulder first, Scott narrowed the space between them so he could whisper. "Tonight is our night, Ian. You and me. I don't want anything to ruin it."

"It won't, love. It won't." Ian rested his hand on Scott's shoulder.

Straining against all his urges, Scott said, "Do you have any idea how hard it is to not pull you into an embrace and kiss you right now?"

Smiling impishly, Ian answered, "Yessss…"

"Fuck." Scott chuckled with him. "It sucks."

"I'm sorry, Scott. You understand why."

"Oh, fuck yeah! I do! Believe me!"

Inhaling and gazing up at the towering buildings, Ian said, "Okay, Mr. Epstein, where to?"

Scott grinned in excitement and gestured for Ian to walk along with him.

"Hi, Mom." Claire brooded for an hour and then decided to call home for some words of support.

"Hello, sweetheart. Happy New Year."

"You too, Mom. You and Dad doing anything tonight?"

"We're going to a dance at the temple."

"Oh. Good for you!"

"And you?"

"Nothing."

"Why not? What's Scott doing?"

Her bottom lip trembling, Claire felt like she was eleven years old. "He and Ian are going to Times Square."

"Didn't you want to go?"

"Not at first. I sort of do now." Sniffling, she dabbed at a tear in the corner of her eye before it fell.

"What's the matter? You sound upset, dear."

"Well," she sniffled again, "I guess I thought they'd want me with them. But they don't."

"What about some of your other friends, then? Where's Jenine?"

"I kind of screwed myself, Mom. It's my own fault. I've been so tired from work and Christmas I told everyone I didn't want to party."

"And now you regret it? Oh, sweetie, I'm sorry."

As Claire dabbed her nose on a tissue, she heard her mother explaining the problem to her father. "Christ, I'm pathetic," she said to herself, but her mother heard.

"You're not pathetic! Look, why don't you pour yourself a

glass of champagne, fill the tub with bubbles, light some candles, and put on some nice music. Then like you really had planned, just rest."

"I love you," Claire blubbered. "You're right. I should. I shouldn't feel left out."

"No, dear, you shouldn't. All your friends would have welcomed you if you wanted to be there."

"Yes, they would have."

"So, don't be upset. I hate you living so far from us when you get this way. Are you dating anyone?"

"No, Mom." That turned Claire's mood into instant irritation.

"Well, if you had someone in your life, you wouldn't feel as lonely. You're thirty-two, Claire, and if you ever want to raise a family—"

"Oh, here we go! Look, if the conversation is turning into this, I'm hanging up."

"Don't get all defensive! I'm just trying to let you know—"

"I'm hanging up!" Claire threatened.

"Fine! Good-bye!"

When it disconnected, Claire slammed it down. "Oh, fuck everyone!" she screamed.

Scanning the area to scope out a good spot to view the ball drop, Scott led Ian into the very heart of the city. A few hundred revelers were already there thinking they could claim their place before the mass of people came flooding in.

"We have a do in Trafalgar Square, but it's just a group waiting to hear Big Ben chime. No fireworks or light display." Ian shivered in the icy wind as he craned his neck up the tower the ball would drop from.

"Nothing, huh?" Scott shifted in the chill from one leg to the other. The frigid air was slowly making its way inside his clothing.

"No, not since the millennium. Nothing at all. It's kind of a shame. But the constables don't even want us in Trafalgar anymore. As a matter of fact, since they've been working on the pavements, they closed it all off. You have to go up to Edinburgh, Scotland for any type of party."

"Scotland? Cool!"

"Cool? No, this is fucking cool!" Ian gestured to the icy air. "My bollocks is freezing off."

"We don't have to stand out here all night. Actually, that was my surprise."

"Surprise?"

"Come on!" Scott grabbed his sleeve and tugged him along.

When they stood in front of the Iroquois Hotel, Ian caught his breath. "What?"

"I've got us a room! A room with a view! So we could either go and celebrate in the square, or watch from up there." He raised his jaw to the tower.

"You what? You mean to tell me, you booked us a room at this hotel? Us two?"

"No! Not as a couple! Use your head. Just under my name. Duh." Scott shook his head at him.

"How on earth did you get a bloody reservation? It must be booked solid!"

"It is! A little trick. Spencer & Epstein have some pull in this town." Scott grinned wickedly.

"You naughty boy!"

"Now you know why I didn't want Claire to come. So? Heat up with room service?" Rubbing his hands together as he puffed vaporous warm breath on them, Scott made the offer very appealing.

"What did it set you back? Blimey! It must have cost some

serious wedge," Ian said, as he eyed the extravagant hotel.

"Don't worry. I had some stored away for a rainy day. Come on!"

They were grinning like demons as the red-coated doorman opened the glass door. Scott made directly for the desk as Ian loitered well behind.

"Yes, I've a reservation. Scott Epstein, co-chairman of Spencer & Epstein."

"Yes. Mr. Epstein. Sign here, sir."

As the key was set out on the counter, Scott signed the credit card slip and was dying to see what Ian was doing behind his back. The moment he could, he spun around, grinning as if he'd just pulled off the perfect bank heist.

Scott noticed Ian was doing his best to be invisible. The minute he realized the key was in hand, he made a path to the elevator, trying to convince anyone in the lobby they were not together. Coming to meet him on a diagonal, Scott stood side by side with him, waiting for the door to open. Neither said a word, hiding their smirks of excitement.

The elevator doors opened and they stepped in. As they closed and the numbered lights illuminated, Scott thought he caught a glimpse of one of his sister's employees, Randy the cameraman. Twisting away frantically, he kept his back turned as the doors sealed them in.

"What?" Ian asked.

"Nothing… Well," he sighed, "Here we go! Welcome 2007!"

"Welcome indeed!" Ian giggled mischievously.

Stealthily they made their way to their room. It was on the eighth floor and faced Times Square and the lighted ball. Fumbling with the key as Ian kept watch behind his back for any human being who may find them, the moment Scott got the door opened they flew in and bolted it, feeling like Russian spies.

Once inside, they panted as if they needed to catch their breaths. "Fuck. We did it," Scott gasped.

"Do you believe real people live like this? With this closet shite?"

As Scott gazed at Ian he said, "Ah, yes, Ian. We are. Duh! You say some of the stupidest things."

"Shut up!"

"No, you shut up!"

"No, you shut up!"

At the third chorus, Ian raced after him. Scott leapt over chairs and tables to the bed and dove on it, landing with a bounce. Ian was right behind him, pinning him to it.

Digging his way out from under all of Ian's long locks, Scott finally found his smile and grabbed his jaw to bring him for a kiss.

Wearing her bunny fuzzy slippers and matching white furry robe, Claire braved the daunting task of hunting through the refrigerator for a snack. There never were any leftovers. Scott saw to that. Some eggs, bread, various green vegetables, bottled water, milk. It looked bleak. Hitting the cabinets next; canned soup, rice cakes, and peanut butter, gave the same outlook. "Damn," she groaned. Scuffing back to the couch, sitting with the Chinese Hunan Chef menu on her lap, she wondered if she could order enough food to hit the minimum she needed for home delivery. Knowing anything leftover Scott would devour, she sat by the phone and dialed anxiously.

"How long?" she gasped. "Oh, okay, whatever. As long as I get fed! Surcharge? Holiday surcharge? Look, mac, I order from you guys at least once a week— What? Oh, whatever. Just feed me." She hung up angrier than before. "I hate New Year's." Staring at the phone, she thought about ringing Scott's mobile, then wondered if he even had it with him or if he bothered to turn it on. Assuming he would just blow her off again, she pouted and flipped on the television. "Life sucks sometimes."

As her mother's words rung in her ears, she thought seriously about whether she should think more about dating. Maybe one of her models was just the thing for a long lasting relationship.

"Ha!" she shouted. "Well, maybe." Ian's face came to mind. He did make a less than subtle offer. "*Fancy a shag?*" he said. Should she take him up on it? Even though he was only twenty-one?

"Naaaa..."

"What time is it?" Ian poured more champagne into the fluted glass.

"Time to fuck!"

"You pervo. You certainly know how to romance a bloke." Ian laughed.

"So? You got a problem with that?" Moving toward him as he reclined on the bed, Scott started tugging at Ian's zipper.

"I may. Who gets shagged first?"

"I'll let you do me."

"Will you? Brave man."

"I know, but, you sucked first. I figure it's only fair." Having accomplished opening his trousers, Scott was intent on taking them off.

"Criminy! You are a bit randy!"

"Randy?" Scott thought of the cameraman in panic.

"Rrrrrandy!!" Ian set his glass down and attacked him.

Squirming in glee at the tickling, Scott burst out laughing and wrestled with him playfully. "Ah! Stop! I can't stand it," he gasped.

Letting up on the torture, Ian leaned on his side to stare at Scott's face. "I'm surprised you haven't gotten any major roles in television. You're quite good looking."

Gazing back at him, unused to the directness of this Englishman, Scott was at a loss for words.

"I mean," Ian continued, "If I was to try anything on with a bloke, which I never imagined doing," pausing, he added, "Not seriously, anyhow. You would be the type I would want to experiment with. Do I make any sense?"

"Yes."

"To be honest, I've really not been the king of conquests. On the contrary, I'm quite shy with the birds. I dated one I met in school. Elizabeth. We were together for six years. I don't know what happened. We just fell out of love, I guess. Other than Liz, I haven't really been handled by anyone. Do you think I'm some kind of a misfit? Telling you this?"

"No. Not at all, Ian."

Ian lowered his eyes to Scott's chest, slowly opening the buttons to expose his skin. "I know I'm a bit feminine looking, especially with the long hair. I've had blokes come on before, chat me up in clubs, but, I've not really thought seriously about touching them. I've no idea why this whole thing began with you, or why I like it."

"A kiss." Scott smiled affectionately, and as that finely boned hand continued to undress him, his primal urges began emerging.

Smiling, Ian spread wide Scott's shirt and smoothed his hand over his pectoral muscles. "Yes. One or two kisses. Still, I do think it was the way you kissed me. I'd expected one thing and got quite another." Rubbing over him gently, he whispered, "You're nubby."

"I know, and itchy." Scott laughed.

"Oh! Not half!!" Ian scratched at his own chest through his shirt. "You never warned me about that!"

"Sorry," Scott tried to get under Ian's shirt to scratch for him. "About what you said, the kiss being something more.

Something different—"

"Oh, yes. Well," Ian paused. "The way you did it. How can I explain? Holding my head that way, opening your mouth, the accident when our tongues touched— Well, all that I suppose."

"Accident." Scott chuckled softly, knowing on his end it was no accident. He hunted for it.

"Did you think you wanted more of me? Were you attracted to me? That day in Claire's office when we first met?"

In instinctive irritation, Scott wanted to shout, NO! But, it wasn't the truth. And Ian was being so painfully honest with him it wouldn't be fair to lie. Maybe being American, Scott could not open up as easily as this man could. Everything he wanted to say sounded in his mind, so awkward, so weak. The sentences just refused to pass his lips.

Ian stared into Scott's eyes impatiently. "I wasn't particularly attracted to you," Ian said. "Well, why should I be?"

"You're not gay." Tongue in cheek, Scott loved the irony.

"No. Or should I say, I wasn't." Ian's light eyes glimmered like a fox.

"How do you explain this?" Opening his arms, Scott tried to communicate, this situation, the both of them on a bed.

"I don't know."

As the smile changed to something darker on Ian's face, Scott wished they had not chosen to speak to each other and stuck with the original plan. "Okay, enough talk."

"What are we doing? Are we mad?"

"Ian!" Scott gripped his arms and shook him. "No one will ever find out!"

"But they do. Inevitably, they do. Don't they? It happens all the time to people. Especially people who are in the spotlight. When that commercial hits, my love, we will just about be outed in public."

"No! You're wrong! When we are on Calahan's show,

137

we'll be able to tell the world we're straight! That's when we can make sure everyone knows that the kiss was acting."

As Scott's powerful hands squeezed his shoulders, his eyes desperately tried to convey what he meant. Ian's face contorted with his thoughts.

Unfortunately, Scott knew exactly what Ian was going through. His situation was a mirror image. But, caring less at the moment what the rest of the universe thought, he brought that mouth once again close to his, and then wrapped his arms around him tightly.

At the contact, Ian's body released its fear and returned the passion twofold.

Seated on the couch with a grease-stained white take-away carton of shrimp fried rice in her hand, Claire stared at the television hoping it would get her mind off her loneliness. Frustrated with the selection, she grabbed the remote control and scrolled once again through the channels in vain. "Crap!" she shouted. "Nothing but crap! A hundred channels on cable and nothing but crap!!" She envisioned throwing the remote, smashing the television screen, and her glee at seeing it smoke and sizzle.

Muting the sound, taking another mouthful of food, she once again stared at her telephone. What if she called Scott? Just to say hi. Maybe ask him where he was. She could still meet him. It was only nine o'clock.

Imagining the brush off, she once again heard his line, "*Our night!*"

Their night? Christ, that was a bit possessive. She wondered if she and Ian had any sort of sexual fling, what would Scott's reaction be then? Would he have a tantrum?

It was all a little confusing. She'd known Scott all his life. The only other time he behaved this way with her was with his favorite toys. Well, quite frankly she couldn't get near his GI

Joes. If she so much as laid a hand on that action figure, (he refused to call it a doll), then she would be attacked violently. Was Ian Scott's new GI Joe? Did they play war games? Fantasize having battles against Afghani rebels?

How exactly did they play together?

Claire could only wonder.

Naked, splayed out, Ian moaned in delight from Scott's rough passion.

Raised to a frenzied peak from tasting every inch of this pretty boy's body, Scott sat up suddenly and said, "Right. You ready?"

"Yes! Let's get on with it!"

As if time were of the essence, Scott hopped off the bed and rifled through his jacket with almost a crazed passion.

Tilting his head in curiosity, Ian leaned up on his elbows and said, "What the bloody hell are you doing?"

When he found what he was looking for, Scott threw it to Ian, who couldn't catch it in time and just watched it bounce on the bed. "Petroleum jelly? Bloody hell!"

"Can you think of anything else? I snagged it from home. I wasn't about to go shopping for lube! Are you nuts?" Scott sat on the bed, gave him a condom, then opened the top. "How much should we use?"

"Again he's asking me like I'm the authority!" Ian laughed. "I would suggest we use as much as we need!" Ian rolled the rubber on his cock.

"Well, in that case," Scott handed him the open jar and scooted next to him to lie flat on his stomach, "Use a lot. You've got a big dick."

"You think so?" Ian stared down at himself. "I've never thought of it as big."

"Shut up and get on with it!" Scott was trying to psych

himself up.

Ian stopped himself and sat up, staring down at Scott's ass. "Up the Glitter. I never thought I'd do it."

"The what?" Scott leaned on his elbows and turned to look back at him.

"Glitter-shitter. Never mind."

"You lost your hard-on. You sure you want to do this?"

"I'm not bloody sure of anything at the moment, mate!" Ian snapped off the condom and threw it on the floor.

Twisting back around to comfort him, Scott reached for him with open arms. And as if his limbs were weighing on him, Ian moved to receive that embrace, then closed his eyes and exhaled a deep stressful breath.

"All right, sweetie, you don't do anything you don't want to do." Scott felt odd telling him that. He had imagined some heavy sexual bout, something he had gone over and over again in his mind every night. The way it might feel to be penetrated. To share his body that way. He was willing, and very eager to experience it. At the moment, he didn't know what was happening or why.

Peeking at the time, seeing it was ten p.m., Scott could only think of one thing, generating that passion once more, getting them to a state of frenzy, and getting what he wanted from this male.

As he nudged Ian to raise his head to his mouth, he remembered that first kiss and the 'accidental' touching of their tongues. A rush of fire, so potent it consumed him, raced over his length. With both hands he found Ian again, and massaged and worked him until he was hard. When he responded, little gasps escaping his kisses, Scott knew it was what they both wanted, and he wasn't going to allow anything to stand in their way.

By ten o'clock, Claire could hardly keep her eyes open.

140

The Kiss

Deciding on that hot soak in the tub after all, she forced herself off the couch and dragged her long-pink ears and bunny nose-covered feet to the bathroom. Her private bath only had a shower, so she filled the second bathroom's tub with hot water and bubbles, then set out some candles. As the water rushed out of the brass tap, she sighed, "Yes, this first, then bed."

Intent on another glass of wine, she found her way to the kitchen to pour herself one. On her trip back to the bathroom, she stared at the phone once more, glaring at it as if it was an object of disdain, then closed herself into the steaming heat.

Trying not to break the momentum, Scott decided he needed to be the one to take control. Keeping Ian face up, his lips occupied, Scott reached for his legs and gently urged them apart and bent at the knees.

Ian kept his eyes closed and his mouth busy. When Scott needed to sit back to continue, he released Ian's lips and then stared down at him as he lay exposed for the first time. "Damn, you're gorgeous."

Ian didn't respond. His green eyes were luminous and wide as he waited. Silent, allowing what was about to happen to continue, Ian stared at Scott as he slipped on a condom and reached for that jar.

His hands slick and wild as he prepared, Scott could not catch his breath as the anticipation of the act was catching up to him. "I won't hurt you, Ian. I promise."

Nothing was said in return, only the widening of his innocent eyes.

Ready, oiled, and about to combust on contact, Scott made his way closer. As he set himself on target, he diverted his attention to Ian's face. Nothing mattered more than what that man thought at the moment. "Ready, sweetie?"

With a tiny movement, Ian nodded his head, never releasing his gaze from Scott's.

As he made his way in, Scott started to shake from anxiety visibly. "Tell me if it hurts."

"No, it doesn't," Ian assured calmly.

As slowly as he could, Scott penetrated. When he was deep inside him, he set himself up better for his hips to move. His vision flicking from Ian's expressions to the act, he felt his breathing rising to a pant. "Fucking hell!

"What?" Ian panicked.

"I'm coming!"

"Oh!"

As Scott tensed his muscles, grunted and gasped, Ian stared at him with so much intensity, it was as if he would burn a hole through him.

Backing away, pulling out, Scott collapsed on top of Ian with a groan. Nuzzling into his armpit to savor the afterglow, Scott closed his eyes and whispered, "I love you so much."

With his gaze a million miles away, Ian kissed Scott's hair and didn't answer.

At the bewitching hour Claire was fast asleep. A hot soak, too much wine, and exhaustion had worked their spell. In her sleepy mind she imagined the noise of the men returning home would wake her. Then she could wish them a Happy New Year, and doze off again knowing they were home, safe and sound.

Drowsing, almost forgetting what time it was, a flurry of explosive fireworks set loose on the city. Propping themselves up, they exchanged glances and remembered just precisely what night it was. Racing to the window, the two naked males leaned against the ledge and shoved back the heavy gold curtains.

After the ball dropped and the shouting from below echoed around the icy buildings, Scott became absorbed in staring at Ian as he reacted in delight to the visions of white sparklers and sonic booms. An enormous puppet of father time on stilts moved precariously through the throng, tipping and weaving its way through a mob so thick, pavement could not be seen under it.

His enthusiasm always contagious, Scott leaned against his side to share the experience with him. As Ian felt the heat of Scott near, his warm breath misting the ice-cold window, he gave him a very affectionate smile.

"Happy New Year, Mr. Epstein."

"Happy New Year, Mr. Sullivan."

Chapter Thirteen

January 1st, 2007, at ten a.m. Ian and Scott made it through the door of Claire's apartment. Still giggling together as if they had been bad boys who stayed out all night and were coming home to mother's scolding, they were surprised to find the place vacant.

Trying not to be concerned, Scott browsed around for a note. There was none. He instantly went to the phone and dialed his sister's mobile number.

Ian, meanwhile, tossed off his new leather jacket and sat on the couch, patting the spot beside him. Immediately taking note, Scott joined him and was embraced in his arms. "Hey! Where are you? We're home."

"Finally! Man, where did you guys sleep? I was really upset when I woke and you weren't there!"

"Ah, we sort of stayed up all night in bars. We'll catch a nap. Where are you?"

"At a café. Want to join me? Or are you too tired?"

"Hang on." Scott cupped the phone. "She's at a café, you interested?"

"Magic." Ian smiled and kissed Scott's cheek.

"We're game, which one?"

"Café au Latte. Our usual. I'll save a seat by the window."

"I'm surprised you found someone open."

"Me, too. It's filling fast. So jog here."

"Ha! Right, on our way." He hung up and returned Ian's cuddle.

"She sound upset?"

"Not in the least. Just a bit worried we didn't come home last night. You heard what I said. So, if she starts prying, let me give her the list of clubs. You play dumb. Okay, cutie?"

"Gotcha." Ian smiled, "It's my easiest part to play."

Scott coiled around him, kissing him, nudging him back on the couch.

"Didn't she want us to meet her?" Ian asked between smooches.

"Yes, and fast. She said it's filling up with customers." But he showed no sign of budging.

"Uh huh…" Ian tilted his head in question.

"I want you again," he purred.

"Do you? Now?"

"Yes, but I'll wait for later," he said as he chewed on his ear.

"You are rrrrandy!" Ian laughed.

"Oh, yes! Randy, dandy and wanting English candy!" Shoving him back against the leather sofa, Ian laughed in hilarity as Scott licked and nibbled his neck.

Checking her watch neurotically, Claire kept a sharp eye out the window for them. If they were jogging they must be jogging backwards! After almost a half hour she found them through the foggy glass, smiling and laughing as they walked in stride.

Being a gentleman, Scott pushed open the door and held it for Ian as he stepped in and scanned the place, searching for Claire.

She waved enthusiastically and gestured to the seats she had saved.

"Hello, Miss Epstein!" Ian grinned impishly.

"Happy New Year, Mr. Sullivan." Leaning toward him, it was obvious she was expecting a kiss. He reacted to her gesture and pecked her on the cheek.

"Happy New Year, Sis," Scott said enthusiastically, and kissed her as well. As Ian scooted out a chair and made himself comfortable, Scott asked him what he wanted so he could go to the counter and order for him.

"Uh...I have no clue. Whatever you're having, love."

With a wink, Scott headed to the counter to take care of the task.

Gaping at them, still stuck on the affectionate word, 'love' and the sensual wink, Claire said, "Ahhh, okay, so— Tell me about last night! How was your first New York New Year's Eve experience?"

Ian said, "Cushty!"

"And?" Claire leaned over to him and grabbed his knee. "How about the crowd? Were they rowdy?"

"No. Not very. A good group, actually." He glanced up at Scott who was just placing his order.

"Did you freeze?" Claire scooted her chair closer and moved her hand higher on his thigh.

Ian cleared his throat. "Uh, no, not too cold. We were blocked from the wind. You know, in the dense crowd."

"Which clubs did you get to? I'll bet they were mobbed!"

"I'll let Scott give you the list. I don't know one from another, really." With her hand making its way boldly to his inner thigh, Ian let out a nervous chuckle, "Miss Epstein! Are you molesting me?"

She drew back instantly. "I was! Should I not be?"

Before Ian could respond, Scott had his coffee in hand and

set it before him on the tiny round table. "There you go! Mocha with whipped cream. You said what I was having, and that's what I ordered. I hope it's all right."

"Cheers, thanks mate." Ian inched his chair back from Claire to give Scott room to move to the remaining vacant spot.

"Where did you guys go?" Claire sipped the last drop of her skinny latte.

Taking a moment, Scott said, "Session 73, Club New York, Danny's Skylight Room, and the Firebird Café."

"Christ!" she laughed sarcastically. "What did you do? Have one drink and keep moving on?"

"Well, I wanted to show Ian a good time." Scott avoided her eyes.

"What did it cost in cover charges? I would think on New Year's Eve it would have been brutal."

"It was. What do you care?" Scott changed the subject. "So? What did you do?"

"Sat home, ate Chinese food, had a bath. A real thrill."

Ian stared at her. When he met her gaze she turned away.

"Well," Scott mumbled, "You did say you wanted a quiet night."

"Not that quiet!" Her laughter was edgy, like crushed aluminum foil against granite. "I would have preferred someone in the tub with me!"

When Ian felt her boot toe enter his pant leg, he jolted in surprise.

"What?" Scott caught his reaction.

"Nothing. Hot coffee." He nodded to his cup and backed his leg away from the curious poke.

Returning his attention to his sister, Scott said, "Look, you have hundreds of friends, you should have called one."

"Naaa, it was too late. I really needed to make that plan weeks ago. I just couldn't think of anyone I wanted to be alone with. Until now."

With those last two words she grinned at Ian's stunned expression. Scott had lost interest in her babbling and didn't even catch it.

Growing hot and nervous, Ian unzipped his jacket and parted it to get some air. His cheeks were rosy from the boiling coffee. While Scott drifted off into the recesses of his mind, Claire reached under the table for Ian's knee again.

"Uh! Right. They have a WC here?" Shifting back so her hand could no longer reach, Ian made a move to get away.

"Yes." Claire nodded, "Back and to the right."

"Good. I'll be back." And without another glance, he escaped.

As he left, Claire stared at him critically. "He is one of our loveliest."

"Hmmm?" Scott came back to the present. "Ian?"

"Yes. I can't wait for the holidays to be over so I can truly get an idea of the impact he's made on everyone. There were a few at the party I feel sure wanted him."

Looking back over his shoulder, Scott asked, "Did any of them ask about me?"

Waiting to get complete focused eye contact from him and not hiding her irritation, Claire said, "Listen, Scott, you barely mingled, you kept your back leaning against the wall in the hall, and no one knew who you were. What do you expect?"

Instantly her bitterness was reflected in his face as he tried not to explode in anger. He said in a restrained tone, "I'm a model! They only need to look at me to see what I have to offer!"

"If you think you don't have to schmooze people, then you're a naïve little twat."

"Fuck you!" he roared, unable to control his temper. "You know, I make the effort to come here and hang out, and look at the shit I put up with!"

"Hang out? You call being here for five minutes, hanging out? Where were you last night when I was sitting alone in the apartment? You could have called and wished me a Happy New Year! You could have let me know where you were! Which clubs! I would have come out and joined you! You think your five minutes of time is some colossal portion of generosity? Come on, Scott. You have to be kidding."

"One evening! One evening, Ian and I do something alone together and you're all bent out of shape! We play the fucking three musketeers every other night."

"One evening? Which evening did you pick, Scott? Gee, could you have found a less important night to blank me?"

As Ian made his way back to the table he could tell by their body posture the battle was on. He had no idea where he would come in on this one or if he was indeed, the topic. Taking a peek at the door, he actually thought of slipping out, leaving them to sort it out on their own. But, inevitably he would have to return to that apartment with the two of them. And after the little pass Claire had just made, he wasn't sure what he should do any longer.

Catching him standing there undecided, his hands deep in his pockets, his long hair covering his eyes, Claire stopped her debate and stared at him curiously. Immediately Scott spun around in his chair to see him. At the sight of his solemn expression, he leapt to his feet and hurried to him.

The reaction stunned Claire. *All right, what's going on*? she said to herself.

"What's wrong, Ian?" Scott delicately brushed the hair back from his face. "Did something happen?"

He sighed and shook his head, "I can't stand the two of you arguing."

"Ian! It's normal for us. You don't have to worry. Really."

"Maybe moving in was a mistake. I had no idea when I did,

149

that we would get involved."

"Stop—" Scott held up his hand. "Please. Not here, not now, and not after the kind of night we had last night."

She was trying to read their lips. But even without the words for support, Scott's posture was unmistakable, invading Ian's personal space, touching his hair, and most of all, appearing to plead. It was something she had seen him do with Fifi on a visit to California years ago.

"Look, we'll just sip this coffee and then go somewhere and talk, okay?"

Biting his lip, Ian said, "No. We need to spend some time with her, Scott. She'll get the miseries, have another row, and that's it for work for me. You see what I mean?"

The conversation was taking a disastrously long time. "Okay. A few more minutes, but, I want to hash this out." Spoken like a warning, Scott led him back to the table.

Claire was glaring at them. Biding her time, waiting until they sat down she went over in her mind how to phrase her thoughts. Outright asking them if something was going on between them was not going to work. If anything, it was going to do the opposite.

Instead of another confrontation, she decided to ignore this mess, then later, at the apartment, at night, do some more investigating and seducing. He was willing only a couple of weeks ago. Why had it changed? It could only be one thing. And they had spent a whole night together somewhere. What were the odds they never slept? But where?

"You okay, Ian?" Claire altered her expression to her mother-care look, and softened her tone.

"Yes, fine." Lifting his coffee, he found it a more tolerable temperature and sipped it down.

"What are your plans for today?" she asked them. "I would assume everything is closed and the weather sucks. You going back to the apartment to sleep?"

Putting on his thinking face, Scott nodded. "Yes. We need to get some rest. Probably after this we'll head back. What are you doing?"

"I was going to call Jenine and see how her night went. If she's available, I'll probably go visit her." Finding her cell phone, Claire tried to make it look official.

"Oh! Good. Well, we can all meet for dinner, if Jenine is available."

"Nothing will be open. We'll have to cook, Scottchula."

Ian laughed.

"What?" Scott asked curiously.

"Scottchula?"

"Yeah, never mind." Laughing as he finished his drink, he was making the movements of someone who is preparing to depart.

Ian tipped the remainder of his mocha into his mouth.

"Right." Claire had her phone in hand. "See ya later. At least a few hours from now. Get some rest or you'll be a mess later tonight."

"Okay. Ready, Ian?" Scott rose up and moved out the chair.

"I am." Ian followed him and they waved and smiled as they left the café.

Watching them with very suspicious eyes, Claire stuck her phone to her ear and waited until they passed the window, waving through it. The minute they were out of sight, she tossed it back into her bag.

"See. I told you she's all right. She must be on the rag or something." Rubbing shoulders as they walked through the pelting sleet, Scott smiled sweetly at him. "That means we have the apartment to ourselves, lover."

"For a few hours at least." Ian grinned back.

"Let's make the most of it!" Scott jabbed him with his elbow and then started jogging back to the apartment, with Ian close behind.

She tapped her fingernails against the table, noticed a couple eyeing it impatiently, and stood up, gathering her things. As she stepped out onto the sidewalk, the wind and snow pummeled her face. Finding her felt hat in her bag and pulling it on quickly, she zipped up her jacket and slid her gloves on in a hurry. Head down, she made her way to the city block where her building stood. There she could wait in the lobby for a few minutes, let them get on with whatever it was they would do, then she was going to go up and investigate this. She knew what she would find. It was only a matter of time.

As they raced into the apartment, laughing and playing, Ian was just out of reach as Scott scrambled to get a grip on him. Spinning away and avoiding the furniture, Ian roared with laughter, ducking and diving under those hungry hands. The moment he ran out of the space to run, Scott caught him, encircling his arms around him and shoving him into his bedroom, kissing him.

As they hummed and groaned their jackets dropped to the carpet, then their shirts.

With Ian under him, Scott fell to the bed, smothering him with hungry kisses.

"You certain she won't come back?"

"No. Not certain. But she did say she was calling Jenine."

"What if Jenine isn't available. What will Claire do?"

As if just realizing that possibility, Scott stopped what he was doing and leaned up to think about it. "Fuck. She'll come back here."

"I reckon she might."

"Shit. I was really looking forward to it."

152

"I know, baby." Ian kissed his slack mouth. "But, think of the consequences. I'd rather not take the chance."

"Ohhh....why does she have to come back?" Scott squirmed on his hips in yearning.

"Look, love, she'll be back at work tomorrow. Surely we can wait one day."

"Yes. You're right."

"And to be honest, I wouldn't mind a siesta. We didn't do much in the way of sleeping last night, did we?"

Scott grinned back at his wicked smirk. "No. I agree. Okay, Ian. Let's just get a catnap. That way if she comes back unexpectedly, we're covered."

"I knew you would see it was the right thing to do. I have a terrible feeling she's suspecting something."

"Do you?" Scott climbed off of him and reached to haul him up. "Shit! Then get to your room. I'll see ya in a couple of hours."

"Okay, love."

They stood and kissed for a few moments, then Scott handed him his jacket and shirt and walked with him to the hall. "Okay. Later. Try and sleep."

"Yes, Mr. Epstein." Ian laughed and headed to his room.

Waiting until he closed himself in, Scott pouted in disappointment, then shut his door in defeat. Dragging his feet tiredly over the short pile carpet, he moved to the folder on his desk and flipped it open. A smile emerged from his lips and warmth filled his chest at Ian's lovely face.

Checking her watch neurotically, she moved from the lobby to the elevator like she was some paranoid half-crazed thief. She'd given them twenty minutes. She imagined that was enough time to just begin something, and not quite enough to finish. As the numbers lit in succession, her heart was beginning to pound. What if?

What if she found them in bed together? What then? Should she make a scene? Or act like she already knew and it was no big deal?

But, it was a big deal! All that homophobic denial! She was sick to death of Scott's overreacting to every line she let loose of her opinion about his sexuality. And if she did know, what about their careers? Well, she would be tight-lipped. There was no other way to deal with it. She'd have to tell Jenine, of course.

As she crept out of the elevator, down the carpeted hall, she knew exactly what she would find.

Her key ring shaking in her hand, she moved as slowly as humanly possible, trying to believe they were in Scott's bedroom and couldn't possibly hear her key moving the lock. As it clicked, she cringed, then paused, waiting. Another click and the door was ajar. Inhaling to calm herself, she pushed it back and peeked in. No one was in the living, dining, or kitchen area. And that tree was still up. They had to take the damn Christmas tree down.

Shaking herself out of distracting thoughts of house cleaning, she closed the door quietly behind her and paused, scanning the room. It was as she left it that morning. She at least expected their leather jackets to be on the couch. Standing in the middle of the room, it was deathly silent except for the water running in someone else's unit and the distant yawn of traffic and airplanes.

Lowering to a deep knee bend to set her purse down, she then dropped her jacket over it, as well as her hat and gloves. Almost forgetting something, she panicked and remembered her cell phone. Finding it with clumsy hands she shut it off, sighing with relief that it didn't ring. Waiting again, listening to every sound, she thought she heard a noise, then couldn't tell if it was coming from inside or out of the unit. Upright, tall and feeling courageous, she decided on listening in at Scott's room first. Most likely he'd take Ian there, where he was most comfortable.

The Kiss

Praying the wood flooring would not squeak and give her away, she cursed herself and yanked off her boots, then resumed her advance.

Both their doors were closed. That in itself should have told her things were all right. But, deciding on seeing for herself, she tried the knob. It didn't turn. Locked! Aha!

Coaching herself, she said, "Okay, now what?" If Ian's door was locked as well, that would be her answer. If it was open, and empty, then that was the other answer.

Moving as slowly as she could, making herself into a snail, she oozed her way down the hall. Holding her breath to stop her chest from heaving, she tried the knob. When it cracked open she was stunned. As she pushed it back, the dimness of the interior came into view. Through the Venetian blinds, the slatted light traveled, across the short pile carpet to the fringe of the bed skirt. Creeping over the top of the spread, that linear shading came to rest on a form. Long, tall, and exquisitely sensual.

In some place in her mind, the relief from the jealousy at finding him where he should be, alone and asleep in his bed, was so great, she felt like sinking to the floor to recuperate. They were straight. She had given them the open invitation to screw, and they didn't.

Knowing she should back out, close the door, and maybe take a nap of her own, she had another amazing impulse. If Ian was not gay, then what did she have to lose? Trying to think back on the last time she slept with a man, it was upsetting her it was such a struggle. Had it really been over a year ago?

Over a year. She had lasted without sex for over a year. It just didn't seem conceivable.

Enter this pretty boy.

Rules were rules. But some rules were made to be broken.

Tiptoeing in, closing the door behind her, she crouched down beside the bed to get a closer look at his face. As he slept, his hair unruly and covering his left eye, she thought to herself she had never seen a man more lovely. And she had seen so many men before him.

As his dreams wove him back to his home, walking the cobbled streets of Hertfordshire, his body was levitating above Manhattan Island. And at this point it was all she needed.

Rising up, unbuttoning her blouse, she let it fall silently over his size ten and a half shoes. As if she were a lap dancer, she slipped her slacks down her legs, and shook out her hair, feeling very sexy, and very ready.

Pinching the blankets between her fingers, she lifted the corner to see his hot skin shining in the dimness, those black and white striped shadows appeared like painted flesh. Trying not to shake the bed to extreme, all she kept thinking of was getting in and holding him close. The rest would take its course.

Groggy from being under a deep sleep, he attempted to open his eyes. "Hullo?"

"Hello, my lovely." Now that he was awake, she curled around him like the coils of a snake, savoring his heat and velvety skin.

"Miss Epstein?" His voice was barely a hoarse whisper.

"Yes, my pretty boy." Light kisses were given to this lovely prince, as he struggled to come awake.

"Why are you in my bed, Miss Epstein?"

"Because I want to make love to you." Licking his neck under his chin, she wrapped her legs around his and dragged him close.

"I thought making love to a client was against your rules?" He raised his chin to back away from her kisses.

"Rules are made to be broken. That's my New Year's resolution."

"Ah!" he gasped as her hand became bold. "You're being very naughty with me, Miss Epstein."

"I know. I'm a very naughty woman," she giggled.

"I don't think this is a very good idea, my love." Gently, Ian tried to back up.

"I don't want any strings or commitment, sweetie. Just your cock."

"Ah!" He slinked back. "I see that. But even without strings, Miss Epstein, there will be problems in our professional relationship. Don't you think?"

Reaching once more into his briefs, she purred, "No problems. Believe me. I won't treat you any differently."

Finding her wrist, he attempted to remove her hand once more. "I appreciate your attention. Honestly I do. But you yourself said this would only lead to trouble. Remember?"

"I remember you telling me I had nice tits, that I remember." Unable to get her hand into his underwear again, she set back to try and make out his face in the dimness. "You really don't want this? Ian, it's just sex. I don't want more."

"Claire…" His tone becoming very serious, he set back from all her contact and tried to get her to listen. "I appreciate it. Everything you're saying. The fact that it is just physical, no strings attached, blah, blah, blah…but— Inevitably strings are attached. And you put me on the spot doing this. If I refuse you, do you hold back work from me out of spite? If we do have sex, do we have it just this once? Or will it be expected of me regularly? You see my problem?"

"You're make it sound so clinical!"

He flinched. "I apologize if I am, but, Claire, look at the position you have placed us in."

"I was hoping 'the position' would be you between my legs!"

"Claire, please. I can see you are already unreasonably upset—"

"Upset?" her voice strangled in her throat. "Do you have any idea how many of my models want to screw me? And here, I offer it to you on a silver platter and you bring up every bit of nonsense you can to blow the mood!"

"This was why I didn't want to do it. You see how unreasonable you are behaving."

About to blow her top, she threw off the covers and climbed out of bed.

"No, wait. Claire, be sensible!" Ian panicked. "I knew I never should have moved in here. This was bound to happen."

"Bound to happen? You conceited brat! You think you're that irresistible?" She grabbed her clothing and was gripping it in her clenched fists. "Your type are a dime a dozen, sweetie!"

"Claire!" He jumped out of the bed to stop her. "Not like this! Please! Sit down. Let's talk this out. I don't want this to jeopardize our working relationship. Please!"

Her chest rising and falling rapidly from hurt ego and pride, she couldn't face the rejection. Never had she thought of that as a scenario when she crept into that room. It was inconceivable to her. He had flirted! He had made overt passes!

"Sit. Please." Getting hold of her wrist, he gave it a slight tug, trying to make her calm down and talk to him.

Coming to the surface of his short nap, hearing the murmur of voices, Scott slipped his gym shorts on and opened his door. As he listened he advanced down the hall. Unmistakably the sound of arguing was heard through Ian's door. With his blood running cold in his veins, Scott leaned his ear against the wood panel to overhear the conversation.

"Are you calm, Miss Epstein?"

"No. Stop calling me that! You make me sound like I'm someone's goddamn mother. It's insulting." She crossed her arms in a huff.

"Fine. I'll stop calling you that. But I never meant it to insult you. It was said as an endearing term. And with all respect."

"I don't want you to respect me! For Christ sake, I'm here to screw you!"

Outside the door, Scott jumped at that comment, then pressed closer to find out Ian's reply.

"And I am flattered! I really am! And in another set of circumstances, I would accept! You have to believe me. You are lovely, and horny, and I'd be a fool to turn you down—"

"Oh?" She softened her tone and leaned toward him.

"But—"

"There's always a but, isn't there?" She sat back and frowned at him.

"There is this time. Look, Claire, I thank you for all your hospitality. Your generosity, your kindness, all of that. I do. I never want to seem ungrateful for anything you have done. Or will hopefully continue to do for me in the future. But I cannot shag you. Please. Though I'm sure it would be an act worth remembering. I can't. But I need reassurances from you that this in no way will affect our working relationship. Promise me."

She let go a long stressful sigh. "I'm sorry, Ian. I should have stuck to my rules in the first place. It's just that you're so damn beautiful I couldn't help but be tempted. You know?"

"I do know. Believe me, you tempt me as well, Miss— err, Claire."

When he chuckled in that silly way, she melted and gave him a very affectionate smile. "I adore you, Ian Sullivan. I would never do anything to harm you or your career."

"Sweeter words were never spoken," he sighed with relief. When she wrapped her arms around his neck and dragged him to her lips, he gasped, "No tongue!"

Scott bristled and went for the handle, barely controlling himself and waiting.

"I bet you didn't say that to my brother..." Claire

whispered devilishly.

"Miss Epstein! You naughty, naughty girl!" Ian admonished. "Now, off with you."

As she stood, she gathered her clothing again into her arms. "You lovely boy. I'm going to make sure you are a star."

"From your mouth to god's ear!" he laughed.

"Ha! My mother says that!"

"Mine, too." Ian winked.

When the door jiggled, Scott backed up quickly, then ran to the kitchen. As it opened he stopped, then spun around to look at her. When he found her with her things in her arms, he shouted. "What the fuck do you think you're doing?"

"Humping pretty boy. What's it to you?"

Hearing her lie, Ian jumped up and shoved open of the door. "Claire! Why are you telling him that?"

"Because I want to see if he's jealous!" she sneered.

Scott smirked. "Jealous? Why the hell should I be jealous? Have I ever cared about who you spread for before?"

"Scott!" she shouted, "How rude!"

"Please, don't you two start fighting again. I can't bear it."

"Don't worry, Ian. I won't let her bait me." Scott continued to the kitchen to get something to drink.

"What bloody time is it?" Ian rubbed his head in exhaustion.

"It's one fifteen," Scott said, then poured himself some juice. "Is Jenine coming for dinner?"

Forgetting she was supposed to have called her, Claire said quickly, "No. She's busy."

"Oh, too bad. Just us three then." He grinned at her as he drank.

"Yeah. Us three." She tilted her head at the odd look of satisfaction on her brother's face as Ian closed himself back into his room to get dressed.

"Why don't you go put something on? I don't want to see your undies. You're grossing me out." Scott cringed.

"Oh, shut up!"

"No, you shut up!"

"No, you shut up!" Claire laughed as she made her way to her room.

When her door closed, Scott felt his chest swell in pride. Ian was his. There was no mistaking that fact any longer.

Chapter Fourteen

As the holidays faded to a memory and the after Christmas sales flooded the junk mail in the post, Ian started classes at Juilliard while Scott reluctantly hunted for a part time job to fill his days. Tired of waiting for Claire to come up with something steady for him, he sat with the want ads and web sites, sifting through the minimum wage nightmare. What the hell was he qualified for? Waiting tables? Stripping at a club?

Back at Spencer & Epstein, Claire was on the job matching the models to the ads. And as she expected, Ian was in demand. With the pile of offers on her desk growing, she wanted to sit with him quietly to go over his options. Somehow he would fit in all this work between his acting classes.

As far as Scott's last job was concerned, he was scheduled to appear on the cover of *Men's World* in a week. With any luck, she may even get some calls for him as well. Meanwhile, the rest of her stud farm was keeping her busy.

"Yes, I realize the taping is live." Jenine nodded her head as her secretary, Patty, sat idle, ready with pad and pen. "Right. You want them Sunday evening after the ball game. I understand. Right." Jenine started waving her hand at Patty for her to write this information down, Patty started scribbling what she overheard. "Yes. One is named Ian Sullivan. He's the

Englishman with the long hair. The other is Scott Epstein."
Pausing to hear the comment, she said, "Yes, he's Claire
Epstein's brother. Yes. Uh, I think Ian is twenty-one and Scott
is twenty-five. Both single. No, no significant others that I know
of. Hmm? No, they're not gay. They just did the kiss for the
ad." She rolled her eyes at Patty at the inane interrogation. "Yes,
we did give their vitals out to *People* when they asked. I don't
see what—" Sighing, she reached out to Patty, "You have their
compcards?"

Patty raised her pad and checked her lap, handing them
over.

"Okay, ready? Ian Sullivan. Six feet tall, one hundred
seventy-five pounds, brown hair, green eyes, born in
Hertfordshire, England...got it? Okay, Scott Epstein. Six feet
two inches, one hundred ninety pounds, brown and brown, born
in Manhattan, obviously American." She waited. "Living? Well,
Scott lives with his sister, and Ian is staying there temporarily.
Yes, that's right. Fine. Are they going on first that night? Do
you know who the other guests are? Who? Possibly the
comedian, Garry Scheffeld? Oh, that's not good. No. He'll tease
them. Why? Be reasonable! I want them shown in the most
beneficial way! Not humiliated and accused of being gay! It's
bad enough Calahan may instigate something. He won't? Oh,
please. I know that man loves controversy! He used to be a day-
time TV host!"

As she handed the compcards back to Patty, she contorted
her face at her as if she was in pain, trying to communicate her
disgust with the conversation.

"Listen, Bob, I know how Calahan operates. He'll do it if
it's good for a laugh and he loves to be a pit bull at times. But
please, tell him not to do it at the expense of my men, okay?"
Biting her nail as she listened to half-hearted reassurances, she
said, "Okay, fine. Yes, I understand. But a lot of damage can be
done in five minutes. Yes, I do want them on the show. No.
Okay. Just go easy on them! They'll be there. Right."

As she hung up she ran her hands through her hair. It was falling out of its clip and annoying her. "Augh! I swear, Patty, they'll all put me in an early grave."

"The guys will be okay. Don't worry. They're not gay, so they don't have anything to hide!"

"Right. I know. I keep telling myself that. But even though they're straight, they can still be humiliated. Scheffeld. Good fucking lord. Like Bert Calahan wasn't enough punishment!"

As Scott surfed the Internet for some ideas, he heard someone at the front door. Curious as to whom it could be, he checked the time. It was two p.m. "Hello?"

"Oi…you all right?" Ian came in, smiling brightly.

"You're early!" Scott closed down the program and hurried to greet him.

"Yes, they let us go. Looks like more snow, I'm afraid. I think it scares the faculty."

Opening his arms lovingly, Scott wanted a proper hello. Ian set his books aside and moved to hug him warmly.

"Mmmm, you feel good," Ian sighed.

"Ditto." Scott nuzzled and sniffed his hair. "You hungry?"

"I am a bit." He released him and slid his coat off, tossing it on the couch.

Grabbing Ian's hand, excited that he'd come home unexpectedly and alleviated his boredom, Scott brought him to the kitchen. "We've got some deli meats. You want a sandwich?"

Ian tugged on Scott's hand, spinning him around to face him, and wrapping around him. "Later."

"Oh?" Scott grinned wickedly. "Hungry for something else instead?"

"Grrrrrrowl!"

"Wow. Okay. Lead the way!"

The Kiss

Ian dipped his hand into the front of Scott's jeans and tugged him across the living room to the bedroom by his waistband. After he had shoved Scott in, he locked the door.

"Don't worry, Claire won't be home till after five," Scott said, pulling his shirt over his head.

"Hey, I get out early sometimes, so can she." Ian was winning the stripping contest, getting out of his clothing quickly.

"Well, she hasn't been home early once since she's been back at the office." Working his way backward, feeling for the bed, Scott fell on it, keeping his eye on Ian.

"No. You're right. No worries then!" Once he was naked, he shoved Scott flat and parted his knees.

"Oh, baby! Whatever you want, take it!"

"I intend to. Been thinking about you all day." Ian felt around inside Scott's nightstand for a condom and the jar. Finding it, he sat up, slid the rubber on, and coated himself as Scott stared, enthralled. Once he had accomplished the task, he tossed the jar onto the floor and said, "Ready?"

"Go for it." Scott smiled, spreading his legs wider.

Needing no further encouragement, Ian climbed over him, pushing in. "Oh, love! That is so tight!"

"I bet you say that to all the girls," Scott whispered wickedly.

Remembering the first time he had said it, Ian laughed and tried not to get distracted. "Shut your gob and let me shag you!"

"Sorry. Shag away." Scott stuck his hands behind his head to prop it up and watched Ian in action.

"You got a minute?"

"Sure, come in." Claire waved Jenine into her office and yelled for her secretary to get the phones for a moment. "Sit, my dear."

As if she were a puppet whose strings were severed, Jenine, dropped into the chair and exhaled in exhaustion.

"Just come for a breather?"

"No. Look, Bob from network TV called. They want the boys to do the show Sunday night after the game, live. They think Garry Scheffeld is booked with them."

"Oh, great. Just what they need." Claire rubbed her face tiredly.

"Well, what can you do? Anyway, I tried to get them to promise to lay off the gay issue. But you know Calahan. It's the hot topic. You think the boys can handle it?"

"I think they can. But we'll see. I can picture Ian going mute and Scott enraged. Wouldn't that be a pretty picture? Oh, my god, the offers would stop dead."

"That's why I'm here. I want you to coach them. At least prepare them for the possibility that their sexuality will be inspected. They're both single males, twenty-something, with no female partners. Ya know? And they're cohabitating."

"With me!"

"Big shit. Think they care? They're fair game. I want you to tell Scott not to get angry. Under no circumstances is he to get baited into a fight. Got it? Claire, I'm counting on you to keep him in line."

"Oh, great." She rolled her eyes at the folly.

"He's your brother! Why did you pick him for the ad if you didn't think he could live up to all the pressure?"

"Hold on! Calm down! I didn't say he couldn't handle it. Let's just keep calm and not make matters worse. He'll be fine. Look, Jenine, they are both heterosexuals who are very secure in their manhood. Don't worry. Okay?" *I hope,* Claire said to herself in a prayer.

"Right. I've got nothing to worry about, right?" Her hair in her face, she tugged out her clip, stuck it in her mouth and started twisting her ponytail again to clip up.

The Kiss

Knowing she had everything in the world to worry about, Claire said, "Right."

"Baby, you are amazing," Ian moaned as he rested between Scott's thighs. Inhaling his scent as if it were intoxicating cologne, he sniffed his way to Scott's ear, then nuzzled and kissed his cheek. "I am so mad for you."

After he coiled his arms and legs around Ian, Scott moaned in agreement, "And I love you, Ian. More than you could ever imagine."

"What would I do without you? I'm so glad we met."

"Really? You really mean that?"

Ian leaned up on his elbows and tucked his hair behind his ears. "I do. I wouldn't lie to you, Scott. This time we've had together, well, it's been the best time of my life. I've never had a friend like you before. One who is so devoted to me and loves me this much. It's really more than I could have asked for."

Blinking his eyes in awe, Scott couldn't believe what he was hearing. Though he'd had several relationships in the past, none seemed to compare to the depth of love this one had achieved. And he was stunned it was reciprocal.

Ian blinked his eyes slowly at him. "I'm a plonker. I said something to make you silent."

"No! No, Ian, don't take my silence the wrong way. I—I've just never been good at words. I feel the exact same way as you do, but I'm not the type to be able to express it. I'm sorry. I just know I love you. More than I have loved anyone else in my life."

Smiling, Ian said, "You know exactly what to say, Scott. Believe me."

"Come here," Scott purred, and brought Ian for more kisses.

"What time is it?" Ian whispered.

"Shit." Leaning over, Scott read the clock. "She'll be home soon. You better get dressed."

After a final peck on the lips, Ian hopped out of bed and grabbed his things. Freezing mid-stride, both of them thought they heard a noise. Panicking, Ian scrambled back to his room to finish dressing. Scott breathlessly was yanking on his clothes, his heart pounding in his throat.

"Hellooo?" As she came in she set her purse down and unraveled her scarf. "You guys home?"

"Hey." Scott hurried out to meet her, running his fingers through his hair. "How was work? You hungry? You want me to call for some food?"

Stopping what she was doing, she paused to stare at him. "Slow down! You okay?"

"Hmm?" He crossed his arms over his chest. "Yeah, just had a shit day trying to decide what to do part time."

"Oh..." Taking off her coat she caught some movement out of the tail of her eye. "Ian? You're home early."

"I am!" He came out of the room. "The snow was the catalyst, I'm afraid. I think the instructors all live in Jersey."

"Ah! Well, they should be a bit wary, then." As she set her coat down on the chair, she waited for something else to be said or someone to move. When they both were in the same posture, arms crossed, staring at her, she kept turning her head from one to the other. "What?"

Instantly they broke their trance.

"You guys are really weird," she sighed and headed to the kitchen for some wine.

Out of habit, both men followed her and leaned against the counter to stare at her.

When she turned around to pour, she noticed them there, like bookends. "You boys are hanging around together too much. You're starting to act alike."

They exchanged glances and laughed at each other.

"Okay, well, I was going to wait until after dinner, but since I have your rapt attention now..." She poured two more glasses and handed each of them one. "Sit, my beauties." She gestured to the couch.

Without a word, they obeyed, which again surprised her a little. As they sat on the couch together with a casual air she was getting used to between them, she set her glass down on the coffee table and curled her legs up under her on the chair in front of them.

"I want to put a disclaimer on this conversation," she warned. "So, before—you—" Her index finger pointed Scott out, "get upset, and—you—" next in line was Ian, "get mute, hear me out and remember whose side I'm on."

"Here we go—" Scott growled.

"Stop! I mean it, Scott, this is for real!"

"Give her a chance, mate," Ian touched Scott's shoulder gently.

Settling himself back in a more relaxed posture on the couch, Scott said, "Okay. I'll behave. What?"

"Jenine got a call from the television network today about your appearance on Calahan. She just wanted me to go over some tactics they may use to embarrass you. Or if not outright humiliate you, to make you squirm."

As if on cue, they shifted in their seats.

"I want you both to take a breath and think before you just respond. Especially you!" Her loaded finger aimed at Scott again. "And you, Mr. Sullivan, don't go mute!"

Ian let a nervous laugh escape and then sipped his wine.

"Now, let's say the worst case scenario occurs. What if some comedian is on with you and tries to bait you?"

"Shit. You know who it is. Who? Which comedian?" Scott

shivered.

"Maybe Scheffeld—"

"Oh, fucking great!" Scott threw up his hands.

"Who?" Ian asked.

"I said maybe, Scott. And he may not even stay once he's interviewed. Most of them talk and leave. So you will most likely not have to deal with it. I'm calling for worst cases here. Okay?"

"Is he quick-witted?" Ian asked meekly. "Like Jonathan Ross?"

"Who?" both Ian and Claire asked in stereo.

Not wanting to be distracted, Claire waved her hands frantically. "Stop. Listen to me! You're both big grown, heterosexual men. Right? You are very certain of your sexuality! Right? So, obviously don't let anything they say bother you! You got it? Hello? You are secure in your sexuality, aren't you?"

"We're not gay! Jesus, Claire, change the record!" Scott shouted.

Ian went into a choking fit as the wine was sent down the wrong end of his piping. Scott rolled his eyes and patted his back. "Great timing, limey."

"Sorry. I'm all right." He held Scott off and kept choking until he could breathe normally.

"Guys! It's not that difficult! Just don't get angry, don't go mute, and think before you speak! Can you do that?"

"I've lost me bottle. I reckon it's too late to back out," Ian whispered.

"Yes! What's the big deal?!" Claire was exasperated. "Look, all you have to do is act like Mr. Straight and Mr. Normal and stop worrying! Can you do that?"

Suddenly she noticed even Scott was beginning to sweat. "What sort of questions will they ask us? Do you know?" he asked.

"What difference does it make? You're not answering my direct question! Do I have to ask again!?"

He growled, "Oh, my god, Claire! Stop asking! We're not gay!"

"Then fucking say so!"

"Claire! I'm not going to repeat it a hundred times! Do you get it?"

"Geeez! Don't bite my head off!! Okay! Now, Jenine said they wanted to know your living arrangement, if you had a significant other, and your vital statistics. You know, height, weight…"

"What for?" Ian tried to sip his wine again.

"I don't know. Stop worrying. If things get heavy, just give a nice polite laugh and answer without spite or irritation, Scott!"

"Me? Oh…yeah, I will. Don't worry." His face lost some color.

"Christ," Claire sighed. "Sometimes I feel like I'm yelling at a brick wall!"

"What a horrid thing to say!" Ian cringed.

"She gets that way, I tried to warn you," Scott whispered out of the corner of his mouth.

Claire heard it, obviously, and threw up her hands. "Okay, whatever. But don't say I didn't try to warn you."

As they undressed for bed, both Ian and Scott looked as if they were sick to their stomachs. Claire thought they were extremely quiet after dinner and knew their nerves were getting the better of them. Before she retired for bed, she knocked on her brother's door.

"Yeah?"

"It's me, you decent?"

"I'm in bed. Come in."

She pushed back the door and sighed. "Scottchula, don't worry."

"Easy for you to say. Look. This could be a very big chance for Ian and me to get exposure. You think I don't know how important it is we come across well?"

Sighing tiredly, she sat down on the edge of his bed and offered him a sad smile. "You will. You've been trained by the best. My dear, you'll wow them. You're absolutely gorgeous."

He blinked his eyes at her and whispered, "You've never said that to me before."

"How can I? You're my freaky brother!" She laughed and smiled sweetly at him. "If I find out anymore about it through Jenine, I'll keep you up to date. Honest."

"Thanks. I know you'll look out for me."

"Yes, it's my job. Good night, Scott."

"Night, sis."

As she stood up, she kicked something with her slipper. "Oop!"

"What?"

Bending down to see what it was, she reached blindly under the bed for the object. When she brought out an open jar of Vaseline, Scott's face went pale.

"What the...?" She studied it carefully.

"It's for my hands!" He sat up anxiously and tried to grab it. "They get really dry in this weather and crack! I put it on every night before I go to bed!" Snatching it from her fingers, he dug out a slather and rubbed it into his hands. "I hate winter. I swear my skin is dry all over. Imagine going to an interview and shaking some ad exec's hand with flaky skin! So that's why I take extra care in winter. You know?"

He was talking so quickly, rubbing the gel on so diligently, she had no idea what to say.

"Thanks for finding it. I was looking for it before bed. I

must have knocked it off my night table. Well, good night, Claire. See you in the morning. Shut the light when you leave, okay?"

Reacting slowly, she nodded, her mouth still hanging open as she tried to analyze what was happening before her brain had a chance to figure it out. Then, mechanically, she closed the light and shut his door, standing still in the hall for a moment to think.

Scuffing her fuzzy bunny slippers to her room, Claire closed herself in and sat on her bed. "I don't fucking believe it! They are! Now what?"

Chapter Fifteen

A bowl of popcorn on his lap, Scott was trying to find something on the television worth watching. As he flipped the channels via the remote control, naked except for a pair of red gym shorts, he paused for a moment on the twelve o'clock news update. George W's face flashed before him, then Tony Blair's. He was about to change the channel when the anchorwoman mentioned a featured story to come.

"...later on the six o'clock edition, tune in to our complete coverage of the war with Iraq as well as the local news. Hear about a daring attempt by a gum manufacturer to get on the map as they tempt controversy with the first gay kiss in television commercial history..."

Gaping at the flickering screen, Scott felt a shock wave rush over his body. "What the fuck have I done?"

"Sit! Sit!" Meeting him on his way in, Claire waved to Ian enthusiastically as he stepped into her office. "I want your input on all these offers. You want coffee or anything?"

"No, don't put yourself out." Ian set his backpack next to the chair and leaned over his knees. "What have we got?"

"All right!" She rushed back behind her desk excitedly, shuffling through a handful of notes. "L'Oreal wants you for their hair products, in print format. *Esquire* wants an interview.

Playgirl—oh, we'll leave that one. Ahhh, oh, here's one for Virgin Atlantic Airlines. That one's a billboard. And the last one is for the cover of *New York Revue*."

"Brilliant!" Ian's bright eyes lit up. "Can I do them all, or do I have to choose one?"

"That depends. If they want exclusive contracts with you, then you can't do them all. Would you rather do several with smaller cash fees, or sign with one larger company and try for a large figure?"

"You know best. That's why I've got you!"

"Do you know you have the greatest dimples when you smile?"

"Thank you, Miss Epstein…but, could we get back to the contracts?"

"Okay. My opinion?"

"Please."

"If someone like L'Oreal offers you a huge contract, like six figures, I'd take it. But, if no one is willing to pay out big, then go for them all."

"Sounds reasonable."

"Good. Oh, about that *Playgirl* thing—"

"Bin it, please." Ian smiled sweetly.

"Right. I have to ask, you know." She sat back and stared at him, grinning. "So, how's class going?"

"Quite well, actually. I do like the instructors, so that's essential."

"Good." She waited, tapping her fingers on her over-loaded desktop. "Is there something important you want to tell me?"

It seemed suddenly as if he were a ghost with green eyes, frozen in fear. "T-t-tell you?"

She knew it. If he were any more petrified he would have been solid wood. "Nothing that needs getting off your chest, Ian?"

175

"Off me chest? No. Why would you say that?"

"No reason. Okay, anything else?" She was short on patience suddenly.

"Oh! No! Am I keeping you?" Ian stumbled to get out of the chair.

"Well, you know, busy, busy, busy. I have to make some calls for you now, my dear."

"Right." Standing up, he grabbed his pack and threw it over his shoulder. "Ah, anything come in for Scott?"

She screwed up her expression and shook her head. "No. Sorry."

"Just thought I'd ask. Right then. See you home."

"You will!" She stood up and shouted to stop him, "What do you want for dinner?"

As he paused at the door, he shrugged. "Surprise me."

Instantly a seductive smirk covered her mouth. "Is that a proposition, Mr. Sullivan?"

"I assure you, it is not, Miss Epstein." He grinned sweetly.

"I didn't think it would be. Okay. See you home."

"Right." Hesitating, he then went on his way.

As Claire watched him go, she wondered what it would be like to screw that lovely male. Only her brother knew for sure. Lucky fucker.

The bowl empty and on the floor, Scott was dozing off when he heard the key in the lock. Rubbing his face tiredly, he checked the time. "Hello?"

Ian stepped in and found him there. "Hullo, baby. You all right?"

"Shit, is it really four o'clock. Fuck, where'd the damn day go?"

As he set his things down, Ian looked as if he had a lot on

his mind.

"What's it like out? I haven't left this couch."

"Cold enough to freeze me bollocks off." Ian tossed his jacket on the chair. "Come on, warm me up. Give us a kiss."

At so irresistible an invitation, Scott forced himself off the couch and into those outstretched arms. Humming in pleasure at the feel of their bodies pressing close, Scott nuzzled into his hair lovingly. "Oh, god, you feel so fucking good."

"Like electricity. You feel it?"

"I do. I have never felt anything like it." Gripping him tighter, Scott arched back and raised Ian off his feet.

"Oi! Put me down, ya git!"

"No! I'm going to carry you off and rape you," Scott purred.

"Well, if you're planning on having your way with me, love, you had better be quick. Claire is expected half past five."

"You're right." Setting him down on his feet again, he found his hand and dragged him to the bedroom.

Completely sexually satisfied in Ian's arms, Scott fought the urge to sleep after yet another bad rest the previous night.

Ian was absently petting Scott's hair. The sweat the contact their skin was making was cooling them off after a very vigorous bout. Ian kissed the top of Scott's head and whispered, "You reckon we should tell Claire?"

His entire body tightening in panic, Scott said, "Tell her what?"

"You know."

"No."

"But, love, she suspects us."

"Let her suspect."

"You certain that's the right thing to do?"

Scott leaned up to stare at his eyes. "Please don't admit this to her, Ian. Please?"

Exhaling a tired breath, Ian nodded. "All right, love. Whatever you want."

As they ate the salad and chicken cutlets that Claire had made for them, she sipped her wine and asked Scott, "Did Ian tell you about what we discussed today in my office?"

Both men stopped eating and raised their heads quickly.

"No. I didn't know he was at your office today," Scott turned to give Ian a very suspicious look.

Ian shrugged shyly. "It must have slipped me mind."

"What did you talk about?" Scott resumed eating slowly.

"We had a list of options for him to choose from. I ended up wasting a lot of time after he left." She finished her glass and addressed Ian, "They are all supposed to call me back. No one gave me any answers on figures, Ian."

"I'm not bothered. They will, I'm sure."

"What companies?" Scott asked quietly.

"Ah, what were they, Ian?" Claire put on her thinking face. "L'Oreal, *New York Revue*…"

Having stopped eating, Ian glimpsed Scott's expression quickly, then poured more wine for him, then himself.

"Oh, right, and *Playgirl*! Ha! But, Ian decided he didn't want to show off his big dick, so we threw that one out."

Silent, Scott went back to his plate of food as Ian stuck his fork into his meal with little interest.

Once again Claire studied their reactions. After the discovery of the open Vaseline container, it was growing more obvious that they at least had experimented together. And those long painful gazes they were exchanging were agony to her. She knew the moment she said she and Ian had a discussion, Scott would instantly suspect Ian had let the cat out of the bag. It was odd to suddenly know what they were both thinking when originally it had been a complete mystery.

On the tip of her tongue once again was the urge to ask. It was right there. About to be spit out. But what for? She didn't mind that her brother was gay, not one bit. As she stared at them both trying to finish their dinner in peace, she knew the coming airing of the commercial and the interview on Calahan's talk show was enough pressure, and now that she knew they were hiding a secret, she understood exactly how apprehensive they both must be. It must be terrible, living in the closet—if only she knew a way to protect them from the ridicule that she feared was coming. But other than sit tight and see what they did, she felt she had nothing else to do but wait, and be there if they needed her.

Chapter Sixteen

With the Super Bowl three days away, Scott was growing anxious. He grew up in this town and went to school here for six years before moving to Seattle. He knew people here. All his aunts, uncles, cousins; they were in Brooklyn and Queens. Then there were his buddies from Seattle to think of. The guys he played football with at Ballard High School and the University of Washington. Every one of his college teammates would be watching that fucking game.

Slouching on the couch, his head in his hands, his elbows on his knees, Scott began regretting ever letting Claire talk him into it. He was desperate for work, but at what cost did he do that ad? If he thought his career was sad now, after the airing, it would be over. Ian could get away with it. He appeared metrosexual. Nothing seemed to be affecting Ian's chances at work. If anything, he was even more in demand.

As he sat, almost doubled over on the leather couch, a sob broke from his chest. Though he had scribbled some names of possible jobs to apply for, he hated the idea of traditional office work or retail. Other than acting, he was trained for nothing. And if it weren't for his sister's generosity, he would be waiting tables right now.

Alone in that apartment day after day while Claire and Ian worked or went to class, he could hardly stand the isolation and sense of failure. He was at his wit's end. What more could he do? He was listed with the best modeling agency on the east coast, and maybe even nationally. It all boiled down to him, and in his mind, he was a complete failure.

Bent in two as he hunched over, his hands over his head, he started to cry. The frustration was almost unendurable. And when that stupid commercial aired and the teasing began, he knew he would crack. How was he supposed to appear on Calahan's sleazy talk show with that bitter host, and possibly a caustic comedian sitting beside him, and endure it? He was certain he could not.

When he heard a noise at the front door, he sat up in alarm. Checking the clock on the wall, he was stunned someone was home so early. Having no idea what to do, he attempted to stand up, intent on running to the bathroom to splash his face, but before he could even get to his feet, the door opened.

"Hullo, love." Ian smiled, closing the door behind him and setting his backpack down. When he didn't hear a response, he paused and checked Scott's face.

In absolute horror to be caught crying, Scott twisted away and started walking to his room.

"Baby?" Ian hurried after him in fear. "You all right? Scott?"

When he felt Ian's hand on his back, Scott shouted, "Just leave me the fuck alone!"

Stunned at his anger, Ian removed his hand and blinked in surprise. "What happened? Did something happen?"

"Just get away from me." His voice cracking from the pain, Scott closed the door of his bedroom.

Hovering outside it, Ian he refused to walk away. He opened the door and stepped in. "What the devil is going on?"

Face down on his bed, his pillows crushed under him, Scott fought for control with all his strength.

"Baby…" Ian climbed over the bed to him and cradled him in his arms.

When he felt the contact and loving warmth surround him, Scott broke down, mortified he was showing Ian how defeated and weak he was.

"Shhh, okay, love. Come here and give us a hug."

Making the effort it took to roll over, Scott accepted the embrace and squeezed him tight.

As he allowed Scott to calm down, Ian rubbed his back gently, kissing his neck and cheek.

And as Scott's tears abated, he whispered, "I'm a failure, Ian. A pathetic fucking failure."

"No. You're not!"

Setting back to wipe his face on his sleeve, Scott found Ian's expression of frustrated anger. "But I am, Ian. Look at me! I sit here every day with nothing to do! No calls, no jobs. I know Claire tries. I don't blame her. But, not only am I not working, soon all my buddies back home in Seattle and here will be laughing at me! I'm scared shitless that that ad will completely destroy me."

Brushing away the new tears as they fell, Ian said, "Now you listen to me. This business is brutal. Both of us knew it before we entered it. If it was easy, everyone would be doing it." He held his finger to Scott's lips to stop his sarcasm. "All you need is one break. One. Just like the rest of us. Yes, I'm working a bit, but it's not a contract. It's an ad here or there. It's not easy for any of us, love. But we don't give up. We keep at it. You know what I mean?" He caressed Scott's face gently. "There is no need to get yourself all wound up about it. And as for that pathetic chewing gum advert, that's all it is, my lovely. An ad. One flash, sixty seconds long. A week from the air date, it will be forgotten. Trust me. Will you do that?"

Their body heat mingling, the gaze of Ian's sensual eyes on him, Scott's emotional outburst deescalated. "I don't know what I'd do without you, Ian. Do you have any idea how much you mean to me?"

"No. Tell me." Ian smiled sweetly.

"I'll show you instead." Scott grinned wickedly and leapt on top of him, pinning him to the bed and smothering him with kisses.

Hanging up the phone, Jenine's eyes were on fire. "Oh, my fucking god!" She scrambled around her desk and across the hall, shoving aside assistants and paper pushers in her path.

Busy, her focus on the telephone call in her office, Claire jerked her head up to find Jenine standing at her doorway, panting in excitement, flailing her arms like she had two flashlights in her hands and was guiding a 747 into a gate.

Losing the direction of her own conversation, Claire waved at Jenine to wait while she completed her call and tried to keep track of the voice on the line.

The pause impossible to deal with, Jenine was wringing her hands and pacing.

The moment Claire hung up she shouted, "What?"

Jenine closed the door and rushed her. "Fuck! You'll never believe this one!!"

"What!? For Christ's sake, Jenine, what the hell is it?"

"Scott!"

"Scott?" Claire panicked. "What happened to Scott?" She jumped to her feet and grabbed the phone to call home.

"Nothing! Shut up and put that down. Let me tell you." Jenine stuck her finger on the button to disconnect the call. "Sit!"

With great reluctance, Claire sat down and set the phone back on the cradle. "What the hell's going on?"

Jenine flopped on the chair and tried to catch her breath. "Okay. I just hung up the phone. That cover for *Men's World Magazine*? With Scott's abs? Well, guess who just called to ask about him and for him to come in and audition for a movie?"

183

Somehow Claire was supposed to make the connection between Scott's stomach muscles and a film. Typical of Jenine, nothing made sense. "What audition? What movie? Who?" Claire tried to keep calm.

"He's big! He's huge! Think Hollywood blockbuster."

"Jenine, do you know how close I am to strangling you? Who, god damn it!"

"Oscar Pullman!"

"Oh, fucking hell! No way!"

"Way! He wants Scott to audition for a supporting role to the lead in this mega star movie, a remake of *Alexander the Great*!"

"Oh, my fucking god!" Claire's mouth hung open.

"The role of Hephaestion! Do you believe this?" Jenine burst into nervous giggling.

"Oh, my fucking god!" Claire grabbed the phone.

"No! Don't tell him that way! Do it in person so you can see his face. Then I want a full report back."

"When's the audition? Where? California?"

"Nope, here! Tomorrow! Pullman sent scouts all over the frickin' world. Scott can audition here. If they like him, then he goes to Hollywood to shoot. I am so happy for him!"

"Well, he doesn't have it yet." Claire tried to come back to reality.

"No, but what an opportunity! Look, get out of here now, go to the bookstore and buy him some books on the guy. Let him read up tonight. Shoo! Go! Bye-bye!"

As if the idea had the smack of brilliance, Claire jumped to her feet and raced around the room for her purse and coat. Before Claire left, she grabbed Jenine and kissed her.

Jenine staggered back as Claire spun out of the door. With her eyes wide, Jenine shouted, "Damn! Was it good for you too?"

The Kiss

Ian was scratching out notes as he sat at the kitchen table, his drama books splayed out in front of him. Headphones on out of courtesy, Scott lay on the couch, reliving their last feverish bout of love making in his head. His expression—one of fierce passion, his lips parted open, his hands on his thighs to prevent his hips rising to the rhythm of sound and the memory of hot sex. He could come just thinking about it.

When Claire burst through the door with her arms full, both men jumped out of their skin and checked the time. As Ian and Scott made eye contact, they exchanged fretting gazes at the thought of Claire popping in unexpectedly, something she had never done before on a work day.

"Ian! You're home, too!" Her enthusiasm was unmatched.

"Yes, Miss Epstein. Here and immersed in my studies. What brings you home so early?"

"Never mind. How did the shoot go?"

Scott removed his headphones, glaring at Ian in jealousy.

With a quick check of Scott's expression, Ian said casually. "It went well."

"Good." Spinning around like a tornado inside a vacuum, Claire stalked her brother as he lay prone.

"What?" He grew instantly irritated with her.

With the plastic bag in her arms, she reached in and threw something at him. He caught a magazine and sat up. "Oh, it's out."

The minute he realized it was the magazine, Ian left his pen behind and moved closer, sitting next to him on the couch. "You're dead gorgeous! Look at you!" Ian leaned against Scott's shoulder, almost on top of his lap. "You are bloody horny, mate!"

"Ian!" Scott choked and gaped at him.

"He's right, little brother, you are," Claire smirked, the bag still in her arms.

"All right! Stop embarrassing me. Thanks for buying the magazine, Claire." As Scott set it down on the coffee table, Ian snatched it to ogle.

Unsuccessfully hiding her excitement, Claire sat across from them on the chair. Scott never stopped staring at her as Ian was getting himself into a lather. "What's in the bag?"

"I think you've too much time on your hands. So I bought you some books." She grinned mischievously.

"I hope they're porno." He laughed sarcastically and then glanced over at Ian who hadn't put the magazine down or even raised his chin to their conversation.

"No, not porno, but they will interest you." Setting the bag between her feet, she reached for a book and brought it out, handing it to him.

His head tilting at her in suspicion, he took it and read the cover. "Alexander the Great? Have you lost your marbles?"

"Or how about this one?" Removing another, she reached it across the table to him.

The same topic appeared on the cover. "Oh, fuck you! Is this some slam again about my sexuality? Giving me books on the biggest homo in history?"

"What?" Finally waking from his trance, Ian gaped at him and grabbed the book out of his hand to examine it. "Biggest homo?"

"Screw you, Claire! Leave me alone!"

"Sit down! I have something to tell you." She dumped out the bag and three more books fell out, all with the same theme.

"I'll only warn you once," Scott pointed his loaded index finger at her. "I'm in no mood for this type of teasing, Claire."

"I'm not going to tease you. But you need to listen very carefully to what I am about to say."

Crossing his arms over his chest angrily, he didn't answer,

only glared at her.

"Jenine got a call from someone who works for Oscar Pullman." She waited for it to register.

Ian said, "The director?"

"Yes. A scout found you on this issue," she pointed to the magazine in Ian's hot hands, "and called us about it." She focused back on her brother's dumbfounded expression. "They want you to audition for the role of Hephaestion. Tomorrow."

"Who? Ian?" Scott's gasped.

"No, you asshole! You!" Claire laughed.

As the blood drained from Scott's face, Ian screamed in delight and reached for Claire's hand as she held it up for a high-five. "Congratulations, mate!"

"What?" Scott couldn't catch up. "Can you tell me all this again?"

As slowly as she could, Claire went over the phone call, the audition, and the role.

"I don't believe this!" Scott was about to explode.

"You see! One chance!" Ian nudged him.

"Well, I haven't got the part yet," Scott whispered.

"But it's a shot. Isn't it?" Ian was brimming with joy.

As Claire sat back to watch their reaction, she grinned in complete pleasure. Her brother had waited a lifetime for this. It just had to happen.

He hadn't slept all night. Completely absorbed in the books Claire had bought, he had Ian highlight every chapter with Hephaestion's name in it, then read it, imagining the man himself. By morning, he was lying in a sea of open novels and scratch paper, Ian snoring as he lay across the bottom of the bed where he had dropped off. Checking the time, Scott jumped up, still in his clothing from the night before, and banged on his sister's door. "Claire! What time is the audition?!"

Coming from a deep sleep, sitting up in a panic, she checked the clock. It was six a.m. "Scott! Go back to sleep. It's at eleven, for Christ's sake. I'll make sure you get there."

"What'll I read? What should I read for them?"

"Didn't you have any favorite play from school? Ask Ian. Now shut up and let me sleep…"

Turning back to his bedroom, Scott rubbed his hands together nervously and found Ian sitting up, awake after his shouting. "Bloody hell. I'm knackered," Ian moaned.

"Go get some sleep. But, before you do— Give me something to read for the audition."

"What kind of part?"

"Hell, I don't know! You read the fucking books! Help me!"

"Christ…I can't think…" Ian rubbed his hand through his hair and yawned. "Shakespeare."

"You think?" Scott approached him.

"Yes. It's what all the 'act-tours' read."

"Yeah, great." Hurrying to his bookcase he thumbed through the titles. Once he found a book of Shakespearean plays, he yanked it out and flipped the pages. "I did this one back in California once. I think I still remember most of it."

"Which play?" Lying back on the bed, Ian yawned again.

"*Othello*. Great monologue. Very dramatic."

"Good…can I sleep now?"

"Yes. Shoo…" Scott reached out to grab him distractedly with the intention of helping him up.

"I want to sleep in here," Ian moaned.

"Okay…sleep here." Not even registering what he said, Scott walked out of the room and went to practice in the living room.

Ian pushed the books off the bed and fell fast asleep.

"Scott became obsessive." She finished the water and played with the empty bottle so it popped and crackled. *"Obsessive,"* she repeated, wanting to stress the word. *"He did that. If there was something he wanted, he hung on like a hungry gator. I am not joking. I'm not saying he was mental. Well, not completely certifiably mental, but, he got nutsy. Forget sleep. Scott was so sleep deprived he couldn't lose anymore. So you get the picture; he wasn't sleeping, his eating became erratic, even for Scott. And I could tell he was breaking inside. Then you have this innocent child,"* she paused and laughed, *"I call Ian that because in comparison to the New Yorkers I knew, he'd be eaten alive. You would have thought this mama's-boy-babe-in-the-woods, would have no idea how to cope with Scott when he was in that state. I would have thought that poor Ian just didn't have a clue. But I was wrong. Ian knew just how to calm that savage beast."*

Chapter Seventeen

"Claire, I'm gonna bomb."

"Shut up! Scott, get a grip on yourself! Everyone's nervous. It's normal." Reaching for his hand she brought him with her into the building and checked the floor plan on the wall to direct them. "Okay, third floor."

"Fuck, fuck…"

"Calm down! Geezus, at least give yourself a chance."

In complete frustration, Scott could not decide what to do with his hands. He ran them through his hair, then stuck them into his pockets, then crossed them over his chest like some demented marionette whose strings are tangled.

Taking the short ride in an elevator that reeked of cigar smoke, Claire once again directed them to the correct room. "Okay, baby. You go in alone. You don't need to be seen with your big sister holding your hand."

"Right. Thanks, Claire. Uh, are you going to be waiting here for me when I flop?"

"Scott!" She hit his head in irritation. "You won't flop. Yes. I'll be here. Go!"

With her persistent shoving, he managed to make it through the door and into a room, smaller than what he expected. The gathering was in the front, directly opposite the door. Several men were seated in chairs before a gaping space made to resemble a stage. Someone was reading while someone else was waiting in the wings.

His leather soles like a snake's whisper as he advanced, someone heard him and stood up to meet him. As they checked his name off the list, they instructed him to be seated and wait his turn.

He was sick, nauseous, and wishing he could simply get up and get it over with. Not knowing when he would be called, Scott removed his jacket and sat down, biting his nail nervously.

His eyes unfocused, hardly even paying attention to the movement in front of him, he was going over the lines in his head. He had it memorized not wanting the encumbrance of a script.

"Mr. Epstein?...Mr. Epstein?"

Completely lost in thought, waking out of a dream, he heard his name being called. Popping back to reality, he stood too quickly causing him to trip over a chair as he attempted to get closer to the man who was summoning him.

"You're up. What are you doing for us?"

"Uh, I have something from *Othello*."

"Fine."

The pause was very long as Scott waited for more instruction finally realizing they expected him to get to it immediately. Positive they thought he was a complete moron by now, he moved quickly to the center of the space in front and faced the wall, gathering his thoughts together. Inhaling, thinking of the look on Ian's face when he got the part, he turned around and began reciting the memorized lines. As his voice exploded out of his chest, he was hoping it wasn't too long, and he wasn't overdoing it. Words from his instructors at Juilliard came rushing back to him as he put all his lessons into practice. "*Imagine you are there! Feel the character! Don't just recite lines! Time your pauses! Say things as if they mean something! With love, devotion, feeling, anger! Use all your senses! Reach out to them! Pretend you are the only live act they will see in a lifetime!"*

When he was done it was as silent as a tomb. Not knowing what to do next, he stood there, staring through everyone as if they were transparent.

"Mr. Epstein, we'd like you to read from a script. Can you do that for us?"

"Of course." Inhaling to calm himself, he took what was handed him and noticed it had been rubber-banded back and highlighted.

"Just from the top of the page."

Again relying on the resources he had from class, he read the line to himself, then raised his head, and spoke it out loud to the small audience instead of hiding his face behind the script. Patiently, completing the rest of the page in the same way, his authoritative voice emerged as if it was an echo far off and hadn't come from a human being.

"Thank you, Mr. Epstein. We'll call you."

Someone stepped forward to take the script from him, then it was dead silence once again.

Giving a last sweeping look at the group, for he knew he would never set eyes on them again, he straightened his back and walked proudly to the chair where he had dropped his jacket, then made his way back to the hallway.

Claire was leaning on a wall, shifting her weight from one leg to the other in exhaustion. It'd been almost an hour since he had gone through that door.

When he materialized, she pushed off the wall and waited for him to say something. Anything. The expression on his face was so volatile, she didn't dare ask. Assuming they had told him *no thank you*, she kept her lips sealed as they walked back out into the icy air together.

In the cab ride home, she hated the silence with a passion.

The Kiss

Not wanting to bring up the audition if he didn't want to discuss it, she said, "I'll take us all out to dinner tonight."

"Fine."

"Where do you want to go?"

He shrugged, his gaze lost on the yellow tide of taxicabs flowing and ebbing down Fifth Avenue.

Feeling sick to her stomach by his reaction, or lack of one, she checked her phone to see if it was on, then stuck it back into her purse. What were the odds they'd want someone like Scott with no prior major acting roles? Pretty slim. He was an unknown with very limited experience.

Ian wasn't at the apartment when they arrived. Scott threw off his jacket, went directly to his room and closed the door.

Watching him disappear like a hibernating bear into his den, Claire moaned unhappily and sat by the phone in the living room, lifting the receiver.

"Hello? It's Claire. Put Jenine on, will you, Patty? Thanks, sweetie... Hey... I don't know, he's not saying. I assume it went horribly. Look, it was a long shot... In his room. I'm taking him out to dinner later. Look, I know it's still early, but do you mind if I start the weekend now? You're a dear. Yes. I'll be at my home number if there's a crisis. Okay. See ya Monday, Jen." She hung up and stared at the blank television set, really worried about him. His big chance...if he'd blown it, he'd be devastated.

When Ian came through the door, he found Claire on the floor in the living area, her photographs of models strewn out over the wooden surface, hard rock and roll from *Led Zeppelin* coming from the stereo, and an empty bottle of wine next to her.

"Hullo."

Raising her head to him as he came in and dumped off his things, she smiled. "Hi, Ganymede."

"Where's Scott?"

"Sulking, I'm afraid."

"Oh, no." Taking off his jacket and setting it down, Ian sat on the floor with her to find out the details. "What happened?"

Pushing her hair back from her face and trying to make piles with the photos she had completed, she sighed. "He wouldn't say. Just came out of the audition with a major attitude. I assumed they told him no way."

"Oh, for fuck's sake." Ian rubbed his face in agony.

"It was a long shot, Ian. We all knew that."

"He really needed this, Claire. You have no idea what he's dealing with."

"I do, Ian. Believe me."

"I should see how he is."

"Yes, go. He's probably sleeping it off, but go to him."

"Right." Getting himself upright gracefully, he walked on timid tiptoes to that bedroom door and rapped it lightly. "Scott?" When he didn't hear anything, he opened it. "Baby?" he whispered.

Groggy from a nap, Scott rolled over and made eye contact with him.

"You all right, love?"

"I'll live."

Closing the door behind him and sitting next to him on the bed, Ian rubbed his side and hip affectionately. "What happened, love? Can you tell me? Or are you too upset?"

"Nothing happened."

"Did you read? Did you do your piece?"

"I did. I did the part from *Othello* first. Then they had me read from a script."

"Did they?" Ian perked up.

"Yeah."

"That's promising, love!"

The Kiss

"Is it?" Scott sat up. "What do you mean, promising?" Hope flickered through his misery.

"Well, if they thought you were shite, they wouldn't have bothered. You see what I mean?"

"Really? When they just told me I was through and said, 'We'll call you', I assumed it was the kiss off."

"Not necessarily. Let's not lose hope."

"Come here." Scott opened his arms.

"Claire's home."

"Just a quick hug."

Needing no more prodding, Ian embraced him and they squeezed each other tightly. "Ohhhh, electricity!" Ian laughed.

"God! I know! Can you feel it? It's like we're vibrating!"

"I don't want to let go," Ian purred and nuzzled into Scott's neck affectionately.

"I love you, Ian."

"I love you too, Scott."

"Thanks for putting up with me. I don't know why you do it."

"Neither do I, mate."

When the line registered, Scott backed up to see his expression. Finding that irresistible smirk, Scott chuckled and kissed his lips.

Chapter Eighteen

Saturday morning the phone was ringing off the hook as everyone wanted to get the details as to when that hot potato commercial was going to be played.

Ian's nerves kicked in when his mother called unexpectedly and said she found the article in the newspaper about the ad. Why hadn't he rung her to tell her about it? She was excited and nervous for him, something he hadn't expected.

"What about Dad?" He knew the answer before he asked.

"I haven't mentioned it to your father, Ian. Well, you know how wound up he'll get about it. I reckon it's best we don't mention it."

"It's just an advert, Mum."

"I know, love, but, just the same."

"Well, the game is on too late for him to see it anyway." Ian sighed.

"Yes, it is. I think the paper said tomorrow about half past eleven at night. He'll be long in bed."

"I'm not gay, Mum."

"I know, Ian. You don't have to tell me. It's just a silly advert."

"Yes. That's all it is, Mum. A silly ad." As he spoke, he found Scott trying not to eavesdrop.

"Well, good luck to you, love. And keep in touch."

"Right, I will, Mum...see ya." When he hung up, Scott lingered closer.

"You okay?"

"Yeah, I'm all right. You all right?"

"Yeah, swell."

"To be honest, I'm a bit sick to me stomach. Nerves, ya know?"

Scanning the room quickly, he found Claire on her cell phone, which hadn't stopped ringing either. "I wish we could be alone. I hate weekends when she's here."

Ian had to step closer to hear since Scott was whispering quietly, almost talking to himself. "Right. I know, mate. Could use a shag. A bit pent up."

"Augh. Stop! I'm fucking hornier than hell. Twice a day to nothing. I hate weekends." Grinding his teeth, Scott turned his back so his sister couldn't overhear.

"Where can we go?" Ian checked her out as well, making sure she was busy on the mobile call.

"Fuck..." Scott sighed.

"We're stuck." Ian shrugged. "Can we send her out for something?"

Snapping his fingers, Scott raced to the kitchen and started opening cabinets and the refrigerator as Ian watched in amazed curiosity.

"Ya know, Claire—" Scott shouted over his shoulder, his head in the freezer.

She cupped the receiver, and shouted, "I'm on the phone, Scott!"

"I know! But we need some stuff for tomorrow. We don't have nearly enough soda, or chips, or wine. Or ice!"

"Then go out and get some!" While Claire was trying to tell the other person on the line to hold on a minute, Scott kept shouting obnoxiously, "But you know what brands to get! How should I know?"

"You're pathetic! You know that?" she growled, and said, "Yeah, Jenine, it's my fucking brother. He's so pathetic he can't go to the store and buy potato chips!"

As the plan went into action, Ian stared in awe and stayed quiet, trying to see if Scott could lure her out.

"I know! Have you ever heard of anyone so incompetent?" she continued. "Will you? Jen, you're a doll."

Biting his lip, Scott said, "You should help her out!"

"Me?" she snarled at Scott, then spoke back into the phone. "Can you hear him? What an asshole."

"Fuck," Scott sighed.

"Right. I will. Five minutes. Bye." She hung up and glared at him. "And if I go with Jenine to get the stuff, what the hell are you going to do, you lazy ass?"

"I could straighten up the place. You know, get the glassware and the napkins all out and stuff."

Glancing back at Ian first, she shook her head, then said, "Fine. You're lucky you had such a hard couple of days or I'd make you go out in this weather and get everything."

"You're going?"

"Don't look so fucking pleased with yourself! Or..." Her expression altered completely as she narrowed her gaze at Ian again, then back at Scott. "If you two just want the place for yourself, just say so."

The dry swallow Ian made was audible as Scott went into a chorus of denials.

"All right, I'm outta here. Jenine said she'll meet me at the market, and she'll be coming back with me! So be quick about it!"

"Wha...? No! You...I mean..." Scott stuttered.

"Whatever!" Grabbing her purse she winked at Ian, "See

ya later, Ganymede."

"See ya," he chirped out in embarrassment.

As she closed the door, they stared at each other in surprise. "Does she know?" Ian asked in anxiety. "Did you tell her?"

"Fuck no! She's just playing her pathetic little games. I didn't say a word."

"Criminy. She certainly seems like she knows." Ian rubbed his forehead in worry.

Scott rushed him like a linebacker, gripped him around the thighs, lifted him up over his shoulder and carried him to his bedroom. Flailing at the suddenness of the attack, Ian was gasping and trying to grapple to keep his balance and not cause them both to fall. When he landed on his back on Scott's bed and his jeans were yanked to his knees. His eyes widened in awe at his lover's hunger. "Bloody hell! Careful, mate, or you'll crush me bollocks!"

Doing his damnedest not to laugh, Scott peeled back Ian's hands as they cupped his precious parts in paranoia, and nuzzled in hungrily. At the feel of his mouth, Ian let out a long slow exhale and moaned, "Christ, I needed this."

"Me too, Ian...believe me. Me too." Scott gripped his hips, wrapped his arms around them, then plunged him into his mouth.

Having spotted Jenine, Claire was waving for her to recognize her in the spattering of pedestrian traffic. When the wave was returned, she waited for her in front of the grocery store. "Hi, lady."

"Hi, Claire...so? What are the boys up to that they wanted you the hell out of the house?"

"Three guesses." Claire entered the store and found a cart.

"I knew it!" Jenine laughed. "You know, the way they look at each other, Claire. It's so obvious that they are in love."

"I know. My brother's such a butthead, he still won't admit it. He's up there humping his pretty boy now, and he won't admit to me he does it. I guess after all the teasing, I can see why, but it's still not fair."

As they pushed the cart down the aisle, Jenine started filling it with junk food. "Well, can you imagine Scott coming out? That just isn't a possibility."

"Cheese puffs?" Claire lifted the jumbo bag back out of the cart to sarcastically question Jenine.

"I love those things!"

"They get everything orange!" Claire tossed them back in the cart. "You're so weird."

"I know. So, anyway, Scott and Ian?"

"I think they should keep it in the closet, Jenine. I mean, think of the stigma and their careers. It just wouldn't be a good thing, ya know? They're just embryos in the acting field. Once they've matured, maybe—"

"Really? You don't think it's what everyone will think anyway, after that ad airs?"

"No. Why should they? And after they talk about it on Calahan and they don't lisp or wiggle, why should anyone think twice about their sexuality at all?"

"I'll tell you why." Jenine stopped their progress to the soda aisle. "Because of the way they act when they are in the same room. Because of the body language and expressions they exchange when they're close to one another. I'm telling you, Claire, Calahan will see right through them. Then he'll have them for dinner."

"Stop. Jenine, you're freaking me out. And please, when we go back to the apartment, whatever you do, don't say a word about this conversation." Claire gripped her arm making her search her eyes. "Promise me. If you knew the amount of stress those two have been dealing with, you'd understand."

"You had a talk with them about how to behave on that

200

show?"

"Yes." Pausing, Claire made sure no one was listening, then said, "I sat them both down and discussed it in detail. They get it, Jen."

After a very deep breath, Jenine said, "Okay. I promise. I just hope you're right. If they deny it and Calahan goes after them and convinces the audience they're lying, they'll really be toast."

The cab dropped them off in front of the lobby while the doorman hurried outside to help them unload.

"Thanks, Max. We went a little crazy at Shop-Rite."

"I see that, Miss Epstein. Do you want a hand?"

"No, we've got it. Just get the elevator started, okay?"

"Sure thing, Miss."

As Max rushed to push the button, Jenine whispered, "You think we gave the guys enough time?"

Over her full arms, Claire tried to see her watch. "An hour? Shit, I should hope so. Guys come really fast."

Clearing his throat, Max backed up avoiding her eye.

"Good one, Claire." Jenine shook her head as she stepped into the elevator.

"He won't know what we were talking about. Don't worry." She watched the lights flash over the door impatiently.

"Well, make a lot of noise and move slowly."

"Check." Jenine nodded.

Claire was imagining what they would be doing. How odd to think of her brother and Ian as lovers. How utterly unbelievable.

Setting down the bags, Claire dug for her keys and deliberately hit the door with her knee, knocking it. "Loud enough, sweetie?" she giggled.

"Christ, I should think so!" Jenine shifted to keep the packages from dropping.

They pushed back the door and paused to listen. Music was being played on the stereo.

"Uh oh." Claire whispered nervously. They tiptoed in, searching around for them, but they weren't in sight.

"Shit. I knew it!" Jenine stopped in the middle of the room.

"Come on! Just act normal!" Putting the bags on the counter, Claire waved Jenine over, like she was coaxing a disobedient dog. "Come here! Now! I said, come here! Jenine!"

And moving like she was a mongrel about to be hit, Jenine kept her attention on the hall between the bedrooms. "I'm freaking—they'll be so embarrassed!"

"I know! Stop it!"

"I need wine."

Even before Claire removed her coat and gloves, she reached into the refrigerator and opened the cork of a previously started bottle, pouring two glasses.

A moment later they caught the sound of a door opening and movement.

"Bollocks!" Ian twisted back to Scott who was tugging on a pair of gym shorts. "They're flippin' back!"

"Fuck...okay, don't panic. Just walk out casually."

"Casually? Are you mad?"

"Ian, just take it easy! We're allowed to be in a room together! I'll just say we were reading those Alexander books again."

Ian paused. "Do I look like I've just been shagged?" he asked bluntly.

"Yes..." Scott chuckled, and tried to tame his hair.

"This isn't funny, Scott!"

"Hey! Calm down! Christ, Ian, it isn't that big a deal, is it?"

"Are you fucking insane?" Ian growled. "You think I want your sister and her partner, my bosses, to know I'm shagging you? For fuck sake, Scott!"

A little surprised at the extreme panic, Scott began to get insulted for some reason. "Just go out there, will you? You can't stay in here all night!"

"Shit." Trying to tame his hair and tuck in his shirt, Ian walked out of his room.

When he turned the corner, both Claire and Jenine were gaping at him.

"Oh, hullo, ladies." Ian ran his hand back through his hair nervously. "Scott and I were going over those novels. You know. The books you purchased, Claire. The ones about Alexander."

"Oh, right." She nodded, thinking, *sure, anything you say, Ganymede.*

"I, ah, have to have a piss...be back." He waved awkwardly and slipped into the bathroom.

A moment later, Scott came out, strutting and bold, as if nothing could intimidate him and he was very macho and manly.

Claire covered her laugh, and twisted away.

"Hey. Hey, Jenine. You guys need help putting that shit away?" He moved to the counter and realized they hadn't touched the bags, yet both were drinking a glass of wine. "What are you two doing? Christ, Claire! You still have your fucking gloves on!"

"Oh? Do I?" Setting the glass down, she yanked them off, shoved them into her pockets and removed her coat. As if on cue, Jenine took hers off as well and tossed it on a chair. Then they both stared mesmerized at Scott again.

"What the hell's the matter with you two?" He reached

inside the bags to see what they had purchased. "Cheese puffs?"

"Jenine likes them." Claire giggled, but it had nothing to do with the snack food.

Again, like two sisters, Claire was about to burst out laughing. It was so awkward it was hilarious. Spinning away with her hand over her mouth, she heard Jenine going into a laughing fit and then broke up, bending over to roar.

When Ian opened the bathroom door, he found the women hysterical, while Scott gawked at them in confusion.

"What'd I miss?"

"Beats the fuck outa me!" Scott growled.

"Cheese puffs!" Claire shouted, trying to come up with something to get them off the hook.

"Cheese puffs?" Ian echoed, tilting his head. "Is that what you're laughing at?"

"Yes!" Jenine screamed the word.

"You're both frickin' nuts!" Scott shook his head and continued to empty the bags and put the things away.

Ian sat down in front of the television after closing down the stereo system. As he flipped mindlessly, the giggling behind him subsided.

With the three of them busy getting the things packed away, only a moment passed before they joined him on the couch, handing him a glass of wine. "Oh, cheers, mate."

Scott instinctively sat on the couch with him, as Claire took the chair and Jenine the love seat.

"Wait! Go back to the news!" Claire waved frantically.

Ian flipped back a channel.

"…the controversy surrounding the homosexual kiss on the Minty Gum commercial has begun a debate by the show's producers on whether to pull it. The ad, scheduled to go on during the half-time of the Super Bowl, has the committee in an uproar…"

"Oh, my god!" Jenine gasped.

"...A spokesperson for Mr. Andre Surah, president of Minty Gum stated the commercial is not offensive in any way, and will be aired regardless of the bad publicity. Since no one has seen a preview of the kiss, the promoters of the Super Bowl stated they couldn't comment either way..."

As they sat side by side, Scott flinched. Peeking over at Ian, Scott noticed him cringing. "Do you believe this?"

"No," Ian breathed.

"I told you it would be great!" Claire reached for the remote control hungrily. "Let's see if it's on any other channel."

"No!" came the male chorus.

"Why the hell not?" She flipped the channels like mad. "It's your big break into stardom!"

About to reply angrily, Scott felt Ian's hand on his leg to prevent it.

Jenine caught the gesture and the intimate spot Ian's hand had settled and lingered.

She exploded with the line, "Do you guys screw each other?"

Claire sprayed out her wine before she was able to swallow as the shock of her partner's naiveté stunned her. So much for a promise.

Though Ian's hand remained on Scott's thigh, it went limp as his eyes widened innocently.

The boiling anger inside Scott's chest was like lava bubbling through soft cracked earth. As his face contorted in fury, Claire tried her best to recover and pass over this faux pas before everyone stormed off to their private rooms to sulk. "Jenine! You silly girl! Of course they don't. They're not gay. Why don't you go get us more wine before Scott punches your lights out for such a stupid comment?"

Blinking wide, turning beet red, Jenine stood up slowly,

mumbling her apologies and went for another bottle.

"I'll kill her," Scott snarled, the blush making its way to his cheeks at the humiliation.

"Stop." Claire reached out to calm him. "She can be a twit sometimes. She thinks she's got lesbo tendencies as well. So ignore her."

Ian craned his neck to look back at Jenine before he whispered, "She muff dives?"

Both Claire and Scott stared at him for the crass comment.

"Uh, sorry. Does she like women?" he corrected.

"She doesn't know what she likes. She's just a failure with men."

"Muff dive?" Scott chuckled and then shook his head.

Claire sighed, "Look, you guys are stressed out enough. Just ignore her. Okay?"

"I do wish she'd be more careful with what comes out of her gob, Claire." When his eyes moved to Scott's lap, Ian removed his hand quickly as if he had forgotten it was there. "I do hope she doesn't make accusations like that about us in public."

"Of course not! Ian! We know this business! Stop worrying. I'll bet she regretted it the minute it passed her lips."

The bottle of wine in her fist, Jenine scuffed back to stand before the men who wouldn't look her directly in the eye. "I'm sorry. I guess it just came out of my big fat mouth."

As they debated inside their heads in silence, the television coverage continued relentlessly, "…and overshadowing the kick off in San Diego is the airing of the first homosexual kiss on a commercial advertisement. Minty Gum has decided to make this monumental decision during the half time break…"

Upon hearing it yet again, aching inside at the reality of it, Scott had reached his breaking point. Like one who is at a crisis level about life, he rose up and excused himself around everyone as he made his way to his room, a black cloud lingering over his head.

Without a second thought, Ian hopped up to follow him, then paused. With a pained expression on his face, he looked back at the two females who were waiting to see precisely what his reaction would be and which room he was headed to. "Oh, bollocks!" he shouted in annoyance when no one would say a word, and hurried after Scott.

Left sitting on their own in the tomb-like quiet, Claire gazed at Jenine and said, "Good one, girl. So much for your promise."

"I don't know what happened! It just slipped out! I mean, Claire, look at them. It's so fucking obvious they love each other." She flapped her arms in the air, her frustrated exaggeration making her seem like an animated cartoon character.

"Fine! But at least support them. We need to find a way to help them deal with this, Jenine!"

"I know! I'm sorry. Oh, look, they have their head shots in the background of the broadcast!" Distracted by the scene on the tube, she pointed in excitement.

As Claire watched the television dully, she kept wondering how much her brother could take before he exploded. He'd become a time bomb of nerves and the fuse was growing extremely short.

"Let me in! Scott Epstein, stop behaving horribly to me!" Twisting the knob, Ian pressed his forehead against the door so he could listen to any movement behind it.

A moment later, it opened.

He stepped into the room and shut the door, sighing when he saw Scott breaking down emotionally. "Don't let what that cheeky monkey says wind you up!"

"No. It's not just her, Ian." Collapsing on the bed, his head in his hands, Scott rubbed his eyes tiredly.

"What then?" Ian sat next to him and put his arm around his shoulder, trying to comfort him.

"The commercial. If I ever even had a chance at that stupid movie part, when they get wind of that stupid thing, I'm done for."

"Not necessarily, love. The role you're auditioning for is a gay bloke."

Pausing, Scott raised his head slowly, met Ian's gaze and said, "Holy crap. You may be right!"

"Of course I am." Ian grinned, very happy at getting Scott to see this mess in a positive light.

"Why should it matter?" Scott began straightening his back, sitting up. "The fucker's gay!"

"Right!" Ian cuddled closer, wrapping his hands around Scott's large biceps. "You all right now?"

Turning in his direction to give him a generous smile, Scott said softly, "Yes, thanks, Ian."

"Give us a kiss."

Scott kissed him gently, and then added, "But the thought of a bunch of people in here watching the game and the ad tomorrow depresses the shit out of me."

"Why should it? And if it does, we don't have to be here, do we?" Ian shrugged. "What time does the game start? Can't we piss off?"

"I think it starts six p.m. here. Three in California."

"Aye. That's almost midnight in England. At least I won't have to worry about Mum and Dad seeing it."

"Not live, any way!" Scott laughed and ran his hand back through Ian's long hair.

"Is there a pub around here? You know, to go to and not have to deal with this shite?"

"A pub? No. Not like the kind you're used to. Just bars.

Smoky fucking bars with assholes that are watching the game. Can you imagine after seeing that commercial, if they recognized us? We'd be beaten to a pulp."

"That doesn't sound promising. Any other ideas?"

"Yeah, another hotel room!"

"All right." Ian shrugged again, willing to do anything to ease the situation.

"Oh, right! I was only kidding. Imagine me telling Claire, oh, by the way, Sis, Ian and I are spending the night in a hotel. Come on, Ian…"

"Oi! Keep your 'air on! I'm just trying to help!" His hands flew up defensively.

"Yeah…sorry. It's just that if we go somewhere else, like a hotel, it will most likely raise their suspicion level even further. So, I'm afraid, my dear, we're stuck here."

"All right. So we're stuck here, how horrible could it be? If we just let their cheeky comments roll off us, we should do all right. Okay, love?"

"We don't have any other choice." Scott sighed wearily.

"Give us a cuddle."

Reaching around him warmly, Scott crushed him to his chest, then they parted to kiss again.

"What do you think they're talking about in there?" Jenine mumbled.

"You, you idiot." Arms folded across her chest, Claire was annoyed completely at her partner's lack of common sense.

"I know! I know! Stupid, stupid. I'll shut up now."

"Too late, sistah!" Claire caught a slight slur in her words and leaned closer to stare at her face. "Are you drunk?"

"Yes. It went right to my head. And I'm starving!"

"Well? Go eat something. The kitchen is stocked." Claire waved at her.

Nodding in agreement, Jenine stood up on wobbly legs and made her way to the food.

Claire heard some movement behind her as the men came back out to join them.

"You all right, cookie?" she asked her brother.

"Yeah. I guess I just need thicker skin, you know?" He sat back down on the couch with Ian.

"You do. You are ultra sensitive. You always have been." She reached out to hold his hand. "Oh, Ian, you should have seen the tantrums this one performed as a toddler!"

"That's Dad's fault!" Scott shouted, "He always knew how to push my damn buttons and piss me off."

"Speaking about pissed," Ian tilted his head to Jenine who was standing near them, her hand in the large bag of cheese puffs her fingers and teeth already orange from them, swaying.

"You drunk?" Scott asked, trying not to laugh.

"I think so. And hungry!" It seemed as if she were stuffing a handful of round, dusty marbles into her mouth.

"Oh, Christ, how can you eat those things?" Ian cringed.

"They're good! Try one." She had singled one out in her sticky fingers.

"No! Get that thing away from me!" Ian cowered in fear.

"Chicken!" she shouted, tormenting him with it.

"I'll eat it." Scott offered willingly.

"You would! You swallow anything, mate." Ian winked at him wickedly.

Just before Jenine popped the puff into Scott's mouth, they all burst into laughter at Ian's comment.

"You stupid limey!" Scott could not stop laughing.

"You flamin' yank!" Ian laughed back, shoving him.

As Claire wiped her eyes from her hilarity, she knew that big changes were on their way. For better or worse. These two

The Kiss

could not keep anything under wraps for long.

Chapter Nineteen

Whether they liked it or not, Super Bowl Sunday had arrived. Twenty stories above the sooty gray remnants of the snowplowed streets, the three members of the household slept until almost noon. Emerging with great reluctance from their flannel sheet cocoons, they fought through the haze of dark seductive dreams to see daylight.

Awake and sipping coffee, Claire and Ian lounged in their sleepwear, completely unmotivated for the small gathering and the game to follow.

"Do you like American football, Ian?"

"Yes, I do, actually. You can't catch very many games in England, though. Not unless you're interested in staying up all night to watch them live. I don't understand your baseball very much, I have to say."

"You don't? It's a very easy game. Would you like to go to see one some day?"

"That would be lovely! The Yankees?"

"Sure! I assume you'll still be here in the spring, won't you?"

"Unless your government kicks me out!" he laughed and sipped his cup.

"Why? Do you have ties to Al Qaeda?" Tongue in cheek, she winked at him.

"I do resemble Bin Laden, I know." He sucked in his cheeks and crossed his eyes.

Giggling at his silliness, she set down her mug and reached with both hands into his soft hair, drawing him close. "Oh, I don't think so, you beautiful Ganymede…"

Ian tensed up. "Uh, Claire—"

"I'm not seducing you! I'm just affectionate. Besides, aren't you taken, Mr. Sullivan?"

Though he tried to gracefully edge back, giving himself some space, her hands held him firm. "Don't start winding me up, Claire. Leave it. I've had enough."

As she held his jaw, attempting to keep his eyes on hers, she moved her body closer so their knees touched. She wanted this out in the open, once and for all. It was getting absurd. "Ian, I'm not a dimwit, and I know my brother extremely well. I also know when he's madly in love. And, you, you beautiful creature, have succeeded in capturing Scott's heart completely."

Once again mute, Ian hardly blinked his eyes.

Unaware of his twisting internal organs at the conversation, Claire continued speaking to him softly. "I'm happy for both of you. I knew the moment I set you up with that kiss, you two would end up lovers."

Enraged, he did pull back from her grip. "Set up?" he snarled.

Catching her breath and not wanting him to get up and storm away before she clarified herself, she gripped his wrist and said, "Don't get angry! Sit calmly and listen to me before you jump to conclusions."

"What exactly are you trying to tell me, Claire?" He bit his lip in rage.

Knowing she had put her foot into her mouth carelessly, something she was getting too good at doing recently, she wasn't allowing him to go anywhere before he understood what she meant. "A month back, when I first learned Jenine needed two of our men to kiss in that ad, I won't deny, I picked you both deliberately. Ian, Scott has had nothing but disappointment in his life, from his career to his love life. I just had a hunch after he stole your photo from my briefcase that you intrigued him. And I knew, given the right circumstances, that he would want to touch you. There was nothing malicious or sinister about it, Ian, just some curiosity on my part about what would make Scott happy. That and the obviously wrong assumption that you were a gay man, Ian. At least judging by the way you're acting, and had behaved before, I assume you are either experimenting with him, or deep in the proverbial closet. Or both."

His anger slow to subside, Ian took his hand back and folded it on his lap. "Claire, I was not a homosexual. Simply because a man has long hair—"

"Shh! No, don't even go there. It isn't the hair."

"Well, whatever reason, I dated a woman before this…this relationship. Look what my curiosity has got me?"

"Got you?" she laughed softly, "It's gotten you one of the most loving, handsome men I know. Gee, that's tough, Ian." She playfully mocked him, shaking her head in sympathy.

The comment softened his rage considerably. His body unwinding, he exhaled to whisper, "You must believe me. We didn't know it would happen. Both of us had never touched a man before."

"I know, sweetie. But, I am really happy it has worked out for you." She brushed his hair back from his face.

"But—what about our careers? Do you think any of this—" He waved his hand around, suggesting the whole circumstance.

"It shouldn't get out. Not now. It would be different if you were both established in a strong career, but not now. I agree to keep it quiet, Ian."

Sitting back as if a load was placed on his shoulders, Ian finally said, "But inevitably it will get out, won't it?" He sighed painfully and ran his hands back through his hair to get it out of his face. "Bollocks," he whispered under his breath, then raised his jaw to meet her eyes once more. "It's better now that you know. Hiding it whilst living here has been very trying, Claire."

"I know. You two want to touch each other and you can't. Or at least you couldn't, before. You don't have to sneak behind my back to screw anymore, Ian. I knew anyway."

A rush of humiliation washed over his face. "You're very understanding, Claire. My family would be a right pain in the arse. I can't tell you how miserable the reaction would be from my father. He would literally kill me."

Claire was having similar images pass through her own mind imaging the scene with her father if he found out. "You haven't met my dad! Ha! No way! But look, you guys can't live for your parents. You have to live for yourselves."

"I do love him. Very much. Actually, he's the best thing that's ever happened to me. He's my best friend, my lover, and my confidant." Recited like the inside of a greeting card, Ian had no idea it sounded so trite.

And being polite to this foreigner, Claire ignored the cliché and allowed him to express his feelings freely without her usual sarcastic wit. "Oh, Ian, I can't tell you how happy I am to hear that. To know Scott has something wonderful and worthwhile in his life. It's fantastic."

Smiling shyly, Ian reached out to squeeze her hand. "Yes, it 'tis." Pausing, looking back over his shoulder to make sure they were still on their own, he leaned close to her once more to whisper, "But, Claire, I am worried about him. At times he seems on the brink. You know what I mean?"

"I do. I've seen him there before. He gets into a terrible tizzy worrying about things. And it's the lack of sleep that really kills him. When he's exhausted, his temper gets shorter."

"These last few days he's been like a different person. He gets himself into a right state."

Claire checked behind Ian once more before continuing their conversation. A conversation she knew would devastate her brother if he overheard. "I know, Ian. He does that to himself. He can't settle down. Hopefully after this thing is aired and over, he'll get back to normal again."

"Yes, and fingers crossed about the movie audition."

"You think he's still thinking he has a chance? I was under the impression there was no hope."

"I don't know. But from what he confided in me about the actual audition, I do think he may still be in the running."

"Is that right?" she mused. "Well, you wouldn't know it from his present state of mind."

Ian sighed and whispered, "Has he ever gone off?"

"Gone off? You mean violently?" Ian nodded, his eyes connected to Claire's with an almost surreal intensity. "No. Not really. I mean, when he was in his teens he did punch a wall, putting a hole in the plasterboard. But he's never hit anyone that I'm aware of."

"A hole in the wall?" Ian sat back in fear.

"Yes, a little one. Dad patched it up fine." The memory of the tiny two knuckle-sized dent came back to her.

"Whatever did he do that for?"

"One of his dimwit girlfriends cheated on him."

"Bloody hell."

"Don't worry, Ganymede. He'd never lay a finger on you. He's hopelessly in love with you."

"I certainly hope so, Claire. I'm really no match for him. I've never been a fighter."

"I can tell. You're purely a lover," she said flirtatiously, but it went right over his petrified head. "Why are you thinking about all this? Is there something you need to tell me?" Suddenly she felt darkness in the pit of her stomach. "Look, Ian, if you're not interested in this relationship with him for the long haul, let him down easy." Thinking of Ian dumping her brother at this moment in time horrified her. Scott could not take it. He'd jump off a cliff.

Snapping back to the present, Ian met her gaze again. "Well, as long as things are secret and no one finds out about the way we feel about each other right now, I have no concern in the future, once our careers are established, but, I've waited my whole life for this chance, you know. Me mum and dad have invested a lot in me being here, in making it. I just don't want to deal with that choice right now, you see?"

"No one will ever find out. So don't worry. Okay?" She petted his hair softly to comfort him. "Let's just take it a day at a time, Ian. Hopefully that won't become an issue."

"Right. Thanks for that."

When he felt the bed shift, Scott peeked from under the fluffy sheep pattern blue flannel pillow to see a very seductive British smile. "What are you doing in my bed, Mr. Sullivan?"

Burrowing under the blankets like a kitten seeking the milk of its mother, Ian shivered at the chilliness of the room. The window was cracked open to let in the refreshing winter air for a male body that ran very hot. Once nuzzled in, he reached out for Scott's warmth, kissing his chest.

"Ian!" Scott sat up and panicked. "Claire's home!"

"I know...don't worry...wanna shag? I'm flippin' randy." He shoved his pelvis into Scott's.

"Are you nuts? Get out of here!" Scott gripped the blankets and brought them up to his chin in fear.

"She knows, Scott, stop worrying." Ian disappeared under the sheets like a mole.

"She knows?" Scott gasped. "Knows what?" Feeling the heat of a boiling hot mouth on him, Scott shivered and pushed back the blankets to reveal what Ian was doing. "Agh! Stop! Knows what? Ian, stop and tell me what the hell you told her!"

Removing Scott's body part from his lips reluctantly, Ian rested across Scott's thighs to toy with him as he spoke. "She knows, mate. About how we feel about each other. I didn't have to say a word. And believe me! I wouldn't have! But she sat there just now and told me how happy she was for us that we love each other. She's really okay with it." Pausing, meeting Scott's eyes for a moment, he then went back to what he was doing.

His mind whirling in confusion, Scott tried to lay back and enjoy the morning blowjob, but though it felt wonderful, he was too baffled to concentrate. "Ian, wait...stop."

"Oi! You're a hard one to please, Herr Helmet!" Ian laughed.

"Are you trying to tell me, just now, out there, she said she knew and was happy about it?"

"Yes!"

"You're fucking lying to me!"

"No! I'm not taking the mick! Honest! You think I'd be in here now, in my shorts, with your helmet in my mouth if she didn't? You really are a rodney."

Settling his head back on the pillow, staring at the light fixture, Scott tried to think of the repercussions of her knowing. Other than her relentless teasing and I-told-you-so, were there any?

"All right? You done with the inquisition? All right if I continue?"

"Huh?" Scott tried to concentrate on what Ian was asking, while his mind was moving backwards in blocks of time. "Well, I guess so..."

"Good!" Ian stuffed him inside his mouth and sucked like it was a white chocolate icicle.

"Ah! Yes, very good!" Scott chuckled at the irony, but something just didn't sit right in his head.

The Kiss

Showered and dressed for the upcoming television event, Claire began making the onion dip and cutting up cheese and vegetables for the guests. Over an hour had passed since Ian had gone into Scott's bedroom. When they emerged, Ian headed directly to the shower while Scott waited his turn, gazing shyly at his sister. Slowly, scuffing his feet on the slick polished wood floor, he made his way to the counter as she prepared platters of party food.

"Hi, sweetie, how you doing?" Claire whispered softly.

"You know?" Snatching a carrot off the cutting board, he crunched on it noisily.

"Yup. You okay with that?"

"Did he tell you?"

"No. But he didn't deny it when I asked directly." She sliced another vegetable, handing him a stick of celery.

"Am I crazy, Claire?" He devoured it as quickly as the carrot.

"No. You're in love. Close, but not the same," she smiled, continuing to slice efficiently.

"I— I'm really embarrassed—" He lowered his head, unable to meet her smile suddenly.

"For what? For loving gorgeous Ian? Oh, come on." She laughed at the absurdity.

"But— what about everything I said—getting angry— denying it…I didn't mean for—"

She stopped him before he apologized for his love life. "Look, Scott, I understand. I know how hard it is for men to come out, accept it, and allow other people to know. You think I don't know what you're going through? It's okay. I won't breathe a word, to Mom, Dad, or anyone else."

"Jenine?"

"Oh, fuck no. She has her suspicions, you heard her yesterday, but, I won't ever admit to her that I know for sure."

A long exhaled sigh of relief came out of Scott's broad chest. "I think my career would suffer if anyone knew. I know it would, Claire. Some guys can get away with coming out. But for a newcomer like me, it'd be suicide to my career. Such as it is."

"You're right. It may. So I won't tell anyone."

"Good."

"Good," Claire echoed, smiling sweetly into his disheveled face and uncombed hair. "I am, however, insanely jealous. Scott, he is a god!"

A warm blush appeared on Scott's cheeks.

"How is he in bed?" she whispered seductively, leaning over to tempt him with a radish.

"Claire!" Scott choked in embarrassment.

"Just teasing you, you lucky S.O.B."

Smiling shyly, taking the radish from her hand and popping it into his mouth, Scott finally met her eyes and said, "I am lucky, Claire. He is unbelievable."

"I know. I'm very happy for you."

Only eight guests were invited for the airing of the infamous gum ad. With the relief of Claire knowing their secret, it was very difficult for Ian and Scott to make the abrupt transition when friends arrived and stop pawing at each other. But, restraining their primal urges, they behaved and mingled. And because some of the burden had been reduced and his feelings supported, Scott seemed more at ease with the coming mayhem.

Jenine's cheese-puff covered laughter was heard loudly above the rest, as the pre-game highlights were playing on the television's large 36" screen while U2 music overruled the sports commentators' dialogue for the moment.

Friends of Jenine's, Keith and Karen, were sipping wine,

standing by the window to admire the expansive view of downtown Manhattan on their first visit to Claire's luxury apartment. Keith, with his shaved dome head and tiny dot of hair under his lip, seemed to Claire right out of Seattle's grunge scene. Worn jeans, bleached out Mets' sweatshirt, work boots, and a pierced eyebrow were in contrast to his wife Karen's school-girlish appearance who was quite the opposite in her saintly white buttoned up starched shirt, black shin length skirt, hair pulled back in a tight ponytail, and make-up free face. Claire thought they were an odd couple indeed.

Two of Claire's closest friends from the New York school system who were in touch with her since she relocated back to the Big Apple had arrived. Bob and Greg were lured over to the apartment with the promise of lager and good food, not to mention the big screen television.

Though no one immediately assumed Ian and Scott were together, the pair of them seemed permanently attached for security in a tense situation. As they continued to find each other and whisper into each other's ear seductively, they became more relaxed. Claire said nothing about them to a soul. She allowed the people present to think what they wanted to think. It wasn't up to her any longer.

As the game began and the darkness of a winter night gathered over New York's unsettled streets, it seemed calmness took over the island as everyone was glued to their sets. Flipping a few inside lights on, Claire attempted to keep out the gloom though the day had been crisp, cold, and clear earlier, promising a very cold starlit night.

Cold beers in their hands, Ian asked Scott, "Do you like American football?" as they stood behind the fully occupied couch.

"Not really. I used to like the Seahawks when I lived in Seattle, and I did play football at the U-Dub—"

"Uni?" Ian tried to clarify.

"University of Washington. The Dawgs!"

221

Tilting his head as he deciphered American slang, Ian did not get what he was attempting to say.

"The Huskies." Scott explained, "That was what our college team was called. And believe it or not, we sold out the damn stadium. More than the damn Hawks did!"

"Did you? What position did you play?"

"Quarterback," Scott mumbled.

"Sorry?" Ian leaned closer, not catching the jumble of syllables.

"I played quarterback," Scott said, as if he were embarrassed by it.

Everyone in the room overheard it and stopped their conversations to gape at him.

"You did?" Bob asked in surprise. "Claire, I didn't know your brother was a football star!"

"Among other things," she teased sarcastically, hiding her smirk behind her glass.

"Shhh!!" Keith grumbled in annoyance as the game had begun.

His wife Karen whacked him for being rude, but the rest of the group obediently settled down because of it.

Claire turned off the music as Keith pressed the mute button on the remote and released the blaring voices of the sports commentators who filled the room like it was the size of a telephone booth and they were sumo wrestlers.

"It's going to be a long game," Ian sighed, sneaking a brush of himself against his lover's side.

"May as well pull up a chair." Scott nodded to the dining room and they grabbed a few to set up around the television.

At the first commercial break they all stretched, took turns in the bathroom, and grabbed more alcohol.

Ian noticed Greg constantly staring at his profile while he tried to focus on the game.

The Kiss

"I love your accent!" Greg finally shouted what it seemed he'd been dying to say the whole first quarter.

"And I love yours!" Ian mocked, using the exact same inflection and body language.

"Mine? What? South Bronx? You're joking!" Greg laughed.

"He is, Greg." Claire smiled at him knowingly. "He just hears it from all us dumb yanks."

"That's not fair, Claire," Ian defended. "I love it here. America is the land of wide-open spaces. Unfortunately, most of the space is surrounded by teeth."

It took a moment for the rest to get it, but Claire was immediately doubled over with laughter. When Scott realized it was a slam, he casually stepped behind Ian and pinched his bottom, causing him to jump and spin around.

"Cheeky!" Ian gasped.

"All right! Game's on!" Keith shouted in annoyance as Karen rolled her eyes in irritation.

As they settled down once more, Scott tilted his head for Ian to follow.

Everyone knew exactly what they were doing, and the moment the men left the room, the rest of the group erupted in conversation about them, much to Keith's annoyance.

"Claire!" Greg whispered, "I had no idea your brother was gay."

She smiled smugly and shrugged as Jenine looked to see some kind of confirmation from her, which she wasn't going to get.

"What a piece of ass that Englishman is! Mama mia!" Bob whispered, exaggerating his facial expression for effect.

"Are they gay, Claire?" Jenine leaned over the coffee table, obstructing Keith's view, and it seemed as if he wanted to strike her to get her to sit back.

"I don't know for sure," Claire said, trying not to give too much away in her face.

"You don't know?" Greg's sarcastic laugh cut her off. "Ah, dear, take it from me. They are."

"Are they? Did they tell you?" Jenine sat up and leaned the other direction, toward Greg and Bob.

"Can we just watch the fucking game?" Keith moaned.

"God! Be a little polite! It won't kill you!" Karen punched his arm.

"Ow!" Keith rubbed it, pouting. "I thought we were here to watch the game!"

"No, actually, we're here to watch a commercial," Claire said, peering over her shoulder before she continued. "Who gives a crap about the game?"

"A commercial?" Keith crunched his face up in annoyance, his chin hair sticking outwards like the tip of a paintbrush. "What commercial?"

Karen almost punched him again. "Where the hell do you live? The one they have been talking about all week! The gay kiss!"

"Oh, fucking sick!" Keith blurted, then slowly found five sets of angry eyes on him. "Uh. Sorry." His bald head seemed to sink in height as he tried to melt into the leather sofa cushions.

Ignoring the obvious slap to his sexuality with an air of quiet dignity and reserve, Greg pretended he hadn't noticed the last comment. "When is it supposed to air, Jenine?" he said, finishing his beer and wanting another.

"Half time."

"Well," Bob giggled, tilting his head in the direction of the bedrooms. "Hopefully those boys will be done playing with each other by then and not miss it."

"Oh, no. They won't miss it, believe me," Claire assured him.

The Kiss

"They're playing with each other?" Jenine's continuous stuffing of orange cheese puffs had come to a stop as her eyes widened in exaggeration.

Claire chose to ignore it and made herself busy by refilling bowls of chips and dip.

"You're driving me crazy." As if they hadn't been allowed contact with each other in weeks, Scott reached inside Ian's slacks hungrily now that they were closed inside their dark bedroom.

Spreading his legs wide as eager fingers made their way down, Ian managed to say, "Same here, love, but, we have guests..." while kissing a very passionate mouth.

Testing the integrity of Ian's zipper, his entire forearm dipped inside, Scott groped him, anxious to get him excited. "I see the way those gay guys are leering at you. You have any idea how much they want to fuck you?"

As Scott grabbed a hold of his cock, Ian shivered, and closed his eyes. "I don't want them. I want you."

Suddenly, released from any inhibition, Scott cared less what the others thought about them disappearing. Touching and teasing what he so much wanted to own permanently, he fell prey to the urge and began tearing open Ian's slacks with an urgency that made Ian wince and shiver in delight. Spreading his slacks wide, Scott dropped to his knees before him.

"Oh, love—you really are too much." Ian leaned back against the door for support as his head spun.

Working him wildly, yearning only to please him, Scott's passion was out of control. All he wanted was to keep this lovely man with him forever. In his heart he knew he'd be shattered if something came between them. Thinking this kind of wild sexual contact which turned them both into beasts must surely be one of the keys to keeping Ian his, Scott knew it was part of the reason why he had made the decision to commit to him. Complete sexual gratification constantly. No arguments, no headaches, no menstrual periods, no pregnancies, no games, no excuses. Just sex, when he wanted it, and how he wanted it. It was a euphoric sense of freedom he'd never dreamed of. And he wanted it forever. Thinking about any other man disinterested him. It had to be this man. This creature that was so wholly beautiful inside and out. And one who was behaving as if this sexual fulfillment was equally as important to him as well. Night after night, Scott tried to determine: love or lust? He'd given up finding the fine line between the two. One thing he was certain of. No matter where he ended up, New York or California, this man had to be with him. With all his heart, he was praying Ian felt the same way.

As Ian's gasps grew, Scott became more determined to please him. Giving Scott what he was after, Ian's legs weakened and Scott needed to prop him up until he recovered.

Staring up at him as the waves of orgasm washed over his fine features, Scott could not think of a lovelier vision. "Was it good, baby?"

"Aye…brilliant."

Panting to catch their breath, they heard a light tap on the door and Claire's voice, tinged with sarcasm, saying, "Commercial time!"

"Okay!" Scott shouted to her, then gazed up at Ian as he calmed his racing pulse. "You ready, limey?"

"I am indeed, yankee doodle." Ian laughed as he zipped his fly.

One last peck on the lips, and they rejoined the others, all of whom were staring at them with smirks on their faces when they came back in, except Keith, who was glued to the set and in a constant state of irritation at the noise and distractions.

Grabbing the beers they had left behind, they tried to pretend they had only been gone for a minute, not twenty, and sat back down. Bob was grinning at Ian in such a comical way, Ian kept laughing to himself and shaking his head at the rudeness.

"Half-time folks!" Claire waved as she shouted. "This is it! Where's the remote? I need to tape it." Snatching it from Keith's possessive grasp, Claire hit the record button and the room grew completely silent. As advertisement after advertisement filled the air, Claire began to wonder if they did indeed pull it and it would not show up, when suddenly, the logo appeared.

"Oh, fuck me," Scott murmured under his breath.

Instinctively, discreetly, Ian reached to hold his hand.

As the commercial began, Scott and 'Gigi' walked down the movie aisle as every person in the nation was glued to the set simultaneously to see this mystery ad.

Not a sound came from a soul in that room. It was as if everyone were holding their breaths.

The lights dimmed inside that on-screen theater, and 'Gigi' made her exit. The camera lens focused in on Scott as he struggled awkwardly to get a piece of gum into his mouth in the dimness.

Ian's mouth opened in awe.

As if on cue with his thoughts, the camera moved to him and 'Bambi' making their way to those empty seats.

Back on the commercial, chewing diligently, Scott twisted around, grabbed Ian's head through his lovely long hair, and planted a very passionate, open-mouthed kiss on him.

"Damn!" Bob choked in amazement, as Greg whispered, "It's fucking them!" pointing in excitement at the two stars. "I knew that!" Bob defended as his lover shushed him.

On screen, when Ian and Scott parted, Ian gave his one word line, "Mmm, nice!" chewing as if he now owned the gum, and to everyone's surprise, they added the little peck Ian gave Scott in the first bad take. The music followed and the logo appeared again as the spokesperson said, "Minty Gum, makes breath worth kissing!"

Then it vanished.

A long pause of silence followed. It seemed as if everyone had to allow their brains to digest what their eyes had witnessed, then feed the information to their conscious mind where it was readily absorbed and available for debate. Finally trying to escape the awkwardness the quiet had imposed, Ian let out a laugh and spun around to Scott. "They put that second kiss in!"

"I see that!" Scott was as excited as Ian.

"I'm gob-smacked they actually put my extra kiss in! They seemed so bloody upset when I did it, remember?"

"Well done, boys!" Greg reached out to shake their hands.

"Claire! You didn't tell us it was Scott!" Bob shouted, his face completely red from the effect the ad had on him.

"It wasn't that big a deal," Keith added. "I mean, all the controversy, the bad press, the media blitz, it wasn't that bad an ad."

"Spoken by the only heterosexual male in the group," Claire blurted before she realized it. When it dawned on her, she shook her head and caught her brother's horrified glare. She didn't even want to see Ian's expression. "Uh, I mean—I—"

"They know what you mean, Claire!" Scott shouted in rage.

"No! Except Scott and Ian!" Try as she might, she could not retract her comment. As if it had been concrete falling from the top of a tower, the thud and damage was beyond her control.

Bob shouted, hoping to distract everyone, "Rewind it, Claire! Let's see it again!"

Floundering horribly, sick to her stomach, she remembered quickly to stop the tape, then hit rewind as Keith moaned about missing the game. The self-flagellation began in earnest inside Claire. She had tried so hard, walked on eggshells, prided herself on discretion, advised them to keep it under wraps, only to be the one who blurted out the truth. It was as if the sickness in her would never move from her mid-section. Out of all the things she was responsible for doing to her brother, this one was the most painful. In front of all those people, Jenine included, she hoped to somehow make it up to him.

"Christ! Stop whining!" Karen was about to hit her husband again.

"Anyone need another beer?" Scott rose up tiredly and headed to the refrigerator.

"Cheers, mate. I'll give you a hand." Ian hurried after him.

"Stop drinking so much, Scott!" Claire shouted after him, but was ignored.

The moment they made themselves scarce, Jenine leaned over to whisper to Claire, "Then I was right. They are gay."

With her head beginning to pound from stupidity and nerves, Claire said, "No. I was just kidding them, you know, because of the commercial..." Where were the sarcastic words she had always relied on? Where were her resources? Here's the strong twenty-first century business woman, wanting to crawl into bed and hide, a box of chocolate truffles as company.

"Oh...right," Jenine sneered.

Feeling the anger and betrayal from Jenine now as well, Claire's helplessness over the situation didn't improve, it worsened miserably. One line. One stupid thoughtless comment and she went from elated to disgusted.

As the ad replayed once more, Ian found the bottle opener and reached for the beer in Scott's hand. "All right, love, don't go into the miseries again. She didn't mean any harm."

"I know. It still stung." He took back the beer and drank it from the bottle. "And this is just in front of five, can you imagine it getting out?"

"I'd sooner die and crawl back to England, mate. I can't handle it. I would flamin' die."

The phone rang and Claire and Scott exchanged looks of

panic. It was as if no good news would come with the outside world knowing about the ad.

"You get it! I know it's Mom and Dad." Scott never took a step toward it.

Claire read the display and picked up the receiver. "Hi. Hello, Mom. Yes! Did you guys see it? I know. I thought it was great. What did Dad say?" Trying to put her anguish behind her, she took a deep breath knowing her mother would notice if she sounded odd.

Scott turned his back to the conversation as the gum ad replayed again on the screen behind him. "I know I don't want to hear this." Scott shivered. "This is so much worse than I thought it would be. Why did we do the fucking thing?"

"Too late for regrets, mate," Ian whispered, his light eyes appeared to fill with water as they reflected the dim light of the kitchen.

Another muffled cell phone ring-tone was heard.

Everyone scrambled to check their mobiles, a hunt for buried treasure or Easter eggs.

Ian started laughing at the frenzy. "Look at that!"

"I know, pathetic." Scott shook his head, reaching for his fourth beer.

"It's mine!" Jenine found it in her purse. "Hello? Yes, this is Jenine Spencer."

"I expect Mum will be ringing up next." Ian sighed, just noticing Scott's empty bottle in surprise.

"Did you tell her when it would air?" Tipping it up for the last drop, Scott finished the remainder of his beer and tossed the bottle into recycling.

"I bloody had to! She read it in the paper! But she got me going on the phone as well. I know she misses me and wants to seem like she's involved in my life. I am across the pond, love. A bit far away." When Scott opened another beer, Ian said, "Should you be drinking so much? We have to be at Calahan's studio in a few hours."

"I'll be sober by then," Scott assured him, spinning the cap into the sink.

"No. No mate, that's enough." Ian took the beer away from him and handed him a bottle of water.

They all started in panic when Jenine screamed at the top of her lungs.

"Fucking hell!" Ian grabbed his chest in alarm.

"What the hell's wrong with you?" Scott shouted in fury.

"Scott! Scott!" Jenine could not catch her breath as she tripped across the floor to where he stood.

"What!" he roared at her in anger. "You didn't have to scare the hell out of everyone!"

"No! Scott, listen! Listen!" Grasping at him from over the counter, she couldn't seem to get him to hear what she had to say.

"You're a fucking loon, Jenine! A fucking loon!" Scott moved back from her in anger, twisting away and slapping her hand down as she sought to get a grip on him.

Ian backed away from her warily.

"Scott! Shut up and listen!" Grasping for him, crawling over the counter where the food platters were, she appeared rabid. Everyone in the living area behind her was frozen as if they were watching the approaching collision of a diesel train and a VW bug.

"I'm listening, Jenine!" Scott was about to strike her. "What the fuck is wrong with you?"

The roaring chaos becoming a distraction she could neither avoid nor ignore, Claire told her mother to hold on, cupped the phone, and stared at Jenine in anxiety for what she was trying to say.

"That audition! That part!" The words were strangled she was squeezing them out so tightly.

"What about it?"

"You got it! You got it!" The syllables emerged like the screech of an owl with talons bared.

"I got what?"

Catching exactly what she was implying, Ian shouted in joy and rushed him, lifting him off his feet. "Oi! Did ya hear that, mate?"

"Wait! Jenine, did you say I got the part?" Leaning toward her from Ian's embrace, Scott asked again.

As Jenine shook her head, struggling to put legible sentences together with her face a big grinning plastic mask, everyone behind them began murmuring about what part he had auditioned for. Managing to get out one word, she screamed, "Yes!"

As he and Ian hopping around the room like a pogo stick with four legs, Claire came back to the phone and said, "Ya know something, Mom? Your son is going to be very famous. He just got a part in an Oscar Pullman blockbuster." Holding the phone from her ear, she waited for her mother's screaming to subside.

"I got it!" Scott held Ian's shoulders to shout into his face as the news finally sank in.

"You did! Well done!"

"It's because of you." Scott softened as their bouncing slowed to a sensual stillness.

"Me?" Ian laughed at his expression, which was suddenly very serious.

"Yes, you were my inspiration."

"Well! That's brilliant!"

Grabbing the sides of his face impulsively, Scott kissed him, the tears of joy running down his face.

Bob, Greg, Karen, and finally Keith, burst into applause, catcalls, and whistles. "Bring out the champagne!" Greg shouted.

As Jenine watched their sparking passion in absolute astonishment, Claire smiled at them and said, "Mom, your son is going to be the next big thing."

Chapter Twenty

Claire stood with him as he was tended. "You'll be okay. Scott, don't worry about it. Just be calm and be yourself."

"I know…I'm okay. Just nervous, that's all."

"That's normal. Just keep a smile on your face."

His hair was brushed, his face powdered, and it was only moments before going on. Knowing Ian was nearby, he tried to find him without actually turning his head. "Is Ian there?"

"Yes, Scott. Will you take a deep breath?"

A man with paperwork in his fist came rushing up to Scott to say, "Line up change. You guys are on right after Calahan's monologue."

A huge butterfly flipped Scott's stomach around like a pancake in a fry pan. "What happened? No Garry Scheffeld?"

"No, he's just running late. He's up after you now." Acting as if answering these questions were below his station, he was about to leave when Scott asked, "Great…how much time do we have?"

"Five. Go wait behind the curtain for your intro." Then he vanished as quickly as he came.

"Shit…okay, Scott. Just relax. You'll be fine."

Pausing to make sure his make-up was complete, Scott stood up and found Ian already there, waiting for him. He was suspicious of the change and knew it was possible the comedian could get a better angle at jabbing them from behind. It only served to bring his nerves to a breaking point.

"I'm okay, Claire..."

"You ready, mate?" Ian's eyes were shimmering brilliant green gems as if he was on fire internally and those two holes were the only outlet for the light.

The mere presence of him standing there, looking glorious in his black silk Perry Ellis suit and mock turtleneck was enough to calm Scott's turmoil. "I am." *With you beside me*, he added in his head, restraining the urge to reach out for his hand for that reassuring clasp.

Another man signaled for them to follow, and they were led backstage to stand behind the curtain they would make their entry through.

"Break a leg!" Claire whispered in excitement.

"Thanks, sis." As Scott struggled to calm his pulse, he tuned in to what was being said on stage by Bert Calahan in his monologue. First the war between Iraq and the US, a slam at Saddam Hussein and George W, then moving swiftly to the results of Tampa Bay crushing the Oakland Raiders. Pausing for the laughter to subside, he arrived at the introduction of his two guests. Before he signaled their entry, a few sarcastic jokes were leveled at the gay kiss. A blush washed over Scott's face. He was hoping this was not really happening. That it was some kind of odd dream. His limbs were completely numb.

"...I'm sure you're aware of the controversy surrounding the commercial for Minty Gum at half-time. We haven't seen so much hot sex on an ad since Britney's belly-button." Laughter was heard from the audience. "...and the word on the street is that one of the men puts her loveliness to shame!" Intermittent applause and laughs followed. "In light of the recent events in the news, it's reassuring to know that Tony and George aren't the only British and American couple to rock the planet!" Predictable applause and laughter rumbled once more.

Scott swallowed audibly and knew Ian was growing pale next to him.

Claire listened, trying to watch their faces carefully.

"But, Mr. Blair and Mr. Bush haven't been caught exchanging spit, merely propaganda! I should think we can now rest assured these men did wonders to unite our two countries in a more—intimate—manner! Screw that shoulder-to-shoulder bull! I'd like to see more mouth-to-mouth!" Uproarious applause and laughter followed.

"Bloody hell!" Ian tried to loosen his collar.

"Steady, Ian," Scott whispered.

"Certainly!" Calahan continued, "Certainly we are glad England no longer considers homosexuality illegal. Imagine coming home after such a world-wide event to a pair of handcuffs!" He paused for effect. "But we don't want to reveal what they do in the privacy of their bedroom!" More laughter followed. "Unless they want to!" A burst of hilarious laughter exploded, followed by applause.

"Enough delaying of the sixty sexy seconds that changed the course of the advertising world. Most of you have already seen it. For those of you who haven't, here and at home, we have that ad for you now...roll it, please!" Calahan's booming voice ordered.

Shaking in their shoes, Ian and Scott stared at each other as they envisioned the clip playing for the live studio audience. A minute later, the applause rang out and Calahan's deep thundering roar was heard above it while Claire bit her fingernails nervously behind them. "...Ladies and gentlemen, welcome our guests—Ian Sullivan and Scott Epstein!"

The man back stage nodded, the curtain was parted, and after almost reconsidering and running away, Ian and Scott went on stage bravely.

As they jogged through, Claire crossed her fingers and prayed.

The Kiss

Calahan was grinning at them wickedly as Ian reached for his outstretched hand and shook it, then backed up to allow Scott to do the same. The applause rumbled on like a hum in Scott's ears. Through his mild inebriation, he caught the gesture for them to be seated on a leather sofa next to the big host's imposing desk.

As they opened the buttons of their suit jackets to get more comfortable, Scott tried to look out at the audience to see how many people were seated there. When he squinted his eyes he was only able to make out the first few rows passed the glaring lights, but, judging by the sound of the reactions he imagined a few hundred.

"Well, boys..." Calahan paused to give them a moment to settle down. "Aren't they lovely, ladies and gentlemen?" He allowed a second rush of applause to erupt, staring at them as they squirmed. When it died back he said, "How does it feel making advertising history?"

Knowing Ian would not speak a syllable unless addressed directly, Scott knew it was up to him to lead the interview. "It doesn't feel quite as momentous as that." Somehow he was going to salvage this mess. He felt confident he would not let this beast bait him.

"No? Oh, don't be so modest, Mr. Epstein! An advertising first! Your sister's modeling firm is famous for delivering the loveliest males in New York for advertisers to snatch up hungrily. The public could not be more delighted than I was to see the two of you made as poster-models for every horny teen!"

Opening his lips to reply, Scott couldn't think of a comment, and then tried to backtrack to find if there was actually a question.

Ian's mouth was sealed tight as he moved his attention from the cameramen, to the monitors, to the audience, and back to the horrifyingly rude man behind the imposing desk.

Calahan smiled devilishly and continued, "You have no

idea what you two have done? What you mean to so many struggling men out there? Men and boys who were afraid to come out and be themselves?"

Realizing exactly where he was going suddenly, Scott shook his head to deny the charge, "But—"

Not giving him the chance to say the obvious, Calahan shouted over him, "You, alone, thought it was unimportant! We thought it was momentous enough to make a special tribute! And I'm sure our audience agrees!" With his puffy cheeks looking like round peach golf balls, Calahan's greedy smile turned to the stage. A curtain was pulled back and a larger than life-sized cutout of the men kissing was brought out by two scantily clad female models.

With Ian squirming in agony next to him, Scott leaned forward around the desk and the corner of the stage to see what they were bringing out that was causing such a wild reaction from the studio audience. The hooting and pounding of hands and feet was unbelievable. Unable to catch it from where he sat, he searched for a monitor and was able to see it up close as the television cameras panned in on it. The audience was literally going berserk. He began to wonder who they had invited into the studio for the crowd to react that way. It reminded him of a group of rabid hounds.

After he figured out what the commotion was about, Scott spun back to Ian to see his face. He was horrified, trying his best not to run off the stage in tears.

The noise slowed to calm, Calahan waited to see their reaction, appearing to absolutely love their terrified expressions, then he shouted to the audience, "Let's hear it for freedom of sexual choice!"

A roar rose up immediately, whistles and catcalls filled the small studio.

Shaking his head in disbelief, Scott was mortified.

"We're not gay!" Ian tried to be heard above the shouting.

As Calahan attempted to quiet the mob, he asked Ian to repeat it.

Clearing his throat, Ian said, "I said, we're not gay, Mr. Calahan."

"No one said you are, young man! It's the ad we're referring to, of course!

"But—" Ian struggled to speak clearly, "But even the blokes on the advert aren't meant to be gay…"

"Maybe it's because you're so androgynous, Mr. Sullivan—" Calahan interrupted him with his bold, embarrassing comment. "I mean— You're prettier than half the starlets in Hollywood!"

A rush of heat washed over Ian's angular face. A few isolated whistles were heard from the crowd.

Calahan continued, "Pretty men are all the rage, Mr. Sullivan. You are perfect for any role. And your character could swing either way." His tongue was planted in his cheek.

The venom was upsetting Scott. He wanted that beast to lay off Ian. "You're not the first male to be jealous of Ian's appeal, Mr. Calahan." Scott tried to jab him where it hurt, his ugliness.

It had no effect whatsoever. "Oh, I agree! The jealousy must be constant! As I assume it is with your wives! I hope they had no problem with it."

Scott knew Calahan was aware of their backgrounds, and now they were going to play right into his skillfully crafted hands.

"We're not married," Ian said innocently.

Mugging to the camera first, Calahan grinned, "No? How about girlfriends?" He sat back in his chair and raised his coffee cup to his lips to take a relaxing sip.

Since Ian had been the one he was addressing, and there was no way to communicate his thoughts to him, Scott tried not to rub his face in agony, instead clasping his clenched hands on his lap.

"Uh, no. Not at the moment—"

"And aren't you two living together?" Calahan grinned with so much superiority it made Scott ill. "Look, boys, I know when a career is young and you're not well established, things are better left behind, in a closet."

"We're not gay!" Ian shouted.

Before Calahan could respond, enflaming that defensive posture, Scott tried desperately to change the subject. "So— Mr. Calahan, it was good of you to ask us on. As you know we're both aspiring actors and models in search of our big break." Smiling bravely to the camera, Scott waved, "Hi, Mom! Hello out there!"

"What other work have you done?" It seemed Scott's tactics worked momentarily.

"I've done some ads for men's magazines, and just recently—" about to mention his good news, he was cut short.

Snapped off from his line again, Calahan waved to his assistants for the next prop. "We know about that one! A cover for a men's fitness magazine!" The monitors filled with Scott's abdominal muscles, chest, and scant attire.

"Do you know you're a gay icon? On every web page! Posters of you are being sold over the internet of this exact cover!"

A sick feeling washed over Scott's skin. The nastiness was almost too much to bear. They were being outed, whether or not they were gay. Everywhere the conversation veered, Calahan was sure to bring it back to controversy.

"And we have one of the pretty Englishman!" Calahan shouted, waving again. "Your attempt at Calvin's!"

Ian posing in his briefs appeared and the audience went wild.

"Bloody hell!" Ian whispered to Scott in agony.

"Shut up and smile," Scott managed to get out through his grinding teeth.

"The two of you have really kept yourselves fit. I can see why you're so appealing..." He stopped at saying, 'to each other', which Scott very much expected. "It's my understanding they've been trying to get an exclusive interview with you in Mister Mo's."

Ian's eyes widened as Scott's throat went dry. He'd never heard of any offers for an interview, and if Claire had one, she most certainly would have mentioned it, even if it were from a gay magazine.

Once again finding them mute, Calahan continued, "Mr. Mo's? The magazine for the gay lifestyle? Surely you've heard of it." As Ian sank lower into the couch and Scott unconsciously began rubbing his jaw stubble, Calahan pushed farther into their personal territory. "What are your next plans?" Keeping both photos visible to the audience on a split screen giving the appearance they were posing together as he continued the interview, both men kept being distracted by the illusion. The two of them, almost naked, side by side, were being broadcast nationwide.

About to crack from the pressure, Scott was suddenly afraid to let out he'd been selected to play Hephaestion, yet another gay implication. "No. I've not heard of that magazine—" Scott mumbled, too low to be understood by anyone but Ian.

As the pause grew to an almost painful measure, Ian blurted, "Scott just landed a role in a major motion picture!"

Boiling hot, unsuccessfully trying to loosen his collar, Scott squirmed in anguish in his seat as Ian began revealing his secret.

"How wonderful!" Calahan shouted, "What picture?" His comments pointed daggers back at Scott.

Struggling to put up with this chaos and not throw up from nerves, Scott sat straight and tried to say with some pride and dignity left, "It's an upcoming new movie from Oscar Pullman.

I don't know how much information I can give out—"

Thinking that may get him off the hook, he was shocked when Calahan added, "You mean the one about Alexander the Great?"

In agony, attempting to hide his awe at how this man acquired so much information, Scott nodded, his heart pounding in his chest. "Why, yes…it is. But—?" He had literally just received the call hours ago. How on earth did this man find out so much?

"You must be very proud of him, Ian." Calahan smiled sweetly at Ian.

"I am! Proud as punch!" Ian said innocently.

"Not jealous?" Calahan pushed. "Wishing you had your big break?"

"No. Not in the least. I'm happy for him." Ian smiled adoringly at Scott. "He deserves it. He's worked very hard for it."

"Why, thank you, Ian." Scott smiled warmly back.

Pausing, waiting for his timing to be right, Calahan gazed at the two of them as they brought their focus back on his pudgy face. Leaning his chin in his hand to get nearer to them, he said, very calmly, "It's obvious how much you two adore each other."

He knew, not admitting it, fighting it, would be useless, so Scott faced him in anger and said, "I won't deny we're close," he continued, as Ian held his breath, "If you want us to be honest about our friendship, fine. Since I met Ian, I feel like we've become best friends. I emphasize the word 'friend', Mr. Calahan."

"It's simply lovely." Calahan sighed. "You two certainly have a 'special' friendship."

"What's wrong with having a friend?" Scott asked him.

"Nothing! It's lovely! Isn't it, ladies and gentlemen? A confession of how close this couple really is may suddenly be coming. Come on, Mr. Epstein, we know it's right on the tip of both your tongues! Tell the world! Be proud! Come on out of the closet and don't be afraid!"

"Bloody hell" Ian cringed and looked at Scott.

When Scott met his eyes, Ian said, "I'm not taking any more of this nonsense!"

Scott felt like ice suddenly. He looked back at that puffy-faced host and found him waiting for some kind of confession. He was completely at a loss as to how to react. Glancing off stage he found Claire biting her lip, her face red from her fury.

"Well, it seems we may have to wait for that confession after the break!" Calahan shouted, "...and now a word from our sponsors!"

The minute they cut to a commercial, Ian shouted, "I'm not sitting through this!" He threw up his hands and stood up.

Scott glared at Calahan in rage. "You crossed the line! What the hell's the matter with you doing that to us on national television?"

"I'm pissing off! I've had enough!" Ian stormed off the set towards Claire.

Scott felt completely wretched as the studio audience tried to hear what was going on over the musical interlude and behind the cameras. A voice coming from above shouted, "One minute!"

Stunned, frozen in his seat, Scott had a million things running through his mind simultaneously and couldn't decide what the best thing to do was. He looked off stage and found Claire trying to calm Ian down. As they counted the seconds to the live camera, he twisted and turned on the leather sofa in agony. The moment they went back on the air, Scott rose up gazing in anguish at the wing of the stage where Ian and Claire were standing as if waiting for him to make a decision. Hearing Calahan's shouting behind him, he began to make the move after Ian.

"Where do you think you're going?" Calahan asked.

"I have to leave." Scott kept heading off the stage, frightened, unsure of what was expected of him.

Waving at him, Calahan gave a very exaggerated laugh and said, "I have a show to do! Get back here!"

Standing still, his mind completely blank as to what his obligations were, Scott knew he had to run off that set to comfort his lover, but some sense of responsibility was looming: his sister's company, his movie roll and, whoever may be watching to see if he cracked under pressure. All this was scrambling through his head, when in reality he knew he could not continue this interview and needed to talk to Ian.

"Come! Come back, Mr. Epstein! Let's discuss what we just witnessed! I'm sure everyone is curious as to what you two are up to in the privacy of your bedroom? Right, ladies and gentlemen?"

Through the roar of applause that in all respect was meant to be supportive, Scott shook his head and shouted, "Look, I don't know what you're trying to do to us, but it's pathetic! Go find another victim, Calahan!" About to explode with rage, Scott raced off the set.

Claire's face appeared pale and worn. Scott raced towards her breathlessly, "Where's Ian?"

"He ran out of here, Scott, I couldn't hold him. I think he went back to the apartment."

"Shit! Come on, let's get out of here."

As they sprinted to the exit, they heard behind them, Calahan sneering, "...you'll have to excuse my two guests, ladies and gentlemen. Obviously they're not ready to expose their love affair. Please welcome our next guest, the comedian—"

Scott stood on the pavement in front of the studio looking up and down the street for him. Hearing footsteps behind him, he spun back to see his sister's stricken face.

"What bullshit, Claire! Did you have any idea that asshole would do that to us?"

"No! Are you kidding me? You think I would have let you do that show? I had no idea the beast would get that dirty! Oh! Grab that cab, Scott, hurry!"

They waved frantically and managed to get the attention of the yellow cab. As they climbed in, Claire reached for Scott's hand to comfort him. "It's okay, Scottchula. He'll be there."

"My god, Claire, I've never been through anything like that in my life. Poor Ian! Can you imagine how he feels?"

"I know! What an arrogant ass! I'm so sorry, Scott. I never would have agreed to let you guys do the interview. Honest. I've seen him do that to only one other person and it was a politician who cheated on his wife. I never thought he'd go that far with you two."

Scott wrung his hands anxiously, wanting the cab to go faster. "I've got to see Ian. Can't this thing move any quicker?"

The minute it stopped at their building, he rocketed out of the back, allowing Claire to pay the driver. Holding his breath, pounding the elevator button, when it opened Claire managed to jump on with him. He felt her watching him and tried not to meet her eyes. He was about to burst into tears.

She got her keys out and they jogged to the door and opened it. Scott heard Claire mumble under her breath, "Thank god."

"Ian! Ian!" Scott found him in his room packing.

When he grabbed him, Ian turned around with tears standing in his eyes.

"Oh, baby," Scott sighed, wrapping around him tightly.

"I can't believe he did that to us, Scott. I'm gutted. I have to leave. I can't stay here anymore. Maybe I need to get back to England."

"Shh...hang on...don't jump on a plane just yet, okay? We'll deal with it. I swear we can handle this."

"What about our careers?" Ian noticed Claire at the doorway. "Claire...will this kill our chances or what?"

"No. Ian, let the dust settle. Look, everyone knows what a pit bull Calahan is at times. They'll most likely feel pity for you, not disdain, believe me. I'm sure it will calm down. Give it time."

Ian dropped down on his bed heavily. "I don't know what to do...honest, Scott, I'm completely lost."

Scott sat next to him and put his arm around his shoulders. "Hang in there, Ian. We didn't admit to shit out there. Claire's right. It was all just his badgering insults. We did nothing wrong."

"Yes. Yes, maybe you're right." A deep exhaled sigh came out of him. Scott cuddled him closer and kissed his cheek. "Don't worry, baby...I won't let anything happen to you."

Smiling, adoring her brother's soft side, Claire whispered, "How about I get us some wine?"

"Thanks, Claire," Scott replied.

She left the room and went to the kitchen.

After she had gone, Scott faced Ian and looked into his eyes. "Will you try not to let it eat you up?"

"Aye. I'll try."

"You know how these things go. We'll be yesterday's news soon. People grow bored quickly with this kind of gossip, Ian."

"Yes, you're right. It should blow over...right."

When they looked up at the doorway, Claire had three stemmed glasses, a bottle of wine, and a big contented grin on her face. "I'm proud of you both," she said. "You'll be fine. Trust me. If anything, it'll make the public adore you more."

"Thanks, Claire." Scott took the glasses from her and

allowed her to pour.

When she had, they lifted up the wine to give a toast. She said, "To some peace and calm."

The men tapped her glass and sipped the crisp wine.

Chapter Twenty-one

The next morning Claire set the coffee maker up and checked to see the supply of eggs and bread for breakfast. When her phone rang she cringed at first and then answered it.

"Hello?"

"It's me."

"Hi, Jenine."

"I had no idea Calahan would do that to them, Claire. If I did I never would have let them do the show."

"I know, sweetie."

"How are they? Did they survive?"

"They did. They're still asleep. I want to let them sleep in a little."

"You coming into the office today?"

"You mind if I'm late?"

"Naa, I don't care. Take care of the boys first."

"My thoughts exactly."

"What do you think they should do? You know, until this blows over?"

"I don't know. I was hoping after having last night to think about it we'd come up with something. But I know one thing, I'll never send another victim to that beast again! Jesus, Jenine, I still can't believe he did that to them."

"I am so sorry!"

"It's not your fault, dear. Oh! I hear movement. I think they're waking up. Let me go. I'll be in later this afternoon."

"Okay. See ya then."

Claire hung up and stared at the hallway between the bedrooms and bathroom. Ian scuffed his way by to the toilet.

She shook her head sadly and put the bread into the toaster.

After they had both showered and sniffed out the fresh dripped coffee, she poured them two mugs full and started frying up the eggs. "You guys okay?"

"Yeah, we'll live." Scott blew on the hot liquid, then sipped it.

"I was thinking...and it's only a suggestion..."

"Go on, Claire," Ian replied.

"Maybe Ian should move out temporarily. You know, until the heat dies down."

Scott looked back at his lover to see his reaction.

Ian paused, then nodded. "Yes. Perhaps it's for the best, Claire. But will it blow over?"

"I'm sure it will, Ian." She smiled sweetly.

Scott ran his hands down Ian's arm. "I'll miss you being underfoot, limey."

"You understand, Scott. Don't you?"

"Of course."

When they kissed, Claire smiled to herself, then said, "You two are so cute together!"

Scott grinned wryly at her and shouted, "Shut up!"

"No, you shut up!"

"No, you shut up!" Scott began laughing.

Then Ian threw up his hands in feigned frustration and said, "Enough already!"

They burst out laughing and Claire felt a warmth fill her

heart. She knew this would work out, just knew it.

Chapter Twenty-two

A week had gone by and it was beginning to feel as if the public had lost interest. Ian had moved into a small one bedroom apartment close to his school, with Claire's financial help, and Scott spent most of his days sneaking his way to it, sleeping there and coming home in the wee hours of the morning to avoid detection. If the media thought they could drive a wedge between them, they were mistaken. If anything it had strengthened their resolve to stay together.

Taking a rare opportunity to get out into the fresh air together, Scott suggested a small out of the way café where they could grab a cup of coffee and some food.

Sitting together quietly, Scott rubbed his face and leaned his elbow on the table towards Ian. "So? Will you come out to California with me? You know, when I make that movie?"

"Aye! I'd love to see that part of the states. If Claire lets me. I have no idea what my schedule looks like, but I'm sure to have a long break from school in the spring. I'll stay there as long as I can, and you know, I'll be here waiting for you when you get back."

Smiling in delight, Scott had a tremendous urge to reach over the table to his hand but restrained himself. "Great. I would love to play on the beach with you. I could use some sun."

"Play? You'll be working, mate!" Ian laughed. "You think the studio would even give you a day off?"

"I don't know. I've never worked on anything this big before."

"I'd imagine it'd be pretty grueling. I would think after you get most of it done, you can find some time for some rest and relax. But don't these blockbusters take years to produce?"

"Christ! What a thought! I suppose some of them do. It depends on the budget. Oh well, we'll work it out. If you can't be out there the entire time, we'll just call every day."

"Right. Don't worry, love, I'm not going out on you. No way."

"I adore you. You know that?" Scott felt his chest swell with pride.

Suddenly Ian's expression dropped to panic. "Oh, bullocks..."

"What?" Scott looked around.

"I can't believe this! We've been left alone for ages. Now look... a bloody photographer!"

"Where?"

Ian pointed to a small conspicuous man in a black coat with a very heavy camera hanging around his neck. He seemed to be honing in on them like a shark to blood.

"I'm leery of us being seen together. You know what I mean? They'll most likely throw us on the front page of some rag and the whole thing will start all over again." Ian stood, grabbing his jacket.

"Why can't they leave us alone? Oh, Ian, I feel badly we can't even have a cup of coffee without some moron ruining it. Should I stop by later? After dark?"

"Aye. Yes. Come by. Let's not let him see us together."

Nodding, Scott looked outside and could tell the man hadn't found them yet but was obvious tipped off they were eating as a couple at the café. Since Ian moved out and they kept their affair secret, things had calmed down to the point where they thought they were free of the attention. This was the first time they had been in public together, hoping the novelty had worn off from the media circus.

When Ian left, the bloodsucker immediately raced after him. Scott bristled in anger and threw some money on the table to cover the tab. He rushed out and trailed behind them just in case Ian needed him.

Ian appeared to twist away, trying to ignore the intrusion, pretending the vulture wasn't there.

When he stood at the corner to flag down a cab, the man seemed to get right in Ian's face.

"Oi! Back off!" Ian shouted, holding up his hand.

It was all Scott could do to not lunge at the man from behind and drop him to the cold concrete.

Suddenly Scott noticed Ian spot him lingering in the background as if only just realizing he was there. Unsure if he should get lost or stand his ground, Scott was torn. For a moment he imagined Ian getting angry at him for following him. To his surprise, Ian seemed to exhale deeply, as if coming to some decision, then he walked right passed the photographer and directly towards him. Scott stood there, silent, his eyes wide as Ian said, "You know, Scott, this is getting on me nerves, all this hiding and sneaking around."

Looking over Ian's shoulder, he could see the man reloading his film quickly, taking shot after shot. "And? What do you want me to do about it? Kill the guy? Steal his camera?"

Ian glanced back once, then stared into Scott's eyes.

Scott had no idea what he was going to do, but he held his breath out of nervousness. Then to his amazement, Ian wrapped around Scott's neck and kissed him, right on the lips.

Scott parted from that kiss with a surprised breath. The cameraman went wild with his shutter.

"What the hell is this all about?" Scott asked in shock.

"I'm out. Bullocks to the world!" Ian shouted, then grinned

devilishly at Scott. "No more hiding, love. What do we have to be ashamed of anyway? Eh? I'm sick to bloody death of seeing you only after dark. If the world doesn't like us, to hell with them."

Scott wrapped his arms around Ian's waist and spun him around in delight. "I love you, you crazy limey!"

"Aye, and I love you too ya, mad yank!"

"So, that's the story of how my brother and Ian Sullivan met," she said, looking at the journalist as he stared back at her. "It's a great romance story, isn't it?" She crushed her empty water bottle. "I suppose someone will make a movie out of it, right? After all, big screen gay love stories are all the rage!" she laughed. "Maybe it's a lesson in bravery. I think both of them learned to just be themselves. I know they took a big chance finally coming out, but, it hasn't hurt either career at the moment.

Maybe the world is beginning to see that love is universal, and it comes in all shapes and sizes...and sexes! I know I've learned a lesson. Be true to yourself. Be honest with yourself, and be fearless. I'm a firm believer in it now...okay? You still need more? Can I just end it by saying, 'and they both lived happily ever after'? Was there anything else? Or is this the end of the interview? Cool. I'm tired of talking! When will it be in the magazine? Okay. Thanks!"

Jenine was waiting for her outside. When Claire emerged, she felt completely drained of life.

"Wow, that took forever! What did they ask you?"

"The usual. I think they just wanted to know what happened to Scott and Ian after that fiasco on Calahan."

"When are they publishing the story?"

"Next issue of the magazine. I'm surprised we're still getting publicity from that commercial."

"Well, it does make an unusual story." Walking down the dirty New York sidewalk, the old leftover plowed snow crunching under her boot, Jenine bowed her head as she walked.

"I suppose," Claire sighed.

"What do you think is going to happen between them? I mean, now that they have admitted to their relationship. You don't think it'll do them any harm, do you? My guess is no. I think the acting and modeling profession is more tolerant than any other in that respect."

"We'll have to take it a day at a time. But I just don't see it turning badly for them, Jenine. I think in some ways, Calahan's attack worked in their favor—have you read any of the fan mail that keeps coming in for them?"

"Yeah, it's amazing. But I worry about them. I wish I had a crystal ball to see if everything will work out in the end. You think the world really is changing, becoming more accepting?"

"Wouldn't that be nice!" Claire laughed. "I'm keeping my fingers crossed for a happy ending."

"Hi, Mom?" Claire sat with her legs crossed under her comfortably in her living room.

"Hello, dear. How are you doing?"

"Good. Things have really calmed down."

"I'm glad to hear it, Claire. How is Scott doing?"

"He's doing great. I think he finally found true love."

"With that English fella?"

"Yeah, Mom. I've never seen him so happy. It seems as if everything is finally going right for Scott. His career, his love life. Now if I can find a man like that, I'd be happy!"

"You will, sweetheart."

"It's really funny, though."

"What's that, Claire?"

"Well, all this over one kiss!"

255

A soft laugh came over the line to her. "Never underestimate the power of a kiss, Claire."

"Oh, Mom, you said a mouthful," Claire replied, then added, "No pun intended!"

The End

About the Author

Award-winning author G. A. Hauser was born in Fair Lawn, New Jersey, USA, and attended university in New York City. She moved to Seattle, Washington where she worked as a patrol officer with the Seattle Polic Department. In early 2000 G.A. moved to Hertfordshire, England, where she began her writing in earnest and published her first book, *In the Shadow of Alexander*. Now a full-time writer in Ohio, G.A. has written dozens of novels, including several bestsellers of gay fiction. For more information on other books by G.A., visit the author at her official website at: www.authorgahauser.com.

G.A. has won awards from All Romance eBooks for Best Novel 2007, *Secrets and Misdemeanors*, Best Author 2007. Best Novel 2008, *Mile High*, and Best Author 2008.

The G.A. Hauser Collection

Available Now
Single Titles

Unnecessary Roughness

Heart of Steele

Julian

Black Leather Phoenix

A Man's Best Friend

It Takes a Man

The Physician and the Actor

For Love and Money

The Kiss

Naked Dragon

Secrets and Misdemeanors

Capital Games

Giving Up the Ghost

To Have and To Hostage

Love you, Loveday

The Boy Next Door

When Adam Met Jack

Exposure

All Man

In the Dark and What Should Never Be, Erotic Short Stories

Mark and Sharon (formerly titled A Question of Sex)

The Vampire and the Man-eater
Murphy's Hero
Mark Antonious deMontford
Prince of Servitude
Calling Dr. Love
The Rape of St. Peter
The Wedding Planner
Going Deep
Double Trouble
Pirates
Miller's Tale
Vampire Nights
Teacher's Pet
In the Shadow of Alexander
The Rise and Fall of the Sacred Band of Thebes

The Action Series
Acting Naughty
Playing Dirty
Getting it in the End
Behaving Badly
Dripping Hot
Packing Heat

Men in Motion Series
Mile High
Cruising
Driving Hard
Leather Boys

Breinigsville, PA USA
06 July 2010
241245BV00003B/37/P